MKLM Library

THE RIVER AND THE SOURCE

Margaret A Ogola

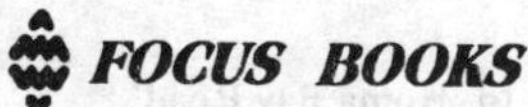

Focus Publications Ltd
P.O. Box 28176
Nairobi, Kenya.

Reprinted 1995

Cover Design
Irene A Ogendo
ICIPE Science Press

ISBN 9966 882 05 7

Printed by
General Printers Ltd, Homa Bay Road,
P.O. Box 18001, Nairobi, Kenya.
G0859

Dedication

In memory of John Felix Odongo
Who filled our lives with love and laughter

To George — my love
and companion upon life's way

To my children
Each of whom has brought something fresh and new
to the table of life

Acknowledgements

The germ of this book was planted early in my life by my mother, Herina Odongo, whose gift as a story teller and acerbic wit are still the spice of our lives.

For the first part of this book, I have extensively borrowed from the life and times of Obanda Kingi nyar' Ang'eyo — my great grandmother, which was narrated to me by my mother and my sister Rose Josiah, who had the fortune of hearing it first-hand from my grandmother Paulina Opondo who was Obanda's daughter.

Of all the living people I know, Grace Hagoma Okumu most closely portrays the spirit of this book — that of the undefeatable womanhood of Africa. Widowed while extremely young, she fought the good fight with great spirit. She is also a natural philosopher, and her sayings, which are apt, witty and often hilarious, have been brought to my attention by her daughter and my good friend Pamela Hagono.

The idea of this book and many other things in my life would have remained dormant were it not for the intensive care I received at the hands of Margaret Roche—Irish by birth, Kenyan by choice. She has a way of bringing out the best in me. Her friendship is something I value.

Pamela Kadenge is the young lady who patiently deciphered my handwriting to type the manuscript. I am very grateful to her.

Contents

PART I

THE GIRL CHILD

Chapter 1

One night, in the smoky hut of Aketch, the second wife of the great chief Odero Gogni of Yimbo, a baby was born. It was about thirty seasons before that great snaking metal road of *Jorochere*, the white people, reached the bartering market of Kisuma. The baby yelled so lustily on its first gulp of acrid air, that the chief strolling around unconcernedly as befitted his station and manhood, thought with satisfaction, 'Another rock for my sling', by which he meant another son. Actually he had already covered himself in considerable glory by siring seven sons. However this time he was wrong because for the first time he was the father of a daughter. Later he would say wisely, with something of a turnabout, that a home without daughters is like a spring without a source; for it was his right as a great chief not only to lead but to utter wisdom as well, change of heart notwithstanding.

This was the season when the leaves of the growing sorghum, now the height of a toddling child, trembled greenly in the wind and the weeders were busy hoeing and chanting in unison a song about the prowess of some long departed hero. The child would therefore have been called Adoyo and indeed she was, but as was the custom some ancestor or other would send a dream to stake out his interest in the baby and therefore like so many others, the little girl ended up with more than one name.

Now these ancestral spirits usually sent such vivid dreams that no one was ever left in doubt. In this case the child's great uncle, recently dead, a medicine man of great renown sent dreams to both the father and the grandmother of the child (the mother was probably too exhausted to dream). She was therefore named Obanda—it not being uncommon to name a girl after a man and a boy after a woman.

When she was two weeks old the baby developed a prolonged bout of colic and screaming that went on all night. Now as sure as the sun rises in the east because this is the home of Great *Were* the god of Ramogi, everything in this world has a reason if only you search diligently for it. Now why would such a little baby, the only daughter of so great a chief cry so bitterly? Had some evil enemy cast a spell? Had she not been properly named? The grandmother was summoned. The father hung around in a rather unchiefly manner, probably afraid that his spring would dry up before it had really begun.

Grandmother *nyar*-Alego came in and began to march up and down with the help of her cane, a rather spritely figure for her age. She started talking in a conversational tone, then with an increase in tempo that eventually reached a complaining high pitched harangue. "Great *Were*, god of the eye of the rising sun, creator of Ramogi, we revere you and prostrate ourselves before you. Is it not you who brings the rain in season to shower our crops and support new life? Oh Rahuma! Great warrior and father of many children, husband of many wives, did you not select a husband carefully for me and did I not as a good daughter agree without a murmur? Oh Achieng! Daughter of the rocky country of Seme, my dearest mother, did you not teach me how to conduct myself as a good wife? Did I ever turn to the left or to the right of the way you taught me? Did I not honour, love and serve the great Chief Gogni

Adinda, my husband, until the day I buried him in pomp and honour fulfilling all the requirements of *Chik*, the way of our people? Did not my upright son, Odero, rule in his father's stead and have I not always guided him to listen to the counsel of the council of *Jodongo*, our elders? Has he not always heard and done everything in its season, offering sacrifices of bulls, goats and rams and profuse libations of *kong'o*, our brew for the safety, health and prosperity of his people? Show us, O *Were* and ye departed spirits of our ancestors, where we have gone wrong so that we may rectify ourselves and save this little one, for a home without daughters can never prosper but is faced with eventual poverty and lack of friendships forged in marriage. Or is it you my dear sister long dead who is doing this to me and mine? But did I not take you as my younger sister and bring you from our country and from my father's house to come and help me live in my husband's house as my co-wife? Oh Akelo my sister, is it my fault that you died without issue...?" And before she could complete that sentence the baby suddenly stopped crying, burped, looked around her dazedly for a little while and then fell asleep. Everybody looked at the other significantly before tiptoeing away. It was the hour of the first cock-crow and one might still catch a little sleep — the rest could wait till sun-up.

The next day a cock was ceremoniously slaughtered and eaten in memory of poor childless Akelo who obviously did not want to be totally forgotten. The baby was then given a third name, Akelo, after her grandmother's sister. Among these people, it is not enough that a child has three names or more, praise names are always added either in memory of the child's namesakes, or to bring to attention some aspect of the child's personality. For example a child named after a brave warrior may spend most of his life being called Wuon-Okumba (bearer of the shield); or another be called Wuod-Lando (son of the brown woman). For little Adoyo Obanda (for her third name was rarely ever used except by her grandmother) that extra name was Akoko (the noisy one) for she had an extremely powerful set of lungs and she did not mind using them. Later she would be a famous singer of the dirge, *gueyo* in its complete range; but for now she was just a temperamental baby. Everybody remarked that she would be a very determined person some day.

Akoko grew fairly slowly but she made up for her lack of height with a brightness and a determination that would be the hallmark of her entire life. She amazed the entire household by sitting without support at four months. She pulled up and started cruising around with the support of anything she could hang on to at seven months and completed that feat by pattering away on her own two feet at seven and half months. At ten months she amazed everybody including her father by uttering not one but two words. These were however not *baba* or *mama* as might have been expected but *dwaro mara*. This she screamed at her older brother Oloo who had dared take away something she was playing with and meant 'Want mine!'

Now, to survive in a household consisting of nine brothers (for it was not until four years later that another girl was born) requires some skill, and Akoko perfected it. First and foremost, puny she might be, but she was physically fearless and could take tumbles and tosses with a determined smile. Secondly with the unerring instinct of a child she sensed her father's affection for her. That a man and a chief at that should even take notice of a girl-child was unusual; after all a son meant continuity and a girl would only depart to go and 'cook' for some other clan, but chief Odero found the child irresistible. He tried to cover it up of course for it would have been unseemly, but was soon clear to everyone that only one thing could be counted on to earn one a severe reprimand and that thing was a complaint from Akoko. In truth Akoko was such a sport that she won not only the affection of her strapping brothers but their respect as well and woe to any village girl or boy who dared cross her! Her brother Oloo, in fact, loved her so much that decades later, he did an unheard of thing by taking her, a widow, beaten and bruised by life back into his house. Such a woman became a *migogo* whose chief appearance would be at funerals and would have absolutely no say in her former home, marriage being such a binding thing. To abandon one's marital duties for good or bad reasons was a very serious matter.

In that place and in those days, life went on at an uninterrupted, even keel. Inter-clan warfare was rare, for *dak* (neighbourliness) and *wat* (a concept that encompassed a brotherhood so far-reaching that it was almost impossible to go anywhere and not find a relative) were valued highly. The warlike Lang'o tribesmen were far away, bordering places like Kano and Nyakach, and would never dream of coming this deep within the territory. The weather was benign and food plentiful for anyone who was willing to work, though even the lazy did not starve, but were referred to contemptuously as *jomifwadhi* which can only be translated as disorganised sluggards. Fish came in fresh from the lake and wild fruit abounded; in fact malnutrition at the rates seen among today's urban and rural poor was unknown; indeed Yimbo was a small corner of paradise.

Akoko flourished into a beautiful girl so fast that nobody could tell where the seasons had gone. It was soon necessary to arrange for a *nak* ceremony during which she could be initiated into the rigours of adulthood by the removal of six lower teeth. She held a special place as the first born daughter and all things had to be done perfectly and in order because nothing could be done for any of her sisters before they were done for her. Therefore the *nak* was done with due pomp and after she healed, two more seasons were allowed to pass and then the chief felt that he was ready to receive proposals. Seventeen seasons was quite young for a daughter of Ramogi to consider marriage, somewhat older girls were preferred, and many girls had approached their thirtieth season still in their fathers' houses as their aspiring suitors struggled to acquire the required head of cattle. On the other hand, Akoko was the great chief's daughter and beautiful as well as spirited. Many a spy had been sent to check her out and the report was unanimous — a young woman with impeccable antecedents who could be expected not only to nurture children but to build a real home. The suitors came tumbling over each other, all of them men or sons of men of ability, from good families without a shadow of *juok* or witchcraft, madness, habitual thievery, laziness or any other undesirable trait against them. One and all they met twenty-one hostile brothers and an impossible to please father. As she approached her nineteenth season and her thirteenth suitor, Akoko was resigned to the fact that *Were*, with all his bountifulness had forgotten to create a man good enough for her.

Chapter 2

One fine morning as the waters of the Great Lake shimmered and trembled at the lightest touch of the breeze and the siala trees swayed gently in the warm air, the harvest having been safely gathered into granaries, a young man arrived in chief Odero's compound. As politeness dictated, he stood outside the central hut which was obviously the *duol*, the personal hut of the chief, and waited to be invited inside. Even without his black and white colobus monkey headdress, he stood head and shoulders above most men. He was obviously a man of *nyadhi*,, that is a man of great style for he had a spear in one hand, a shield in the other and splashes of white war paint across his body. His face was ritually tattooed, his head set proudly on his shoulders and he wore only a tiny piece of leopard skin which barely reached his mid thigh, from under which two powerful legs protruded. On his right was a wizened old man and on his left a young man who closely resembled him, as well as six other men.

Odero's eldest son Okumu was sent outside to inquire into the nature of their business. The wizened old man spoke: "We have come to see Odero the son of the great Chief Gogni Adinda for the purpose of betrothing our family to his for even as far away as Sakwa we have heard of the beauty and the spirit of his eldest daughter. We would have come earlier had we not been mourning for our Chief Kembo K'Agina who died last moon, but we came as soon as we could for my nephew Owuor Kembo, now chief in his father's place, urgently seeks a wife. It is unthinkable that a chief should be unmarried, a situation which has arisen only because of the sudden death of his father — the young chief himself being only twenty seasons old."

Now, that lengthy speech had two main purposes: to impress the father and his sons, for a girl's father was all powerful and capable of turning away the prospective suitors at their first meeting and secondly to indicate to the great chief that Owuor Kembo, though not such a great chief, was wifeless and therefore whoever he married would hold the envious position of *mikai*, the first wife, whose house would hold the centre stage directly facing the gate and to whom all other wives and also her husband would defer. Rumour had it that Odero Gogni had set his heart not only on his daughter marrying a chief but also that she be the *mikai* of such a chief. Okumu went back into his father's *simba* and repeated the message. Odero came out and bid the visitors enter. *Kong'o* was brought and as the council of *Jodongo* trooped in one by one the pot of tangy brew was passed from hand to hand, to be sipped through a long reed-like straw, after first offering libation to *Were*. Pleasant questions were asked about the state of the harvest and the cattle and no one had ever seen the great chief being so nice to any suitor including some wealthy ones who had offered to pay double the bride price.

"And how, may I ask is the savanna country of Sakwa? Were the rains adequate and the harvest plentiful? I have heard that a strange malady has killed many cattle in that place." Owuor Kembo's uncle was a seasoned broker who not only knew *Chik* but knew the loopholes and traps that might be set for an unwary suitor. He answered wisely. "The rains were adequate and the food in the granary will feed us well after the next harvest. The rumour you heard was true but *Were*, praise be his name, protected most of our cattle, and besides the dead chief had only two sons and many daughters who will continue to bring in more wealth."

At this Chief Odero could not help being somewhat envious as he had only eight daughters to his twenty-one sons. He had never quite mastered the art of siring daughters. He decided there and then that he would not make things easy for these arrogant upstarts. After all, of late he had to go easy on his wife-marrying spree because he felt a little alarmed at the number of his sons. His father Gogni Mboji, had had vast wealth and only six sons. So rich was he in fact that he had paid dowry for two wives in as many seasons for his elder son Odero, chief-to-be, before his twenty second season.

As the brew continued to flow, Odero called the council of *Jodongo* outside for consultation.

"My fathers," he began, "This is my eldest daughter and as you know I have dispatched twelve suitors, but I like this group of people as the young man is obviously of good stock and his uncle a good spokesman. However, I would like to trim their arrogance a bit. You Aloo K'Olima have been my spokesman all along and you will remain so. Set the bride price at thirty head."

"Thirty head." exclaimed Aloo in disbelief.

"Yes thirty head," declared the uncompromising chief.

"But that is two and half times the usual bride price." Even for Akoko, it was too much.

"Let them show us that my daughter is not going to starve in that wasteland they call a home." They trooped back into the hut and the negotiations began in earnest.

"Brothers, people of Sakwa, we are pleased to welcome you to Yimbo. It is customary, because of the good *dak* between us, for you to marry our daughters and we yours. We are therefore more than neighbours, we have great *wat* between us because of the intermingling of blood though this has not occurred between our two lines so there is no danger of brother marrying sister — a great taboo. Since therefore you are our brothers we will not make things difficult for you." Here he stopped to take a sip of *kong'o* and you could have heard the ants talk, so great was the silence. However nobody was fooled by his sweet words.

He continued, enjoying immensely the tension he was creating. "Our daughter, Adoyo Obanda is a great beauty whose assets have been praised and sung by many a *nyatiti* singer from here to Chumbu Kombit, from Sakwa to Loka Nam. She is as fleet as a gazelle and her flying feet have been incorporated into the sayings of our village so that mothers sending their daughters on errands tell them to run like Adoyo of the flying feet. She has been carefully brought up and has been taught all the requirements of *Chik*. She is a very apt pupil, and will therefore not bring shame and ruin to her husband by improper conduct.

Her antecedents are peerless for she can trace her bloodline clear to Ramogi our great father and her blood is pure for we have always taken care to marry correctly. She is also the eldest daughter of our great chief, a man whose fame is known throughout this land. After careful consultation we have therefore decided that thirty head of cattle should be the proper bride price." Was that an inaudible gasp from someone at the back? Chief Owuor Kembo signalled to his uncle and the old man spoke.

"Brothers, people of Yimbo, we have listened with great care to what you have to say. Since the contract of marriage is a matter of great import, we wish to beg leave to consult with each other outside before we return our verdict."

"Feel free to do so," Aloo said magnanimously. They moved some distance away and Akoko watching from her mother's kitchen thought amusedly to herself, "I should ask father to give me a piece of land to settle on because at this rate I shall never leave his house."

Among the suitors was controlled pandemonium; controlled because an *or*, a son-in law, always had to comport himself with great dignity (even if escaping from a house on fire) when in the presence of his in-laws, especially the *maro*, mother-in-law, whom they were sure was watching them from some chink in a wall.

"Thirty head!" exclaimed Otieno, Owuor's younger brother. "That is enough to marry three wives. Women are all the same Owuor — let's get out of here."

"I think he is right. Why should these people rip us off like this? Who do they think they are? They can keep their daughter, let's be off, chief." The conversation went on in that vein while the young chief remained entirely silent. A rather irrelevant thought came to his head and the corner of his mouth twitched a little. His *jawan'gyo* (the spy he had sent to inspect the girl) had told him that she had a most beautiful neck, long with lovely creases tracing their way around it. She also had a long hooked navel on which two whole rings of beads could fit. These were aspects of feminine beauty much valued among the people.

"My father, my brothers, I think you are greatly mistaken. Not all women are the same. This woman is going to be my *mikai* not just any wife. Besides I have set my heart on marrying her. We shall do as they say."

"What? Are you crazy? Not even a bargain?"

"Please be careful how you address the Chief," reprimanded the old man. "Owuor, my son, I see what you mean. An *or's* honour is a great thing and if your in-laws despise you, it is something that is very difficult to live down. Let us shock them by accepting their offer without bargaining. That way your name will be repeated from mouth to mouth for years to come. You will be Owuor Kembo, a man of style, the famous *or* who paid up without demur. Let's go in." He led the way and everybody had to follow him including those who thought that both he and his nephew had been bewitched by these Yimbo people.

"Brothers, people of Yimbo; Odero great chief, son of Gogni, we are aware of the honour you have accorded us, having listened to our suit with patience. May *Were* shower you with many blessings. My nephew and I have consulted and we have decided that on the fourteenth day of the next moon, thirty head of cattle will be driven by our young men into your homestead so that the marriage may take place."

Odero looked confused for a moment, having expected a spirited fight to reduce the number to at least twenty head. However, he was not a great chief for nothing. He rose beautifully to the occasion. After all style had to be met with style, *nyadhi* with *nyadhi*.

"*Ayie*, I have accepted your suit. May the young girl be called so that people of Sakwa may see what a jewel we are giving them." "Giving us!" thought Otieno in annoyance. "At this rate there will be no cattle left for me to pay bride price with."

In a little while Akoko walked in, in the company of her mother. Traditionally the girl at this point should have been the picture of demure shyness, her eyes fixed firmly on the floor, her hands held together in front of her mouth. Not Akoko. She walked in, steps measured, head held high, hands at her sides. Her head swivelled around a bit and then her gaze rested on Owuor. Let him see what he was getting.

"What a brazen lass," thought Otieno, "Thirty head indeed!"

Owuor experienced an indescribable sensation. What happened, of course was that he had fallen deeply and irrevocably in love. Since that was not considered particularly important for a successful marriage, he did not understand or appreciate what was happening to him and that it would change his entire life and outlook.

She turned and left the room. Her mother remained for the rest of the ceremony.

"People of Sakwa," continued Aloo, "We are pleased that we have reached an understanding and we hope that a friendship will spring up between us now and into posterity. Let us pour more libation to *Were* and drink more *kong'o* to gladden our hearts. Mother of Akoko, please bring us some food."

The feasting went on into the late afternoon until about the tenth hour. Then the suitors had to leave, for *Chik* did not allow them to spend the night.

Chapter 3

On the fourteenth day of the next moon as promised, the cattle were driven into the compound by young men splashed with war paint, whistling and calling out at the top of their lungs and chanting in turn, the names of great warriors of the past such as Lwanda Magere and Gor Mahia.

Once in a while one of them would step up the tempo and start chanting his own personal praise name.

"I am Ochieng Suna, the mosquito
Tiny I am, but when I bite,
Even the great elephant
Flaps his big ears."

and another

"I am Oloo Polo, the sky
When I rumble
And send signs and wonders
Even the brave tremble."

and yet another

"I am Ong'ong' Jaber
So handsome am I
That when I pass
Girls gape and drop their waterpots."

They were received by the local young men, some of them drove away the cattle and others guided the young men into a hut where they feasted late into the night. One by one they passed out literally where they sat or squatted. However, at the first cockcrow, a piercing whistle was heard followed by a blood-curdling whoop. There followed a mad rush to the hut where Akoko slept with her grandmother and sisters. The flimsy door was pushed aside, two young men grabbed Akoko and dashed out. The others put up a spirited fight against her brothers and other young men, mainly in *amen*, that is wrestling duels. Akoko let out one piercing yell after another. Let it never be said that she left her father's house willingly. It was interesting that nobody actually got hurt in the melee, its purpose being purely ceremonial, but the uninitiated might have thought that all were intent on actual bodily harm if not murder.

Eventually the Sakwa men broke away with their prize and with one last war cry, disappeared into the bush. By daybreak, they had journeyed quite some distance away and they stopped for rest and food at the nearest homestead. They were granted hospitality without question according to the dictates of *Chik*. As they waited for the millet gruel and sweet potatoes to be brought, they told the tale of their vanquishing of Yimbo men with such embellishment that one would have thought that the girl had been grabbed from the jaws of a determined dragon.

After eating, they continued their journey at a brisk pace and by the late evening, at about the last hour, with the orange flaming orb of the sun just about to take its dip into the great lake, they approached the first homestead of Sakwa. The guides posted to await their return let out a yell fit to awaken the ancestors. This was answered by a whoop from the young men and a bitter wail from Akoko. They all started to run for all the world as if they had chased the bride all the way from her old home to the very outskirts of her new home. The women came out ululating at the top of their lungs and there was general commotion. Everybody wanted to see with his own eyes this bride who had cost the chief thirty head of cattle. All spoke at once, but eventually the consensus was that never since the days of Nyabera *nyar* Nam had such beauty graced the land. Her eyes were set far apart and neither too small nor too big, her teeth were white and even with a bewitching gap at the centre of the upper set. Her ears with earrings dangling from tiny holes were perfectly shaped standing just at the right angle from her head. And that neck! It was fit to inspire praise songs from *nyatiti* players! And were those two whole rings on her navel? It could not be! And the way her *chieno*, traditional skin, hung gracefully from her tiny waist, swaying so beautifully at the back! As for her legs, *Were* must have carved them out personally rather than one of his apprentices. It was agreed that thirty head was rather high, but the chief had chosen well. Besides the young men reported that he was held in such great awe by the Yimbo people that should he so much as glance in their direction, another girl would immediately be given to the chief with such great *nyadhi*. The people were therefore well satisfied with the *miaha*, the new wife of their chief.

Akoko was duly installed as the *mikai* of Chief Kembo and people started to count the days and the moons. At the third moon whispers were heard, for one never speaks of these things loudly in case some evil spirit hears and causes trouble. By the fifth month everything was obvious to even the most unobservant dullard. People waited with bated breath and ten moons from the day she arrived wailing Akoko delivered herself of a fine son. Piercing ululations were heard as people rejoiced for the continuation of the chief's line. This was a good omen indeed. The child was tentatively called Obura, the counsellor or wise one, while dreams were being awaited. On the second night after the birth, the child's father dreamed of no less than Kembo K'Agina, the late chief. He dreamt that Kembo was handing him a baby boy from his right hand side — a sign that the old chief's spirit was well pleased with his son and grandson. The child therefore became Obura Kembo.

Obura Kembo was a boy to gladden any father's heart. Swift of mind and body like his mother, he was big like his father. His rate of development would have caused comment were it not that the people did not want to bring bad luck to the chief's son by talking about his prowess. For most part they marvelled silently, except for a few ill mannered types who forgot themselves to the point of mentioning some amazing aspects of the child's character. His parents' hearts swelled with pride within them, but even they kept a severe check on their tongues. In fact he was reprimanded more than any other child, and to hear his mother, one would have thought her son a good for nothing, slow witted, lazy bones. It was just as well that Obura was a cheerful fellow and was rarely ever put out — least of all by his mother whom he loved. As had happened with her father before, he probably saw right through her.

When he was about three and a half seasons old, Obura's mother became pregnant again. At this point the chief was under great pressure to marry another wife, especially from his mother who felt that the rate at which he was reproducing himself was too slow. It is to be noted that she had nothing against Akoko, in fact she liked her daughter-in-law. But children were wealth and she remembered how her husband, the late chief, had agonised over the fact that he had only two sons out of six wives.

He on the other hand had twenty two daughters — a feat which caused him to fume with silent fury. Besides, Otieno, Owuor's younger brother had wasted no time in marrying two wives one after the other and already had two children and was expecting two others. The fact that his children were completely lacklustre and unlike Obura was completely beside the point. His wives were completely colourless as well but since he firmly believed that all women were the same this did not matter either.

Nyar Asembo, Owuor's mother even got the council of *Jodongo* to meet and advise her son over the matter. He smiled in his usual enigmatic manner, thanked them and informed them that he would ponder over the matter. How could he tell them that since he married his wife, he had profoundly lost interest in all other women? She was unafraid of him, and spoke candidly on almost any subject. She also had an acerbic but witty tongue, which unless she was angry with him, rarely ever failed to make him laugh. Besides her advice on most matters was sound and he formed the habit of going over to her hut after the evening meal just to hear her talk. However, a monogamous man was an unknown animal and every man worth his salt tried to marry at least two wives. The chief had vast cattle wealth, so he could have any number; but he seemed more eager to get wives for his brother and an assortment of poor cousins than for himself.

Obura came home one morning from his grandmother's hut, where he had fallen asleep the night before expecting that somebody would carry him home as usual. Apparently they had placed him carefully on a pallet and then forgotten all about him. He arrived home still sleepy and very hungry and found commotion.

"Where is my mother?" he demanded.

Nobody heard him.

"Hey! Where's my mother? I want my mother! I am hungry!" This time somebody heard him and put a gourd of gruel and sweet potato in his hands and ordered him to go back to his grandmother's house.

"I will not! I want my mother!" he screamed.

"Will you take that child away from here!" yelled his grandmother from the other room. One of his many aunts grabbed him and ran out with him, legs and arms flailing. He was thereafter held prisoner in his grandmother's hut for another two hours. He wisely gauged the situation and decided resistance would be useless. However, he refused to eat his breakfast despite much pleading from his aunts.

Later his grandmother came for him and informed him that he had a sister.

"A sister?" Other people had sisters and brothers. He was over four seasons old and had been alone all that time. He dashed out past his grandmother and made for his mother's hut. There she was, carefully placed on some soft skins in a corner. He smiled in wonder and touched the baby.

"Careful!" hissed the ubiquitous aunts.

"Let him see his sister," his mother said gently. She was exhausted. She had not had an easy time with Obura but this particular delivery had been a nightmare. The baby had lain badly and was trapped. She lay there gripped in agony as the midwives tried to turn the baby. After an eternity, they succeeded and the baby arrived blue and puffy and with the cord around its neck. That was terrible. They struggled to release it, sweat pouring from their faces. Then the baby would not cry. It lay there terribly blue and simply would not cry. Someone grabbed it, turned it upside down, slapped its bottom twice and eventually she let out a yell to equal her mother's twenty four seasons before. And then the mother began to haemorrhage. The midwives struggled with her and when they were about to give up, the flow slackened and eventually ceased. Everybody heaved a sigh of relief. For a while there, it had looked as if both mother and daughter were goners.

The great chief Odero Gogni had recently died and his daughter had felt really cut up. Therefore when *Were* provided her with a daughter she did not wait for a dream. She took a unilateral decision and named the baby Odero, much to the consternation of her mother-in-law who had a relative or two lined up. The baby was not only pretty but had her father's even temper. Indeed it was only when she was quite ill that her voice could be heard in anything but happy laughter. She met one and all with such a sunny smile that she soon earned herself the name Nyabera, the good one. Her mother did not have to worry about baby sitters for young girls lined up to hold the baby. Obura was very jealous for he would have liked to have more of his sister to himself. So protective was he that he once nearly bit off the finger of a villager who had joked that he would take the baby away.

Nyabera thrived and had a personality to charm the birds off the trees. She was also very bright and in no time at all was giving the hitherto unchallenged Obura a run for his money in riddles and story telling.

Chapter 4

So Akoko had two wonderful children but the chief was still under pressure to marry especially when it became clear that she was one of those women who found it hard to conceive regularly. "The first time must have been a lucky shot," grumbled Nyar Asembo. The pressure became very intense when Nyabera turned four and her mother remained confoundingly slim. She still had a beautiful figure which of course went totally unappreciated.

"My son, what if some ill-wind took your only son!" Nyar Asembo was now reduced to wails, lamentations and dire predictions. Once she so forgot herself as to declare that Nyar Yimbo (Akoko) had bewitched her son. She would never, ever live long enough to forget that terrible day. Her daughter-in-law, a relentless worker, had been out in the field all day, so it was not until evening that she got wind of the matter. She calmly made the evening meal for the children, cleared up and everybody went to bed.

At first light, as was her wont — for she was an early riser, she woke the entire village with wails and screams. People rushed out of their houses to the chief's homestead thinking that it was the chief or his son who had died, for in either case it would have been Nyar Yimbo's duty to raise the alarm. When a good sized crowd had gathered, she stood just outside her house and spoke with a loud voice.

"I Akoko Obanda Nyar Yimbo (daughter of the people of Yimbo) came to the homestead of Owuor Kembo, chief, as a pure girl nineteen seasons old. In all that time I was taught nothing but the ways of *Chik* and how to conduct myself as a woman of impeccable birth. Never in all that time did my mother or my father take me out in the dark for the purposes of showing me how to cast spells or to brew love potions to snare the hearts of men. I was taught that the way to keep a man was by the work of my hands and the words of my mouth. Obanda my grand-uncle was a great healer, after whom many children are named. He was known to harm no man and frequently sent off those who sought trouble for others with a flea in their ear.

Has anyone ever seen me gossiping with other women at the water hole? Do I always not rise early to till my lands? Have I ever begged for food from you my mother-in-law as all your daughters-in-law do? Do I not always have enough to eat and more left over to barter in exchange for cattle, goats and sheep? (Indeed the size of her herds had become quite impressive).

Children are a gift from *Were* both to the deserving and the undeserving. Do not even murderers, witches and sluggards who cannot even feed themselves have children? Should I spit in the eyes of *Were* like a snake and deny that he has given me children? *Were* creates a child in its mother's womb in secret, in his own time and at his own volition. I have not stood in the way of my husband and other women. He is the chief and I can not order him either to marry or not to marry.

Much has been said by the daughter of the people of Asembo (*nyar* Asembo) and her son Otieno about the thirty head of cattle that were paid to my father as a bride price. It causes them much bitterness that I have not borne thirty children in exchange for those cattle. Indeed my continued presence here is bitter aloes to them. Therefore I shall lift their gloom and suffering and depart from here to go back to my father's house. Be it known that my father was a wealthy man before receiving those cattle and would have remained wealthy without them, for none of my twenty-one brothers is wifeless. Be it noted also that the wealth I have created in this home is more than double the number paid for me. This everyone knows. Therefore when I reach home, I shall request the council of *Jodongo* to convene proceedings for a separation. My people will give back your cattle and you will give me back mine."

The crowd hissed; such a thing was unheard of. Didn't a man own a woman body and soul? Marriage was sacred and *Chik* saw to it that it remained that way by a series of taboos that made it almost impossible to sever the union. However, the insult had been great. To accuse someone of *juok*, witchcraft, even in jest was an unforgivable crime. And there had been precedents, if the woman and her people were determined enough to get a separation. The people of Yimbo were a proud lot and their love for their daughter was known all round for they always came out in massive support of her at various ceremonies and functions. The only saving grace would be the high esteem in which they held their son-in-law, Owuor Kembo — the chief.

"And where might he be?" Inquired someone, so taken up had they been by Nyar Yimbo's oratory that they had failed to notice his absence.

"He went to a friend's funeral the day before yesterday and is due back today. Meanwhile I will teach this she-wolf a lesson." This from Otieno her brother-in-law. She looked at him straight in the eye and hissed "Just you dare!" He retreated at the pure venom in her eyes. Besides, he was afraid of his brother who had added scandal to all his other sins by failing to ever lay a finger on his wife.

She left without further ado and her children, forgotten in the confusion ran after her. This would never do. She turned and gently but firmly ordered them to go back and await their father's return.

"But mother..." started the argumentative Obura.

"No buts! Just go back and do as I tell you." She left them and went swiftly on her way. The crowd stood mesmerised for a while before departing also.

When Owuor Kembo returned from his journey he found an empty house. His mother and brother tried to bluff it out but he eventually got the full story from willing villagers and his children. Nobody, but nobody had ever seen the chief so angry. He almost struck his mother, a great taboo, and throttled his brother half to death before reason reasserted itself. Then he locked himself in his *simba* for a day.

His mother muttered to herself about such unseemly behaviour in a full grown man, but was careful to keep her voice low. The following day he called for the council of *Jodongo* to convene.

"My fathers", he began. "It is a shameful thing for my wife to leave her husband's house and return to her father's house. This outrageous thing has occurred only because I was not here to prevent it."

"Our chief, we are all saddened by this unfortunate state of affairs, but you must admit that your mother has a point or two. Long have we pleaded with you to take another wife for yourself and you have adamantly refused. Now she has left you, you are like a *misumba*, a bachelor which would not have been the case if you had another wife. We beg you take another wife for yourself." This was from Oyier, a grizzled old man who had been his mother's greatest champion in her quest for a wife for Owuor. He realised that the old geezers were going to give him a hard time of it, so he changed his tactics.

"Fathers, you are the wise men of this community. That is why you sit in the council. Is it that you have forgotten the ways of *Chik* or that your determination to get me to marry other wives has clouded your judgement? Do you not know that a man's *mikai* is the greatest jewel that adorns his compound? That her position is maintained and protected by taboos imposed by the ways of *Chik?* That if I die, *Were* forbid, my body can only lie in state in her house, before I am buried on the right hand side of her hut? And this would be so even if she herself were dead? To lose one's *mikai* is to lose one's right hand."

The *Jodongo* nodded sagaciously at the wisdom utttered by the chief. It is true that the *mikai* is the centre post that holds up a man's hut. Without her, or if she were stupid, only *Were* could rescue such a man from being blown away from among the people like so much chaff. She it is who saves a young man from the follies and stupidities of youth. Indeed the people of Ramogi had a saying which declared that 'The medicine for stupidity is marriage'. Yes the chief had spoken wisely. But Oyier would not give up so easily.

"Son of Kembo and father of young Kembo, what you say is only the truth. But can a house be built with only one pole however strong it is? Others are needed to give it support. What would you do if an animal attacked you and you had only one arrow in your quiver and you missed with the first and only one? Consider the welfare of your people. If not for yourself at least get another wife for their sake so that you are assured of enough heirs to guide them in future."

"Fathers," countered Owuor, "I already have an heir and besides, Otieno, my brother has six sons already and he also is the blood of the first chief, Maroko Otuoma our great great grandfather."

"Son of Kembo, our chief. May I first of all point out that even though Otieno is of the blood, the spirit of Maroko, great and fearless warrior and a just man, just does not rest upon him. Besides you know that fullness of spirit usually rests on the first born who is therefore empowered by *Chik* to receive all the good fortune which will naturally overflow to the people."

"In that case, I have every reason to thank *Were* for he has not disappointed me in my first born. Let us therefore make haste and send a delegation to Yimbo to plead our case so that the mother of Obura may return to her own house. I am certain that we will have to take a sizeable fine to appease her people, but I do not begrudge her this as the wealth in my house has multiplied under her care."

The council dispersed with Oyier muttering something under his breath; something about the uselessness of wealth without children.

The following day four young men were given a cow and an ox, a he-goat and two nanny goats to drive to Yimbo to smooth the way for elders who would later go there. They were told to take a message of good will and gratitude to the people of Yimbo for the good *dak* which had hitherto existed between the people of Yimbo and the people of Sakwa and the great *wat* which had been forged. They were to inform their hosts that a delegation of elders would arrive on the twenty third day of the moon to discuss the serious and unfortunate thing which had occurred.

They were received cooly and were it not for the fact that *Chik* stated clearly that a messenger should not be victimised in lieu of his senders, something terrible might have been done to them. After the lightest of meals, they took their leave and returned to their clan.

Chapter 5

On the twenty third day of the moon, the chief and seven *Jodongo* arrived in Yimbo to negotiate the return of their wife. The reception was chilly, but everything concerning as delicate a contract as marriage had to be handled according to the most stringent dictates of *Chik*; and *Chik* clearly stated that both sides of the story had to be heard before a decision could be made.

They were shown to the council hut, a grass thatched round building whose walls were only half way covered. The entire council of *Jodongo* was there, waiting. The absence of *kong'o* was evident for this was a grave matter and no drinking was allowed, unless and until an agreement was reached. Aloo K'Olima, now a very old man was still the spokesman.

"Brothers, people of Sakwa, we greet you. Never once did I imagine that I would have to sit in such a distasteful council and of all people, over the eldest daughter of our late chief, an exemplary woman. However, it is not for mere man to know what disappointments the future holds; but before I am found guilty of favouring one side over the other, let me call the woman to speak first as she is the complainant."

Akoko was brought in, with her mother and aunt in tow.

"My granddaughter, fourteen days ago you arrived here alone and unaccompanied from Sakwa. You made a complaint concerning them to your brother, the new chief, who in turn reported it to us, but you have to repeat everything here before us so that all may see that we are open and have nothing to hide. You may speak."

"My fathers, from Yimbo and Sakwa. I thank you for your kind patience. May I state from the outset that leaving my house was a great wound in my heart and that I had never even thought about it until the night before it happened, and this in spite of the abuse and insults heaped upon me by my mother and brother-in-law.

I have always been taught that honour and pride in oneself and one's people were of the utmost importance for one's sense of being, for as the wise men tell us, 'How can you know where you are going if you do not know where you come from?' I therefore felt it was a great insult to my honour and pride to be accused of witchcraft against my own husband who has been good to all of us and has conducted himself most honourably as a good *or*. I have nothing against him and I know that he is by nature not a contentious man; but we cannot live in peace unless he finds a way of curbing his mother's and brother's tongues. I have been accused of having wasted their wealth because I have only two children. Now who in this assembly can tell me how to create a child within my womb? Is that not the premise of *Were*, god of the eye of the rising sun? I have been accused of standing between my husband and marriage to other women by weaving a spell over him; but as *Were* is my witness, I have never trodden on the path of charms and love potions. I did not find it necessary. It is not my place to order the chief to marry or not to marry. I am pleased, of course, that I have found favour in his eyes these ten seasons, but he is free to get a co-wife whom I shall then treat as my own sister. Who knows but that *Were* may favour her with more sons than he has me? My fathers, that is all I have to say." She sat a little aside from the gathering next to the women who had accompanied her. There was a hush during which the only sound that could be heard was that of weaver birds busy at their task. Then Aloo cleared his throat in a manner to suggest that a pot of *kong'o* would have come in handy to smooth his voice at this point.

"*Ahem!*" said he. "My child you have spoken clearly and well. Brothers you have heard for yourselves. The accusations include *juok* and uncalled for insults from the in-laws. The first is a very grave matter as it reflects on the character of our daughter and ourselves. The second is unpleasant but insults never break bones. May the *or*, chief Owuor Kembo please stand and tell us what has so displeased him with our daughter as to cause him to allow her to leave her matrimonial home? No man should allow his wife to leave her house without at least trying to prevent it, so you must tell us your side of this sad affair."

"My fathers, wise men of Sakwa and Yimbo; I am profoundly apologetic over this whole matter. On the day when your daughter left my house I was away on a journey, otherwise this terrible thing would not have occurred. However, I have always treated her well and we have lived in peace and friendship. For this reason I find it difficult to believe that she could leave her home without at least waiting for me to return, however great the provocation — since she knows I have always stood by her over the last ten seasons. This behaviour was very rash and irresponsible especially since she left in full view of the children. I have already dealt with the two people who are responsible, but I think that should you find it in your hearts to bring this matter to a speedy end, then you should warn your daughter about the dangers of rash decisions. That is all,my fathers." Owuor sat down again.

There was a short silence as everyone had expected him to continue for much longer with many protestations of innocence. Then everyone started talking at once — one side less indignant and the other side feeling that Owuor should have used stronger words. Aloo clapped his hands loudly twice for order.

"Brothers! Brothers! Let there be peace and understanding. We have not come here to throttle each other but to listen to each other. Owuor has spoken words full of wisdom. That we must accept if we are to be fair. He has neither said too much nor too little — the sign of a truly wise man. The insult to us and our sister was grievous; but it is now clear that it was from people who do not matter to us directly. After all who knows the goodness of a tree but he who sits under its shade and eats its fruits? Besides Owuor assures us that he has dealt with the ones who brought this matter about. I hope he has found a way of preventing a similar episode from occurring again.

As for Akoko, I have known you since childhood. I know all your virtues, but your weakest point is your temper and impatience. You must know that you are no longer a child to follow your temper wherever it leads you. Soon you will be a *maro* with a son or daughter-in-law of your own because children grow so fast. You must exercise self-control. The fair thing to have done here would have been to wait for your husband to see his stand before making a decision. In future please think before you act.

I, Oloo son of Olima, have listened to both sides of this matter and I have decided that the son-in-law shall bring a goat to appease the *maro* — Akoko's mother, and that tomorrow morning Akoko shall go to Sakwa with her husband. May *kong'o* be brought so that libation might be poured to *Were* god of the eye of the rising sun."

They thereafter feasted and drank together and good spirits were restored to all. The following morning they started out at dawn for their matrimonial home.

Chapter 6

By great good fortune and to the relief of the chief, Akoko conceived soon after her return. He had hoped that he would get some respite from the many oblique statements about his monogamous and one-son state. Not of course that anybody talked about it openly and definitely nobody referred to his wife about the matter, for events were still fresh in the people's memories and everyone knew that there was no wrath like the wrath of an even tempered man; but one can talk without talking, and the people of Ramogi were masters of that wily tongued act.

The pregnancy was uneventful but once again the birth was harrowing and Owuor found himself wishing fervently that no more children would come. The child was a boy and everyone uttered a sigh of relief for the chief. Two rocks were definitely an improvement on one. They named him Owang' Sino after a famous warrior of the clan and he bore a startling resemblance to his father with whom he became friends from the first moment his eyes opened and he saw that black face with its wide cheekbones, big nose and brilliant white teeth. The baby crowed with pleasure whenever his father came within vision and predictably his first word was *baba* — daddy. Compared to his chatterbox brother and sister, Owang' was a welcome respite for his mother. His demands were few and he was as easy to please as his father.

Even by the standards of the time, it was a close knit family, with the father standing resolutely between the world and his little band that everyone so longed to enlarge. In fact he was well pleased, for his father before him with many wives also had what he had achieved with one wife — two sons. His brother on the other hand had made up for Owuor's reserve. He had four wives and eighteen children. The gap between the brothers had widened considerably. This was worsened by the fact that Otieno was a weak man who seemed to have a knack for marrying one shiftless wife after another, with the result that he was almost entirely dependent on his brother. This he took only as a rightful due which could not have been too bad had he not been extremely jealous of his brother whom he also hated with venom. In his heart, in spite of his many wives, he desired his brother's wife who seemed to get younger every year instead of older. Even his youngest wife who was still in her teens could not compare with Akoko, with her flawless skin and still very trim figure kept so by hard work. Otieno treated his wives like sluts and they did not fail him. Owuor treated his wife like a queen and she did not fail him either.

The seasons ran into each other swiftly and silently and soon the children were half grown. However, the world was no longer a quiet, peaceful and predictable paradise. Rumours and whispers had reached this far, of happenings which were strange, to say the least. A footloose wanderer by the name of Ambere K'ongoso who went as mysteriously as he came had brought stories of *Jorochere*, white skinned people who now ruled most of the land. Their magic was incomprehensible for they could kill with a mere puff of smoke and a bang from something that resembled a pipe. Instead of walking they used swift moving little metal houses which had eyes that shone like the moon at night. And wonder of wonders, they were building a long snaking metal line in which it was said that a contraption which looked like a caterpillar carrying many goods could move. They were on the whole a strange people, avid and arrogant.

People only half believed Ambere's stories. When he next left, a young man called Nyaroche left with him. He stayed away for almost a season. They came back with many exciting stories about something called *pesa* made of small flat round pieces of metal which could be used to buy anything.

"And where does one get this *pesa* from?" asked Obura now a strapping lad of sixteen just on the threshold of manhood. He was already six feet tall, very quick on his feet and with his mind. He was curious about everything and learned everything with equal avidity. But he was very restless and were it not for his mother who did not take kindly to people who dodged their duties, he would have spent the whole day listening to the exciting stories of Ambere and Nyaroche.

"Well you work for a white man or for an Indian and he pays you with *pesa*." How easy. Obura was not afraid of work — his mother had seen to that. His questions flew thick and fast until Nyaroche said to him,

"Why don't you come with us next time?"

"What, me? What nonsense! You know that I am next in line to be chief; I can't just leave my duty and go walking about!" All the same he was curious and he kept coming back for more. One day he broached the subject with his mother to whom he was very close.

"Mother do you know that I am almost seventeen seasons and I have never been anywhere except

Yimbo to see my uncles?"

"And where do you want to go, my son?"

"Oh anywhere. See the world and what other people do, how different from us they are," said Obura chewing reflectively on a blade of grass.

"Then I advise you to marry a girl from Chumbu Kombit. I understand you have to walk for almost five days before you reach there," said his mother in jest.

"Oh mother you know very well I don't mean that. I won't marry until I am at least twenty four seasons old. There is no hurry. Besides I won't marry until I meet a girl exactly like you. Girls can be so empty headed."

"Obura," remonstrated his mother, "It seems I don't give you enough work. Only an idle mind can think up such nonsense. You are the chief's son. It is your duty to marry as soon as you can and provide grandchildren for me. Besides, only *Were* knows where this world begins or ends for he made it; you could walk for the rest of your life and not reach its end. Now go and help the herdsmen with their task. You have become such a lay-about."

That evening Akoko spoke to her husband about their restless son.

"My chief, do you know that that shiftless Ambere and his useless friend Nyaroche are filling your son's head with idiotic ideas about seeing the world?"

"Seeing the world?"

"Yes, he has decided that this place is not world enough for him."

"Is that so!" exclaimed Owuor, rather startled for like most fathers his son's fast growth had crept on him almost unnoticed. The next day he took Obura for a walk, ostensibly to go and examine a distant herd of cattle.

"My son."

"Yes father?"

"How old are you now?"

"Almost seventeen, father."

"Really! And look at you — you are a man already. You have grown very fast my son."

"Thank you father."

"I think you should start looking for a girl, my son. I will send out *jawan'gyo* to all clans of Ramogi which are not consanguineous with us, to look around for a suitable *mikai* for you."

"Oh no father!" Obura was quite taken aback, he was just not ready for marriage.

"Yes my son. I myself learned the hard way. My father died and left me a bachelor, a sad state of affairs indeed for I had to go and negotiate by myself for your mother. Believe me the sooner the better."

"But father! I am so young. I don't know anything. I feel it would be better for me to go out and see the world before I settle down." There! It was out in the open now.

"My son," Owuor tried to swallow his disquiet. "You are practically my only son, for your brother is hardly seven seasons old. Do not take your duty so lightly for the chiefdom has been in my family for generations. All young men feel as you do. It will go away and you will realise that what I am saying is true."

"Father, even if I go away, you can trust me to come back. I would like to see the *Jorochere,* the white people and their magic. Maybe I might even make some *pesa* and bring many useful things from out there. I hear these people also have powerful medicines for any fever. Please give me your blessing and let me go."

"No my son. Anything else but that. It would be tempting fate. Maybe when you are married and have children, I might consider it. Now you are too young to know what you are asking of me. Please forget these things that those two lay-abouts are filling your head with."

Later the chief called Ambere and Nyaroche and warned them of dire consequences if they did not stop filling his son's head with their stupid talk.

Chapter 7

Obura never brought up the subject again, but his parents were uneasy for he was not himself. He had moods which could not be explained away by his imminent manhood. He was increasingly reflective with eyes turned either inward to his thoughts or outwards and far away to things which no one else could see. His mother prayed fervently to *Were* to make the evil spell pass, to give her back the happy boy she had known before.

A season passed. One day Obura came home very late and for the first time in months he was friendly and relaxed. He appeared to have reached a decision. His mother was too thankful to mention the hour. She gave him food and he went to his hut.

The next day, the sun rose and hung warm and red in the sky, but Obura who had lived under his mother's adage that the sun should never rise and find a man still asleep and was therefore an habitual early riser, did not make his appearance. His mother thought that maybe he had slept late because he had gone to bed late and was therefore not alarmed; but as she was getting ready to leave for the fields, there still was no sign of her eldest son. She sent Nyabera to go to his hut to rouse him. Nyabera went and stood just outside the door and shouted.

"Obura! Obura! *Chiew* !" There was no answer. She shouted louder, but still there was no answer. She then banged on the door. No answer. She pushed on it with her hand and it flew open easily. There was no one in the hut.

"Mother!"

"Stop shouting you mad child! What is it?"

"He is not here." Akoko arrived on the spot almost before the words were out of her daughter's mouth. Sure enough, he was not there. His things were neatly put away as usual, almost as if nobody had slept in them. Maybe he had left early for the fields; but he had the appetite of a starved lion and had never been known to miss breakfast. Besides he always informed his mother of his whereabouts or likely whereabouts before leaving so that a messenger could find him easily.

The chief came out of his *simba* at the sound of the commotion.

"What is all the noise for so early in the morning?" he asked alarmed.

"Obura is not in his hut," said his mother.

"And he has not eaten his breakfast," supplied his sister.

The chief came to see for himself as if other people's eyes were not good enough, but there was no denying it. The boy was gone.

"I would not worry," said he as if to reassure himself. "A boy his age can be very thoughtless. Maybe he decided to go hunting on the spur of the moment and forgot to tell us." He led the way out of the hut. Akoko was so afraid she could hear her heart drumming away in her chest.

"Great *Were*, please spare my son. Protect him. Remember all the sacrifices I have offered you on his behalf and be merciful." She prayed fervently to herself fearing to raise her voice in case the very air grabbed her words and made her fears a terrible reality.

The chief sat in his hut for a while in deep thought for he was not one to act rashly. Then he called his herdsman and briefly gave him some instructions.

The herdsman came running back within an hour.

"My chief! My Chief! They are both gone. They left last night before the first cockcrow. And, and…," here he stammered and then stopped.

"And what you fool! Tell me!" The chief, a man never known to raise his voice almost screamed at the hapless herdsman.

"Yes my chief! Their families said that they heard them talking to a third man just before they left, but they did not see him because it was very dark."

Akoko fell down in a deep faint. Nyabera ran to her mother screaming and held her head. The chief started barking orders to a group of people who had now gathered to find out the cause of the commotion.

"Get the scouts, except those on watch. Tell them to prepare two search parties — one to take the route of Gem and the other to follow the route of Asembo. Maybe we can intercept them before they reach very far."

The search parties were hastily formed, each consisting of twelve men well trained in tracking game. The groups started out together but separated at the edge of the village.

They were gone for two nights and two days and while they were gone, Akoko lay prostrate on her papyrus pallet. She dared not sleep for she was haunted by nightmares. She was beyond even praying to *Were* and she lay there hour after hour staring, dull eyed , into space. Her children hung around her, trying to make her eat but to no avail. Sometimes she said something to herself but try as they would, they could not catch her words. The older women watching her feared for her sanity for everyone knew that this was her son just like the younger was his father's. He had been the only seventeen year old in the whole village who ever obeyed his mother without question.

On the evening of the third day the scouts trooped in, dejected and beaten. They need not have talked for their failure was evident in their very bearing but a report had to be made nonetheless.

"We greet you our chief," they said formally entering the chief's *simba.*

"I greet you, young men," he also answered formally. "What news do you bring?" he asked as if it was not self evident; but good manners is the fabric that holds the community together.

"We, that is those of us following the route of Gem found their trail. We followed it up to the second village of Gem and lost it there. The people told us that white men came there every three moons to get people to work for them. They put people into those moving metal houses you have heard about, which move so fast, there is no knowing where they might be by now. So we came back because there is nothing further we could do." A low moan from the direction of the main hut was heard, the first sound in three days from that poor suffering woman. Her voice rose as she keened in a high tone, a lonely, lost sound; terrible to hear. It was almost as if the boy was dead, not just lost. The fearful premonition of doom that only a mother, closely connected as she is to the child, can sense , was in the air.

Chapter 8

The days came, dragged slowly by, and eventually went as days are wont to do when misery and apprehension hang low and oppressive in the very air. The children crept by, hardly daring to make a noise, sensing without being told that what had happened was too terrible to be talked about. The mother hardly said a word, and the chief at the best times a man of few words was no better.

The relationship between a chief and his people was usually not authoritarian. His main job was to lead the council of *Jodongo* in their arbitration and their final word was law. He was also a sort of priest, for on public worshipping days he led the whole community in sacrifice and libation. The people held a good chief in high esteem and usually sent a son to help in the chief's household especially in herding cattle, but this was voluntary. The women once in a while gathered together to help the chief's wives till the land. This was also voluntary, but people did it gladly. In turn their chief was ready to listen to their problems at any time of the day or night. He also led them (not sent them) to battle, or if he was too old, his eldest son.

Apart from the people's sheer incomprehension at their chief's stubborn monogamy, Owuor and his wife were held in very high esteem and were much loved by their people. Everybody shared in the chief's grief and fear for his son. Besides they loved Obura in his own right. He was open, bright, cheerful and was never known to take advantage of his position and to lord it over others. He did not shun work. He was also very brave and on the whole everybody had been secure in the knowledge that the next chief would be a good man. To get rid of a bad hereditary chief was possible but not easy and might involve actual bloodshed. For the people of Ramogi, bloodshed even in battle, was a great taboo and required much cleansing, for the angry dead know no barriers, and they might come to confound you long after you had forgotten them. So it was good to know that the future would be in the hands of a good man. His disappearance was a cause of concern for all.

A whole season passed. Another one also marched inexorably and was almost drawing to a close. In the world outside, which Obura had wanted so much to see, the white man whose avidity led him to even count seasons and what's more to remember them, said that this was the one thousandth, nine hundred and eighteenth season.

"Since what?" someone asked.

"Since their god had a son," replied one in the know.

"Their god had a son!" exclaimed the ignoramus. "What sort of madness is that?"

"You don't know the half of it, my friend. This son of their god died to save them."

"Save them! From what? I think you are leading me on. Where did you hear this anyway?"

"I keep my ears open, my friend, I am not like you who sleeps on both your ears. I keep one open and sleep on the other one!" The man in the know laughed mysteriously and went away. What a strange place the world was becoming with white people and their dying god! The man in the know did not tell his ignorant friend that the white men of the tribe of *jo-ingreza*—the English had been hard at war with the white tribe of *jo-jerman* — the Germans for the last four seasons. What's the use of talking to a man whose sole occupation was to sleep on both ears?

One day, when the warm humid air lay too wet and heavy even to breathe, with hardly a breeze from the great lake to stir it, a strange man in a long garb reaching down to his ankles and a red head dress that for all the world resembled a *tao* — fish dish — arrived in the village and asked for the chief. He was accompanied by another one whose mode of dress defied description for nobody had ever seen shorts, leggings and a skull cap before. The children, clothed in nothing but the love of *Were*, god of the rising sun, and a string of beads, came running to see for themselves these weird creatures. They were at first amazed, then amused. If it wasn't for the ugly looking stick that the second one was wielding, they would have tried to touch the strangers' clothes for their fingers were obviously itching to do so.

The heavy air was split with sounds of amazement and laughter.

"*Wololoeloyaye !*"

"*Mama yoo !*"

"*Biuru une!* Come and see!"

The strangers were taken to the chief's house and the older people saw that their faces were solemn. They couldn't be bearers of good news.

"We greet you, O chief Owuor. We are people sent by *sirikal*, the government, with a message for you," the white garbed one who was obviously the spokesman declared.

"And who may I ask, is this *sirikal* ? I've never heard of him," said the chief baffled.

"You may have heard that the country is being ruled by white people now. They with the help of some black people have formed something like the council of *Jodongo*, only much bigger, to make sure that everyone lives in peace according to the new law. This is *sirikal*."

"Is that so?"

"Yes that is so. Now over the last few years, a clan of white people called *jo-jerman*, started a war with everybody in the world joining in and taking their side or the side of our white people the *jo-ingreza* who have eventually won this war. Now to help them, many young men from all over this country were taken. Three of them came from your village and we have brought tidings of them." Everybody held his breath. Now perhaps they might hear about Obura and those ne'er do wells who were the cause of all this. The man waited but the chief said nothing, he just sat there looking at them. Only three men were missing from his village and one was his son. What could he possibly say?

"The names of the three are Obura Kembo, Ambere K'ongoso and Nyaroche Silwal. They went to fight the *jo-jerman* in a place called Tanganyika, a country of black people ruled by *jo-jerman*. Of the three only Nyaroche Silwal survived and he is..." The chief stood up too stunned to talk, but his jaws were working and the mouth frothing. A wail went up and was caught by those who heard. The rest came rushing to find out what was amiss. Above and between the sound of wailers an eerie sound was heard once again. It was the keening mourn of the bereft mother. The chief finally found his voice.

"I will kill that son of a dog. Where is he? Tell me where he is. He has killed my son. He has to die." The man seemed to know what exactly the chief was talking about.

"He lost a leg in the war and is now a beggar in the great market of Kisuma. I doubt he will ever come home again." They then presented the chief with a bracelet which they said was sent by the white people as a thank you and in memory of the fallen men. He hurled it aside and it was later picked by Nyabera who hid it. The two men left and disappeared back into the bush from which they had arrived so unceremoniously.

The village went into mourning for the chief's son. It was made worse by the fact that there was no body to mourn over and to bury. The people traditionally gave vent to their emotions during funerals but this was not easy without an actual body to keep one's fury up. However, when the mother came out of her son's hut with his spear in her right hand and his colourful ox-hide shield in her left — the traditional salute to the fallen warrior — the whole village raised its voice as one. They wailed, sang dirges and young men staged mock battles with each other in his memory. This went on for four days after which a banana trunk was symbolically buried and the people dispersed to their homes except for the close relatives.

There are two ways to deal with pain — either bear it until time heals, for time is a master healer of even the deepest wounds; or commit suicide. Since the latter was a great taboo and would have brought a great curse among the people, for after all *Were* gives life and only he should take it, the bereaved family had to bear their loss as best they could; but it was not easy for so much hope had rested on their fallen son.

Chapter 9

Nyabera who was fourteen at the time of the news of her brother's death was deeply affected by it. She would not weep or grieve for him and she wandered away by herself, mute and quiet, for days on end. She was at a particularly difficult period of life for she was pubescent. So silent did she become in her sorrow that her mother had to snap out of her personal grief to pay some attention to the living. She herself had lived long enough to accept that there was nothing permanent in this world, that even the strongest were so fragile as to be blown by the merest puff of wind.

Her therapy was simple for there is no greater psychologist than the one who graduates from the hard school of life. She simply talked about her son loudly and within the earshot of her daughter. She narrated his birth, the inexpressible joy of being a mother, what a demanding baby he had been, how clever he was, how delighted he had been when his sister was born, how he had carried her out to play as soon as she could sit; how he had taught her to walk with many tumbles, falls and tears; how fun-loving he had been. "Remember the day he came home with a beetle with its legs tied up with a string? The poor thing buzzed madly trying to escape and you laughed so much that you got hiccups!" A strange strangled sound — a cross between a moan and a gurgling laugh rose from the corner where the young girl had been sitting mutely for the last hour. Then the releasing tears came at last and she wept with heaving pain for her lost brother — cut off midstep, in the full flower of his youth. What manner of people were those *Jorochere* to take such a young man, hardly more than a boy, to go and fight in a war he knew nothing about? He had probably thought it would be a great adventure, and a chance to see the 'world' he so longed to see. Dead and gone, never to be seen again, or engaged in an argument or verbal wit, laughed with or just taken for granted knowing that he was around somewhere. She wept late into the night and only dropped off, exhausted, at the hour when the crickets sing loudest and fireflies flit here and there flashing their glowing torches.

Even the heaviest rain eventually ceases and after four days Nyabera ran out of tears and looked around her to discover with some amazement, that life went on as if nothing had happened. *Were* looked down at the world with one fiery eye; the ancestral spirits stirred in the air, whipping it into a playful whirl that picked up sand and leaves and hurled them into people's faces. There were colourful butterflies, light as feather, but so awkward in their flight as if drunk on *kong'o*. She noticed these things and wondered. How could such common place things continue to happen when the chief's heir lay dead and unfulfilled in some strange land? *Were* should stab the world with lightning, the sun should hide its face, the very trees should moan in misery. She herself should die, for of what use was this life if one could be snuffed out like a poorly lit fire, never getting a chance to blaze into a flame?

But she did not die, slowly but surely the wound healed and soon there was only a scab and even that fell in time leaving only a scar — for there must always be something in memory, a little disharmony, a barely visible break in the continuity of the weave of life. She unearthed the bracelet from where she had buried it and took to wearing it on her arm along with her bangles. There were some marks on it which held no meaning for her, but had she known how to read, this was what she could have deciphered:

OWUOR, OBURA KEMBO: KAR MIA 1918

The initials for Kenya African Rifles and missing in action in 1918 — the first big war.

The family had been touched by tragedy and tragedy can sometimes be a habitual drunk who keeps coming back for more. Things would never be the same again though the girl did not realise it then.

Growing up under the tutelage of a woman such as Akoko was a demanding job. She believed that a young woman had to be intelligent, fast on her feet and hard working. Intelligent because according to her, stupidity in a woman was a sin only greater than stupidity in a man, for a man can always find an astute wife to cover his folly, but there is no man born who can cover a gaping hole left by a foolish woman; fast because *Were* in his wisdom gave only so many hours in which to get one's work done and time never waited for any one. And hard working because the greatest eyesore in the world was an idle woman.

"My daughter, should it ever be said of you that you are as lazy as your mother, I will turn in my grave."

Nyabera was a very popular girl for she was generous to a fault. She always had a gang of children at her heels who she insisted should share her meals. God knows there was enough, for by now her mother's wealth was staggering even by the standards of today. Her herds were so vast that it was necessary to build a special dam for them separate from everybody else's. It was said of the herds that should they get to the water to drink before you drew your water then you had to wait for almost two hours before they drank their fill. And to this day if you go to Sakwa near Ndwara Village and ask for *Yap* Obanda (Obanda's dam) it will be shown to you.

Not only was she rich in cattle but her granaries were full to bursting so that during the lean season, people coming to barter their cattle in exchange for food were rested and fed fully before they were given grain to take back to their villages. Everything Akoko Obanda touched simply thrived and multiplied. It could therefore be noticed that her jealous brother-in-law and his entire family hated her to an epic degree. They could barely hide their joy when Obura died and their fingers itched to lay hold of that coveted wealth. Otieno by now had twelve sons, the eldest of whom was ready to marry. He had married off his eldest daughter at barely sixteen but the bride's wealth paid for her simply evaporated in that greedy household. So eyes were being cast on Owuor to provide the cattle. After all he practically had no sons of his own so why not extend the largesse to his nephew?

As Nyabera approached her eighteenth season, suitors started to call. Some arrived with good intentions, but some who knew the situation of the family were simply young men on the make — for human nature is the same the world over.

Akoko decided that she would not allow her daughter to go through what she herself had gone through. Besides, the death of her son, the apple of her eye, was still too raw on her heart. Three suitors came and went. The fourth one, a young man from the next village by name of Okumu Angolo, nice enough but whose main attraction was that he would not take his bride too far away from her mother, was chosen; and Nyabera left to start her own life and hopefully a large family.

Nyabera and Okumu got their first child within the season. The baby did very well for the first six months. Thereafter she sickened, with many bouts of fever, jaundice and swelling of the tummy. She died at the age of two years in spite of herbs, poultices and potions.

The second child was a boy, Sidande and he appeared to be well. The third child was also a boy who though sickly was still hanging on to life and appeared to be getting stronger with time.

Okumu was a good man, rather overwhelmed by his wife for he had never expected his suit to be accepted, as he was not rich and he could barely raise the bride price with a great deal of struggle. He would have had nothing thereafter, but his bride came with a sizeable herd of cattle, sheep and goats as her dowry. She was very pleasant about it and never rubbed in the fact that he was poor. He suspected, correctly that his main attraction lay in his proximity to the bride's home. He did not mind so long as she did not neglect her duty to go traipsing off to her old home and this she never did for she was very industrious. Besides every time she needed to go, she would ask him in the nicest possible way; not of course that he could have said no. He was a lucky man and he knew it.

With the birth of her third child, Nyabera's marriage settled onto an even keel and she began to lose the sense of insecurity which first developed at her brother's death. The two surviving children were very well and life rotated between work, family and the much looked forward to visits from grandmother Akoko.

Meanwhile her younger brother Owang' Sino, who was almost nineteen seasons old and now the chief to be, had had spies sent out in search of a suitable bride. Though lacking in the abundant charisma that his brother had had, Owang' Sino was a good steady lad with a level head and a lot of personal strength. He tried to the best of his ability to step into his dead brother's shoes and to heal the sorrow in his parents' hearts. One of the things he wanted to do was to marry as soon as was practicable and get children to gladden his mother's heart—for with his brother dead and his sister married he was alone at home. Besides, the old chief now approaching fifty was mysteriously ailing. He had never really been well since his son's death nine years before, but he was now getting worse.

A suitable girl was eventually found in Uyoma and a delegation was sent to negotiate but before the bride price could be paid the ailing chief Owuor Kembo died and all negotiations were suspended as the clan went into sixty days mourning mandatory for a chief. Akoko mourned her husband with solemn dignity. She donned his monkey skin headdress that he had come courting in almost thirty years before, took his spear in one hand and his shield in the other. She sung dirges in his honour with her powerful voice carrying well into the village. She sang of his famous courtship of her, the great honour he had accorded her throughout their life together, the friendship that had existed between them.

"Women have given birth to sons
But none are like Owuor
The son of Kembo, of the line of Maroko
My friend, my husband.

Men live with their wives
Like cats and dogs, ravens and chicken
But not the son of Kembo
My friend, my husband.

When I first set my eyes on him
So tall. So handsome. So full of *nyadhi*
My heart was smitten within me
By my friend, my husband.

My father demanded thirty head
And the son of Kembo did not demur
Paid up like a real man
My friend, my husband.

Yes women have had sons
But none will ever be like Owuor
The son of Kembo of the blood of Maroko
My friend, my husband."

This and many others she sung throughout the day and the night until they buried the chief. She was forty-seven and strong with it.

When the mourning was over, the negotiations continued and at the end of it Alando *nyar* Uyoma was brought home to her husband. Akoko, remembering her own mother-in-law, welcomed her daughter with open arms. She leaned over backwards to accommodate her weakness some of which she found very irritating like her tendency to idleness. Had they made a mistake? However, all was soon forgotten in the excitement that followed her becoming pregnant, and when she delivered a son, the first baby in that house for over twenty years, all was forgiven. They named him Owuor after his grandfather.

One night, when the baby was just starting to walk, a commotion was heard from the direction of young chief Owang' Sino's personal hut. This was followed by a scream then another. Akoko dashed out of her hut and made for her son's hut. The sight which met her eyes made her blood run cold with pure horror. There he was sprawled on the floor, both hands around his neck, face contorted beyond description. It was obvious he was choking. His meal of fish and *ugali* lay spread out before him. His wife it was who had screamed after her various attempts at intervention including the swallowing of chunks of *ugali* and banana to dislodge the stuck fish bone failed. His mother just stood there completely petrified. A herdsman dashed in, turned him over and started thumping him between the shoulder blades all to no avail. Owang' Sino died with his disbelieving mother staring at him.

Which is worse, to have a son die away from home or to have one die before one's very own eyes? Like her daughter before her, she was beyond tears, beyond action. She stood in that hut for two hours, not moving, not talking, as people milled around her, trying to comprehend the magnitude of her loss.

Nyabera was summoned immediately, dark as it was, to keep her mother company. She in her turn was not tongue tied this time round and she kept up a bemused, if angry soliloquy.

What has she ever done to deserve this? Does *Were* really exist? Why does he permit such terrible things to happen? She who has never looked at anyone with an evil eye, never denied food to anyone; has she not been generous in sacrifice and libation? Does it not pay to lead an upright life? Why does *Were* give children only to strike them dead at the threshold of life? What has Mother ever done to deserve this. She looked at her dead brother — still her baby brother in her mind. He had been chief for less than two years; had tried hard to live up to a duty he was never trained for. A good man, so like his father; steady, dependable, unassuming and always there.

They buried chief Owang' Sino with due honours and he rested with his ancestors, and for the first time in seven generations, the chiefdom descended on the shoulders of the younger son — Otieno Kembo as *Chik* did not allow a baby to rule unless he was on the threshold of marriage. A chief had to have a wife and it would be many years before the happy toddler Owuor, even understood the meaning of marriage.

Chapter 10

Otieno Kembo took over the chief's stool with glee and sat on it with heavy arrogance. He appropriated his brother's wealth and tried to grab his widow's personal wealth as well. He married two new wives almost in a breath and his excesses were surpassed only by his folly. He dispensed even with the venerated Council of *Jodongo*.

When the struggle for wealth and power reached bitter proportions, Akoko decided that the time had come for the battle lines to be clearly drawn. She knew that as a woman, a widow and a sonless mother, the only male in her direct line being a little baby, she was greatly disadvantaged. She had to get support, massive support from elsewhere, and not being one to forget things easily she remembered now in her hour of need that at the time of her eldest son's death, a messenger had been sent by *sirikal* — the government. Once or twice since then, tentative messengers had been sent to try and make contacts with chief Owuor Kembo, but being full of bitterness because of his dead son Obura, he had sent them away without a word. Young chief Owang' Sino had started to make overtures on his part towards the outside world, but had died before his efforts could bear fruits. The new chief was interested in nothing but his stomach and his pleasure.

She felt the weight of injustice that women have felt since time immemorial in her male dominated world. Even a half-wit like her brother-in-law could rob her of her hard earned wealth, and her grandson of his rightful position as the chief, for in all truth Otieno should have held the chief's stool only until the infant Owuor came of age, but it was now clear he had no intention of ever giving up the chiefdom and after his death, his numerous sons would make sure that it stayed in the family. Owuor would be outnumbered practically by infinity to one. As it was, his grandmother feared for his life and watched him like a hawk. It was disquieting to have all one's eggs in this one tiny frail basket.

After pondering over her predicament at length Akoko decided to make contact with the *sirikal* and seek their intervention. The first thing she did was to remove her two year old grandson and take him back to her brother, Oloo in Yimbo. His mother had meanwhile married one of the numerous cousins. In any case she was not the sort of woman to fight for her rights, leave alone her son's. All she wanted was a husband and some security, and who could blame her? After all not everybody could be like Akoko.

Before she left she went to see her daughter Nyabera who was in mourning again having lost both her sons to a ferocious outbreak of measles which had raged through her village during the last harvest. She was pregnant again but so downcast and depressed that she stayed in her house, rarely going out and hardly eating. She needed help and her mother decided to spend some time with her before leaving.

She found her daughter thin to the point of emaciation with her belly sticking out before her like an appendage. When she saw her mother still unbent and uncowed by suffering, looking like a woman half her age, she just broke down and wept in her arms as if she was a little girl again.

"Cry my child, for one does not bury a child without burying a part of one's soul with it. It is good to cry for who can comprehend the ways of *Were?* It is for us men to wash away our painful confusion with tears and then to carry on, perhaps there might be some meaning in it all that only glimmers like a firefly in a dark night. Who knows but that one day *Were* will give you a child that lives and grows? Yesterday is not today and today is not tomorrow for each day rises fresh from the hands of *Were* god of the eye of the sun, bringing with it gladness and sorrow, sun and darkness, the two faces of *Were;* for how can we appreciate light unless we understand darkness? Weep my child and do not hold pain within yourself for it will turn into a snake that devours you from the inside."

When Nyabera eventually calmed down, she sat her mother down and gave her some food. As she ate, Nyabera talked to her about this and that, her face and eyes looking animated for the first time in months.

"You know mother, I've been having the same dream almost every night."

"What dream, my child?"

"It's about Obura, we are both children and he comes with that funny beetle on a string and as I start laughing the beetle escapes and lands on my shoulder. I try to brush it off but it turns into a beautiful bird the colour of the sky and then flies off. As we watch in amazement, the same bird comes back leading many others which fly around our head, but as I turn to look for my brother, I find he is gone and I am alone at which point I wake up. What do you think it all means mother?"

"How long do you say you have had this dream?"

"Let me see. I would say soon after Sidande died. I was in the sixth moon of pregnancy then, so it must be about two moons now since it all started."

"I think your brother is trying to tell you something. To bring you a message of hope from the spirit world. However, an ancestral spirit does not pick on a pregnant woman without a reason. So the dream is intimately concerned with the unborn baby. May *Were* find it in his heart to fill our hearts with laughter again."

"In that case should I come safely through, I shall name the baby Obura."

"A good thought my daughter. May both your brothers and father watch over you to bring about a safe delivery of a fine child," invoked Akoko. "My daughter, I have decided to go on a journey."

"A journey, mother? Where to?"

"A journey to the bartering market of Kisuma."

"That is a long way away mother. I hear that it is at least a seven day journey from here. And it is a strange place with odd looking houses and some *Jorochere*, who must look very funny indeed. How can you trust one who is so white like the clouds. Maybe they are not even human, mother."

"Now Nyabera. I don't believe a daughter of mine could sound so foolish. Of course they are human, that is why they are called white people, not white animals. And trust is something to give to people who have earned it and therefore you have to give them a chance to do so. I would not trust your uncle Otieno although he is as black as the bottom of the pot I boil maize and beans in. Finally you'd better know that I aim to get some help from them against Otieno. The future of your nephew Owuor is in their hands so start praying."

"Oh, mother! Please don't go! What if something happened to you? I am afraid mother, I am so afraid! And how can you leave Owuor alone considering the kind of irresponsible mother he has? Oh, mother, sometimes I feel as if this family is cursed. What if something happened to him, to you?" Nyabera wailed, her tears running in full force. Akoko stood up to her full height which barely reached her daughter's shoulders. Her eyes were blazing fit to send sparks to set the thatched roof ablaze.

"Nyabera, you are not the woman I brought you up to be. I know you have suffered, but suffering is the lot of many. To suffer is not a curse unless you have earned it and I have never done anything to earn a curse. Both the evil and the good suffer. How you come through suffering is what will make or break you. Please think, my daughter. At least you can have children and you have a good husband. One day *Were* will give you a child that lives; I am sure of it after what you have just told me. But to have a child is one thing, to bring it up to be a human fit to live with others is something else altogether — and the way you are going, I doubt if you will be fit to be a mother when the baby comes. You may be just like Alando your sister-in-law. You have known me all your life. How could you ever imagine that I could leave my grandson at the mercy of your uncle? I've taken him to Yimbo to live in the house of Oloo, my brother. Are you happy now?"

"Oh mother! Why didn't you bring him here to stay with me? Don't you trust me?"

"Of course I trust you. I thought of bringing him here, but I decided it was too near the nest of vipers who now occupy the stool of Maroko, the first chief. Please can you show me a place to rest? I will be staying with you for a few days before I leave for Kisuma. That way no one will know or suspect my motives." Nyabera conducted her mother to her mother-in-law's house as *Chik* did not allow her to spend the night in a married daughter's house.

The next few days passed pleasantly enough, with mother and daughter chatting for hours about their lives, their people, their past, their future, their hopes and all manner of things. On the fifth day she embarked on a journey which would bring her and her scant offspring to a new era; for the great river starts its journey as a little stream which at first meanders around without any apparent direction, sometimes disappearing underground altogether, but always there, always moving towards the sea.

Chapter 11

In those days any long journey was hazardous for the world was untamed and wild animals abounded. Also one might wander accidentally into hostile territory. Especially feared, much more than the animals, were the Lang'o tribesmen who enjoyed killing and maiming, for its own sake. Oloo therefore sent two of his sons to accompany his sister for whom his heart constantly bled. Her strength and courage in the face of blow after devastating blow left him full of painful admiration.

"You Opiyo and you Odongo, you will accompany your aunt Akoko on her journey. If anything happens to her please don't come back for I'll hold you responsible. You will go a day before she leaves your cousin Nyabera's house, join up with her there and travel with her to and from Kisuma. You understand?" Of course they understood. When old Oloo spoke, it was wisest to understand; and where his sister was concerned it was mandatory to understand immediately.

"Yes father. We understand. We will do as you say." Odongo the younger twin was the mouthpiece of the identical duo. Opiyo the older twin was the man of action. They were twenty and not yet married. They made haste to Sakwa to meet their aunt who was far from delighted to see them.

"And what, may I ask are the two of you doing this far from home? Have you turned into vagabonds or something?" she asked.

"Er, er...," began Opiyo trying to find his tongue.

"Actually, father ordered us to come. We are to keep you company on your journey to Kisuma," said

Odongo smiling at his aunt whom he liked greatly.

"What! Are you crazy or is he? I will have none of it. Go back this instant before I throw something heavy at you!"

"Apart from the fact that we would like to come with you, we cannot go home because your brother has made it quite clear that our lives would be in danger. So throw whatever it is you want to throw and then we'll get on with it," replied the unflappable Odongo smiling even more broadly.

"Actually, aunt you know you need protection and I promise to keep Odongo quiet so that he doesn't annoy you too much," Opiyo eventually found his tongue. Akoko had to laugh at their youthful enthusiasm.

"Oh, all right, though I think Oloo has gone crazy. I am an old woman of no consequence to anyone. He really shouldn't have sent you."

"Aunt you will never grow old. I think you will die young. And you will always be of consequence to everybody back home!"

At cockcrow the next day, the usual hour for starting a long journey, the three started out on their epic journey. It was still very dark but they walked surefooted as only those who live in the bush country can. The dewy grass slapped moistly against their swiftly moving legs and trees and tree stumps rose suddenly out of the darkness making grotesque shadows out of the great shadow of the night. The trees whispered conspiratorilly at each other and once in a while an owl hooted, or some animal called its mate, or a hyena laughed hysterically at the night. For all their bravado, the young men would have been at least a little afraid were it not for the calm confidence that Akoko exuded.

When there was a little light and one could reduce one's vigilance a little, Akoko started to recite the history of the people of Ramogi. This was not just a pastime but a bounden duty — for the history of the tribe could only be transmitted by mouth from generation to generation, else how can you know where you are going unless you know where you are coming from? Therefore whenever an elder was alone with a young person, he or she always recited the history of the tribe or clan.

"In the beginning, *Were* was alone in the world which was beautiful. *Were* is a spirit and a spirit is like a flame, you can only see it, but you cannot get hold of it. It is like air which you know is there but which you cannot touch. It is like the wind which can uproot a tree and hurl it afar but has no substance. It is like lightning which is seen in many places at once but is in none. Yes, it is like the essence of man which makes him all that he is yet departs from him quietly and suddenly leaving only a dead image. *Were* is a great spirit. He saw that the world needed more than spirit forms. So he created Ramogi and his brothers who were men. Man has a form which is spiritual. *Were* sent the men he had created to various parts of the world to settle in it. Ramogi he sent to the country around the great lake which was a great favour for he had more spirit than his brothers. The wife whom *Were* gave him was called Nyar Nam who embodied the spirit of the great lake. They had many children including Rachuonyo, Sakwa, Asembo, Yimbo, Gem, Uyoma, Nyakach, Seme and Ugenya among others who settled around the lake, tilling land, taming animals and catching fish. These are the children of Ramogi from whom we all arise.

Of the children of Ramogi many great brave men

have arisen. They are called, *thuondi* the brave ones. These men of renown include Lwanda Magere. So strong and brave a warrior was he that it is rumoured that the sharp spears of Lang'o warriors could not pierce his skin. Then there was Gor Mahia, the wily one who could change his form in to anything at all, thus confounding the enemy. There were many others, great leaders and warriors and women of renown such as Lela Kabanda, the mighty warrior, Onyango Randar—man of war, Ogutu Kipapi, great warrior and my direct ancestors, Tawo Kogot, Obando Mumbo, Oracha Rambo, and the woman Nyamgondho of mighty wealth. There are many others whom we should aspire to imitate."

She continued in that vein with the twins interjecting a question now and again until they reached the borders of Gem where they rested for the night. They started out again from Gem through Asembo and Seme and on the sixth day they were in the outskirts of the Market of Kisuma. There they saw what they thought was a white man. His hair was straight and black and his skin was nut brown. He was sitting inside a tin structure within which were rows and rows of strange looking items.

"He is not very white, is he?" asked Odongo.

"Er-no, he is not" replied Opiyo.

"Our cousin Alando is much lighter than he is. Why do you think they call them white men then?"

"I don't know." The man in question was an Asian. Akoko summoned a passer-by.

"Greetings. May the day be light."

"May the day be full of light."

"We are strangers, all the way from the savannah country of Sakwa."

"Welcome strangers. What is your destination?"

"We are going to look for the big chief of the *sirikal* in the market of Kisuma."

"Oh!" he noticed that she was dressed in the traditional skin called *chieno* and the young men in skins covering only their loins. They both had spears and shields. He himself was in a pair of long shorts and a singlet— the height of civilised fashion. He had also gone to a mission school for one year so he was an educated man. The year was 1930 according to the white men who kept such a close track of seasons. Enlightened he might be but he was still African enough to accord hospitality on demand. These were evidently primitives straight out of the bush.

"Oh I see, but we no longer call the place Kisuma. The *sirikal* has changed that to Kisumu. Also the big white chief is called a DO he..."

"A *diyo*?" asked Odongo mesmerised.

"Yes, just about that my young friend," replied the man condescendingly. "He rules with the help of a tribunal of elders. Mother, why don't you and your sons come to my house then I will take you to see the DO tomorrow. I work there but to day is a Sunday, the day of rest so the DO is not working." They followed him silently quite overwhelmed by events. What could one say faced with a chief called *Diyo* which meant squeeze? What might he want to squeeze, their brains? So they followed the man quietly until they reached his house which was, thank *Were*, a round mud hut with a thatched roof. It however had square windows made of wood and a neat wooden door all painted bright green. Evidently, here was a man who was really with it. His wife fed them, made them comfortable and finally provided them with papyrus pallets to sleep on.

They rose early the next day for it was still a long trek to the centre of the town. As they walked the buildings grew larger and odd looking. Most had white walls and red roofs. Others had tin walls, and rusted roofs. Some were traditional. There were many people milling about in the streets, some of which were paved with small stones. Their host had advised them to leave their weapons at home.

"Nobody is allowed to carry weapons anymore."

"Why is that so?" asked Opiyo who felt lost without the weight of a spear in his hand.

"Because the *sirikal* has *askaris* now to protect everyone and keep the peace."

"And what is aska — whatever you called them?" asked Odongo. He whose tongue was so swift did not take kindly to words around which it couldn't get.

"Oh, the bottomless pit of ignorance," thought the man to himself.

"*Askaris* are men who are armed and given authority to arrest anyone who breaks the law. They wear special clothes so that everyone can tell them apart from the rest of the people."

Eventually they reached the District Officer's office and were stopped by two *askaris* at the gate.

"What business have these people with the DO?" asked one of them rather brusquely.

"They have a complaint to lodge with the tribunal. It is a very serious matter involving a chief so they have a right to see the DO". Their host must have been sent by *Were* himself to smooth the way. How else could they have managed, handicapped as they were with their lack of words? They were eventually let in and their host led them to the clerk who filed their case for the tribunal. Now if their host was with it, this clerk was quite beyond it. He wore a dazzling white shirt, a thin black tie and *khaki* shorts. On his feet were brilliant white shoes. His hair was parted sharply down the middle almost as if he had used a geometrical instrument to do it. Stuck in his hair were several pencils and pens. He was a creature completely beyond comprehension although his skin was black and the words from his mouth recognisable. Later they would learn that he was an erudite man with four years of white man's education behind him. He could speak the language of the white man as well as his own and was therefore an interpreter — an ego boosting job for he held both sides in his power. After he had lodged the general nature of their case, they were told to return in three days.

Chapter 12

The big white chief, the DO, sat on a chair apart. On his right hand was the tribunal and on his left the complainant. In the middle stood the all powerful interpreter.

"May the proceedings of this tribunal begin and may God save the King," intoned the DO. The twins looked at him with interest. He was actually white — not cloud white, but an undefinable translucent colour with spots of red on the cheeks, the ears and the tip of his long nose. His hair was an amazing yellow and wonder of wonders his eyes were blue. Nevertheless he was human and spoke with a human if strange voice — rather resonant with an unusual timbre, somewhat harsh to the ear.

"Great chief, I am a widow. My husband was the chief of Sakwa. We had two sons. The first one who would have been chief died in the big war of the white people. His brother also died accidentally soon after taking over the chief's stool. He left one child, a son who is but a toddler. For this reason my late husband's brother has taken over the chief's stool supposedly in custody for my grandson. However, it has become clear that he has no intention of relinquishing that seat; what is more he has grabbed all his brother's wealth and is now at war with me, trying to grab my own personal wealth as well. He feels that being a woman I deserve nothing. Now if this is allowed to happen, what will my grandson use to pay the brideprice and reclaim the chief's stool? May *Were*, god of the rising sun (the interpreter translated that simply as God) give his wisdom to you so that you can decide this matter fairly. Thank you." She sat down.

The DO was lost in thought for a few minutes. He had lived in this part of the country since the end of the war and he was well aware how deeply these people were steeped in their tradition — they called it *Chik*. *Chik* governed every aspect of the life of the people. It was the glue which held the people together, thus preventing disintegration of the fabric of society, and chaos. Without *Chik* to tell each person where he fitted in the exact order of things, where he came from and where he could expect to go, there would be confusion and apprehension. Very few rebelled and were outcast, cut off from the people like a branch from a tree. The majority were glad to avail themselves of the surety it offered; to do and to be done by.

According to *Chik* the brother should have married his brother's widow and become guardian of the grandson and custodian not owner of the chief's stool. Animosity must run very deep in that family for this not to have been done. He cleared his throat and spoke.

"This is a very deep and serious matter which cannot be decided in one sitting. May a team be dispatched to the village to further investigate this matter. Then the woman may bring her appeal in three months to the visiting District Commissioner. Next case."

Akoko and her nephews left the tribunal and went back to their benefactor's home. They discussed the DO's decision.

"You mean there is a bigger white chief than this *diyo* ?" Odongo asked.

"Looks like it," replied the twin.

"Don't you think he should have decided? Aunt's case is after all so clear."

"Maybe he should have taken a longer time to think."

"He probably does not understand the way of *Chik*. After all he is white."

"My sons," said Akoko. "Do not decide the wisdom of a man by the brevity of his quiet or the multitude of his words. It is only a wise man who can decide quickly that he doesn't know and needs to seek more knowledge. A fool knows everything. It is only a wise man who does not hide his folly behind many words. I think this *Diyo* will help me."

Later that evening their benefactor whose name was Otuoma told them of the DO's conversance with the ways of the people.

"Have no doubt, he will deal fairly with you because he knows right from wrong which is more than you can say for some white people. The DO has lived in this place for thirteen years. It is customary for difficult cases to be heard more than once, so that the truth can be fully ascertained. You just go home and come back in three months. People will soon be sent to hear for themselves what has been happening in your village."

So at dawn the following day Akoko left for Sakwa with her nephews who later would relate the tale of their adventures to their less lucky peers, later still to their own children and grandchildren. The tale took on mythical proportions in the telling, with their aunt assuming the greatness of the foundress, Nyar Nam, and they themselves joining the great braves of the tribe, at least in their own imagination.

"When my brother and I took my aunt to make an *apil* (appeal) to the big white chief whose name was *Diyo,*" would begin Odongo to some round eyed grandson many years later, "we found and overcame many dangers on the way for our courage was boundless. Our aunt walked with her head high for she was the daughter of a chief and the spirit of her ancestors rested fully on her. She faced the white chief unflinchingly, and told him her story, the greed and arrogance of her brother-in-law Otieno, chief by default."

When she got back home, Akoko found that the plunder of her cattle had reached major proportions, the chief having taken advantage of her heaven sent absence. Her first impulse was to storm out and do murder, and be done with it, but reason soon reasserted itself. There was no advantage in knocking one's head against a tree trunk, at best one may chip off a bark but in return get a large bruise on the head. If you want to cut a tree, take time to sharpen an axe. So she bided her time.

The DO kept his word and within twelve days, his messengers arrived. They came so unobtrusively that even Akoko did not get wind of their presence until two days later and the careless chief four days later for most people did not bother to keep him informed due to his extreme arrogance. By the time the chief heard that there were people nosing around his affairs, they were on their way out. He was furious. He summoned Akoko who declined to go. Having no sense of the dignity of his position, he went in search of her and stood fuming and frothing at the door of her hut.

"Are you behind all this you stupid woman? Are

you? Tell me, are you? I will kill you. I will whip you and send you back to your village!"

"Go away you fool," answered she, quite calmly. "Are you the village chief or the village fool? All the same if you want to fight I am willing to oblige. You may be twice my size, but I have three times your courage."

The chief had never gotten over his fear of his brother's terrible wife. He believed that she had powers, else how did she hold such sway with his late brother? He retreated yet again, still frothing at the mouth. Who knows, he might yet do everybody a favour by having a fit and dying! She smiled enigmatically at his retreating back.

Thereafter Akoko did not have to wait for the three months decreed by the DO for he sent a messenger and two *askaris* to escort her to Kisumu to make her appeal before the DC within the month.

The second journey was much easier for the quest was now supported by the *sirikal*, and the messenger knew the quickest way to Kisumu, but Akoko insisted on staying with her old host Otuoma.

The DC was a white man all right but was as different from the first one as east is from west. His hair was reddish brown and his eyes were very pale grey. His skin was tanned so deeply that it had almost taken on the hue of some light skinned black people. His voice was a loud trumpet— almost as if shouting would make people understand him better. He exuded power and authority, for a section of the country almost the size of Wales from where he came was under him. He embodied law and the government. The tribunal was brought to order.

Akoko was asked to stand and repeat her

complaint which she did. The messenger was called to give his findings and he cleared his throat importantly, rubbed his fat nose and said:

"Bwana District Commissioner, Sir, I went to the village of this woman. It is the seat of the chief of Sakwa and all its subclans. I found everything just as the woman said for the chief is bad and is hated by his people who were more than willing to talk. The chief was supported wholly by his brother, having dissipated all his inheritance. Tradition decrees that he should be nothing but guardian to his brother's name and property and if his brother left a young widow, to sire children on behalf of his brother so that the name of his brother may continue to live among the people. He has done none of these but instead has plundered his brother's wealth and the only male offspring of his brother, the grandson Owuor has to live in exile with his granduncle for fear of his life. I think that the chief should be made to give back what he has taken and be removed from the chiefdom. That is all sir. Thank you."

"How old is the grandson?" inquired the DC

"He is only two years old, sir."

"Who else has the power to rule apart from the chief."

"In fact a chief only rules through a Council of Elders, not directly. However, chief Otieno has done away even with this council and makes decisions by himself."

"How does tradition provide for the removal of a bad chief?"

"*Bwana* DC, Sir. The chiefdom is hereditary and passes from father to his eldest son. If there is no son, the closest male relative. If the son is not yet of the age of marriage, then the chiefdom is held in custody by the closest male relative with the council of elders. When the rightful heir comes of age, he ransoms his seat with twelve head of cattle, the price of a bride, payable to the custodian. If he cannot ransom his seat within two years of getting married, then the council of elders may decide that the seat remains with the custodian, for the chief must be both married and a man of some means. A bad chief may only be removed by a unanimous declaration of the council. If he does not leave peacefully, force may be used. That is all, sir."

"The complainant Obanda Owuor, also known as Akoko has convinced this tribunal that an injustice has been done. Therefore a contingent of *askaris* shall go to the village and forcibly remove the chief. He shall be made to return all that he has grabbed from his sister-in-law and his grandnephew. A council of elders shall forthwith rule the village until such time as the rightful heir comes of age. The council may elect one man to be a custodian of the chief's stool and their spokesman. The matter is ended. Next case."

In spite of the DC's decision, it was only a matter of time before the hereditary chiefdoms were done away with totally. It was a changing world.

Akoko returned to her village having won more than a victory for her infant grandson. She had opened up new vistas for her family, which showed another world and the possibility of a different way. She talked about her journey to her daughter Nyabera, who sat on a mat nursing her new born daughter; she drank in her mother's every word.

"You know my child, human beings are all the

same the world over, with good ones and bad ones. The bad ones serve to high-light the goodness of the good ones. To allow oneself to sink unresistingly into evil is a bad thing. Take those white people, they are not of my colour, or of my blood but they are just; but your uncle is ruled by his stomach and directed by his loins. He forgot everything that his brother had ever done for him and his greed turned into vindictive hatred. It would have been something if he had worked to support his appetites, but he is lazy. Laziness opens the door for evil to rule one's mind and body. Work tirelessly my child. It is a shame for an able bodied person to feed off the sweat of others. It becomes like a sickness of the blood which transmits itself to generations and becomes a curse forever."

Akoko left the clan of her husband Owuor and returned to Yimbo with all the property she had salvaged from her brother-in-law, Otieno. It was a mighty herd which moved in three cohorts. Of the three children she had borne, there survived only one; of the grandchildren only two still lived; and she dwelt in the household of her brother Oloo. She was fifty seasons of age, a middleaged woman. Sometimes she remembered how it had been and this was painful, for now she, a *migogo,* was reduced to living with her brother. She wondered how long it would be before his wives started making insinuations, but she did not allow herself to descend to bitterness; for yesterday is not today and today is not tomorrow. Each day rises fresh from the hands of *Were* and brings with it whatsoever it will.

PART II

THE ART OF GIVING

Chapter 1

At the time Akoko went to make her appeal to the DC her daughter Nyabera gave birth to a little girl whom she promptly named Obura after her brother, but she had already lost three children so a little ceremony was performed to confuse the evil spirits and to enhance the child's chances of survival. The midwife took the baby, wrapped it up in a soft kid skin and placed it at the main gate then kept watch at a distance. Sure enough an old woman soon came up the path and found the baby. The woman knew immediately the significance of the phenomenon for those were not the days when babies were left to die by the roadside or worse, thrown into pit latrines. She let out a wail:

"*Uuwi! Uuwi!* I have found a baby! Someone has thrown away a baby! *Owite! Owite!*" She picked the baby up and came with it into the compound.

"I have found a baby just near the gate. Someone must have thrown it away. Since it was near your home it must be the will of *Were* for you to keep it. Here." She handed the baby to its mother. The baby was forthwith named Awiti (feminine for Owiti—the one who had been thrown away). Even with all that Awiti's mother was still afraid for the baby, but year came and year went and the baby, plump and sturdy grew and survived every childhood insult and illness. She appeared determined to live. Nyabera got pregnant again when Awiti was three years old but she miscarried. Then real disaster struck. Her husband Okumu, went down with a sudden fever. He complained of severe headache, pain and stiffness in the neck and he could not retain any food. He died within three days of the onset of the illness.

Nyabera mourned her husband in shocked disbelief. Her mother arrived with the speed of lightning to her daughter's side. She was afraid, extremely afraid for her child, but she need not have been, for this time she had an ally who brooked no resistance — the little girl Awiti, who was approaching four. She asked questions and demanded answers. She had a trick of staring straight at one, with eyes which startlingly resembled her grandmother's until an answer was forthcoming.

"What's wrong with *baba*?" she asked. No answer.

"Mama, what is wrong with *baba-na*?"

She could repeat one question ad infinitum until an answer was given.

"He is dead!" choked her mother.

"What is dead?"

"It means that he won't come back again. He is now a spirit"

"Is a spirit a good thing to be?"

"Yes!" Choke! Choke!

"Then why are you crying *mama*?"

"Because I miss him!" Choke!

"Then why don't we become spirits— you and I? *Baba* must be missing us also." Nyabera looked at her daughter and had to smile in the midst of the disaster — her entire life seemed one big disaster. She was twenty-six, a widow and sonless. It was her mother's life all over again. The word 'cursed' insinuated itself again in her mind but looking into her daughter's eyes she had to push it away. She was a beautiful child, full of vivacity and spirit and even at that age vitally alive. "I must fight. I cannot give up! I must! I must!" thought her mother. She might never have another child, but for this one everything had to be done for it was clear that she was determined to live.

To be a widow and young was an untenable situation. A husband had to be found from close relatives of the dead man, but such a man had no real rights over the woman, his job being that of siring children to maintain the dead man's name and to keep his widow from wandering from man to man (a scandal). This was called *tero*. Even the children he sired did not belong to him — therefore he was under no obligation to provide for them. His duty was to his own wife. So in reality instead of being protected the widow was left in a sort of limbo. Nyabera felt that here *Chik* had erred, the first time such a thought had ever passed through her mind. However, she had not reached the point of rebellion. A husband was found — a second cousin to the dead man. His name was Ogoma Kwach and he wandered in and out of her life as the spirit and his wife directed him. They had two children both of whom died—this time if they had known it, of sickle cell disease.

Nyabera was an attractive woman and once she had made up her mind to fight, the spirit of her mother descended upon her. The man sensing strength started to spend more time at her house than his wife's house. Besides, Akoko had given her daughter a considerable portion of her wealth before taking the rest to Yimbo. The man had hitherto been quite poor and he was determined to at least give Nyabera a son if it killed him. That way he felt that he could at least have a foothold on all those beautiful herds. She would be beholden to him. He therefore neglected his wife shamefully. The wife reported the matter to the Council of *Jodongo*. The man was called and reprimanded.

Nyabera felt full of bitterness and she decided that a change was necessary. For her there was obviously not meant to be the comfort of a husband and children around her knees. When it came to making ruthless decisions, she equalled her mother. She would cut herself off from her people. She would seek another life, a different way. She had had enough. For the first time she felt quite lucky to have a daughter. A son held one under much more obligation than did a daughter for he must be firmly rooted in his people from whom he would inherit land and from whom he was inextricable. You might wander the world with your son but in the end you had to take him back to where he belonged — his father's people. A girl, on the other hand, was a wanderer who would settle anywhere and marry anywhere. Nyabera felt free to go.

Now in that village, a man had once come dressed in a white robe and speaking of a new God who made meaning out of sorrow and suffering and who particularly liked the poor, the orphan and the widow. The man said the latter two were poor in spirit, for having no earthly support, they could better trust in God. In fact he said that this God so loved people that he had sent his only son to live, suffer and die like man. Nyabera had had to leave at that point to attend to her chores. In any case she had only listened with half an ear, but having a retentive mind, she had occasionally mulled over his words wondering what he might have meant. Two villagers had gone with the man — one a barren woman who was totally neglected by her husband; the other a man, one of the footloose types found in every village. The man returned a year later sporting a new name — Pilipo —but what he said made no sense and no one took him seriously. The woman never returned.

Nyabera looked up this man and talked to him at length using his new name, much to his delight. His tongue was further loosened by a pot of beer and a tough looking cockerel which rolled its beady eyes in disbelief each time the man launched into the different parts of his tale.

"Pilipo," began Nyabera, "I know you are a much travelled man. You have learned the new religion of the white man and in gratitude they have given you a new name."

"Yes, yes!" replied Pilipo reaching eagerly for the pot. "But I can tell you it is hard. Very, very hard. I failed several times to answer the questions they asked me but eventually I got the hang of it."

"Were they kind?"

"Yes, very kind but they made me work so hard." Pilipo did not like work at all.

"What did they teach you?"

"Hard things my sister. I doubt a woman could understand them."

"You mean there were no women?"

"Er...er... of course there were women. In fact there were more women than men."

"So what did you learn?"

"Er ... about a God-man called Kristo who was the son of God, his father. He came to die for our sins, to save us. His mother was called Maria — and she was very pure. They said something about God being three but only one but I didn't understand that very well."

"What else did you learn?" asked Nyabera relentlessly.

"Er—I don't remember the rest very well. There were laws which said not to kill, not to steal and to take only one wife. The laws were too hard for me so I came home."

Nyabera tried to get an accurate direction of the mission from him and eventually left him to his beer, much to his relief. The unbelieving cockerel was executed soon after and placed in a pot of stew for his supper.

She made several arrangements. Most of her cattle she left to her mother-in-law who had been a good friend; she took the rest to Yimbo to her mother along with her daughter Awiti who was about seven. She consulted at length with her mother.

"Mother, I have decided to seek the new religion which you have heard about. You know my life is a painful wound to me and much as I try my heart fills with bitterness — for me, and also for you."

"My child, do not feel bitterness for me for I am an old woman who has lived her life. As for you it is better that you seek this new way. It might give you hope and rescue you from bitterness. Bitterness is poison to the spirit for it breeds nothing but vipers some of which might consume your very self. Pain and sorrow all humans feel; but bitterness drops on the spirit like aloes—causing it to wither. I give you my blessings my child. If you are walking along and you find your path leading nowhere, then it is only wise to try some other path."

"Thank you mother. I will bring you news as soon as I can. May *Were* protect you."

Nyabera left the two dearest people to her with a heavy heart but determined feet and made her way to Gem to the already famous mission of Aluor to hear the words of the new religion of Kristo. Life is a puzzle and a mystery and the living human mind spends it in yearning, for what it knows not; but search it must.

Chapter 2

The journey from Yimbo to Gem was through thick bush. Nyabera started out at dawn and did not reach the mission until dusk. Earlier, she had joined herself to a band of travellers for safety, but the journey itself was uneventful. She was taken to the chief catechist's house where she spent the night. People like her in search of a different way of life were a common sight in that house, so food was provided without much ado.

The following day Nyabera spoke to the catechist.

"Teacher, I have come a long way to learn the new religion. I am a widow with only my mother and my little daughter for relatives. What do I do to learn this new way?"

The catechist, a tall bony man with jutting eyebrows, deep set eyes, a full beard and thick fleshy lips looked at her, not unkindly.

"Woman, many come in search of the new way but few can keep it for it is not easy for the faint hearted. It will mean that you live under a different *Chik* from the one you know. However it is not for me to discourage you for God loves us and has called all of us to listen to his Son Yeso Kristo whom he sent to live with us as a man and to show us the way to God. The teaching of religion is done every morning. Every once in a while, the teacher will test you to see whether you have understood. Naturally, some people understand faster than others. When you have fully understood and you agree with those things which you have been taught you receive the *batiso* (baptism), during which you will become a child of God. Because each child born has to receive a name, you will be given a new name."

"Teacher, I have come a long way for this. I doubt there will be a going back. I have nothing to go back to."

"In that case I will take you to the school right away."

As they made their way to the school, Nyabera drank in the new sounds and sights. The houses were made of stone, some whitewashed, and some bare, with red and green metal roofs. The church was beautiful with coloured glass in the windows and a tall cross, which the teacher called the sign of Kristo, towering above it. There were bells in the steeple for *Angelus* — the prayer which the teacher said reminded men three times a day that God had chosen to be born of a woman just like us and had dwelt among us. It was being said in a strange language which she would later learn was called Latin — the old language which once united all Christendom.

Suddenly listening to all this Nyabera knew that she had made the right decision. She was filled with hope. She was only thirty and had been on the threshold of despair. It did not matter that she did not understand the language. Some feelings go beyond words.

Later this affirmation of the central teaching of Christianity would become her favourite prayer, her consolation and her source of strength. That God would deign to be a man! That He should choose to be born of a woman! A woman! One would think that He would have chosen to be born of the unilateral efforts of a man; but no, a woman it was. Further, that he should dwell among us, just exactly like one of us! Eating, breathing, touching, loving, sorrowing, weeping! A man like other men!

Were had been benevolent; but this God was a loving Father. It was the only explanation.

The school house was built of undressed logs with a cement floor. There were four rooms, one for the catechism of adults, another for the catechism of children and the other two for the learning of reading and writing.

Because the great majority could not read, catechism was learned by rote which required no mean memory and will. To aid the memory the answers were given in a sing song voice.

"Who made us?" the catechist would ask.

"Go-od ma-de u-us!"

"Why did God make us?"

"To-o sho-ow fo-or-th hi-is go-odne-ess.!" The enthusiastic answer would come.

Nyabera was an apt and avid learner. Her childhood capacity to spin long tales and remember the most obscure riddles stood her in good stead. In a fortnight she was way ahead of the class and asking the catechist such challenging questions that he decided she was uppity. In truth she just wanted to know and understand better, for catechism is a bare skeleton and she wanted the flesh — something she could sink her teeth into. Why for example did an all powerful God choose such an ignominious death? Could He not have just willed our salvation thus bringing it about? Why so much suffering? If God was good and all powerful, why allow so much suffering?

"You don't question God!" blustered the teacher. Nyabera subsided. After all she was just an ignorant woman. Far be it from her to question the Almighty's representative — the catechist.

After she mastered the basics of religion she started attending Mass every morning before class. She found it intriguing, then absorbing and finally when she got to the point of understanding its full meaning, captivating. The whole process took much longer than the catechism for the Mass was said entirely in Latin. The ritual had translations but since she could not read she was entirely dependent on the catechist's explanations — all the more reason not to annoy the man.

"Now he is washing his hands to signify that Kristo has washed away our sins. Now he is blessing the bread and wine," whispered the catechist as their avid eyes followed the priest, resplendent in white and purple. "Now this is the most important part of the Mass for we are all back on Calvary and the sacrifice is being made again. See how he gathers himself to make bread and wine into the real body and blood of Kristo. He is with us just as he was with Peter and John so long ago — in his actual body." They watched all this in awe and somehow were touched by the breath of the eternal.

As time went by, Nyabera was shown a place to put up a house, being a widow and away from home. It was a very lonely place but then beggars cannot be choosers. She had come so far to seek a new way and something as insignificant as location could not deter her. Was she not the daughter of a chief? Was her mother not Akoko, daughter of the great chief Odero? Far be it from her that she should succumb to cowardice and fear. She would learn all she had to. She would get her baptism and become a member of the one, holy, apostolic and catholic church. One day, and may the day come quickly, she would partake of the body and blood of Kristo and become a branch, finally grafted to a tree.

She had also decided that the first thing she would do after her baptism was to go for her mother and daughter. She suspected that her mother would take to the new faith like *ngege* (fish) to water. It offered such consolation for one could identify oneself easily with the desolation of Mary (a sword shall pierce your heart), with the joy of Elizabeth (whose barrenness was removed by God), the warm love of weak Peter (Lord you know everything, you know that I love you!). And that after he had just denied him to a little slave girl! What ignominy!

One law she knew she would find very hard to keep was the church's law on marriage. The Church taught that one man should marry one woman and there was no compromise in that matter. Now who would want to marry a widow such as herself as his first and only wife? No one. She knew her people well enough not to deceive herself. Her problem was that she wanted children so badly. Children were consolation, laughter and security. Children were everything. At least *Chik* had provided for that particular contingency by the institution of *tero*. It was only a kind of half marriage and not very fulfilling but at least children would be forthcoming. Nyabera knew herself well enough to know that if she ever failed, it would be because of this. However, only a fool tries to peer into the future; enough unto the day were the problems thereof and the problem of that particular day was to give satisfaction in catechism and get baptised.

Everything that has a beginning has an end. One fine Eastertime morning, Nyabera was baptised. She wore a long white robe (on loan) with a white scarf on her head. Her feet were bare. She held a candle in one hand. The priest made the sign of the cross with oil on her forehead and the chest for wisdom and courage, put salt on her tongue (for purity of heart). He then poured water on her forehead and intoned:

"I baptise you Maria in the name of the Father, and of the Son and of the Holy Spirit."

The ritual and symbolism of the Catholic Church were balm to her wounded soul.

Chapter 3

So proud was Nyabera of her new name that when she went back to Yimbo, she insisted that both her mother and child call her Maria, and Maria she became to them, and later to her grandchildren and great-grandchildren. She was the first of a kind and her reaching of the new was placed at par with her mother's famous journey to appeal to the DO and the DC and both were placed in the realm of the mythical.

"Maria! Maria! Tell us about the Angel and Maria!" piped her daughter Awiti, now eight years old and her nephew Owuor aged ten.

"Tell us about the escape to Misri (Egypt)."

"Tell us about the bad King Herodes!"

"Yes tell us, tell us!" The children loved stories surrounding the birth of Yeso Kristo. Their grandmother sat quietly in the background smiling enigmatically from time to time. Maria watching her closely, could only guess her actual thoughts. Six months later when Maria started showing signs of restlessness — she longed to go back to the mission — her mother spoke:

"My child."

"Yes mother."

"I have heard the longing in your voice when you speak of Aluor." She knew her daughter so well.

"Yes mother. It is true, I feel like an uprooted tree which cannot reach soil or water."

"Far be it from me to put obstacles in your way, for this new way sounds very good. However you are unlike me, still a young woman. You need children. From what I see this is not going to be possible with this new religion. What are you going to do?"

Her mother, listening and never asking questions, had gone with one stroke straight to the heart of the problem. It is the way of two souls caring for each other as deeply, if undemonstratively, as these two did. Maria was quiet for so long that Akoko almost regretted having asked the question, but she had never been one to back away however sticky the problem. Eventually she spoke.

"Mother, your words have reached deep within me. I can hide nothing from you even now that I am an old woman! I thought about this at length and I know that this is where I might fail. Denying it is no use — you have spoken only the truth. What can I do except place myself at the feet of the mother of God who lived with Josef in purity? I cannot and will not anticipate the future. And mother, I had hoped to take you and the children with me, for I am very lonely. I know you will live as a poor person for you cannot take this wealth with you, but at least you will be away from the cutting tongues of your sisters-in-law for when all is said and done you are living in exile. You will never belong, while there everybody is welcome. Nobody asks which clan one comes from. Please come with me mother." When her daughter had finished her spirited plea Akoko burst out laughing.

"What is so funny, mother?"

"Ah, child, I thought you would never ask! Of course I will come with you."

Mother and daughter made their preparations in haste as if now that the decision had been made no grass should be allowed to grow underfoot. The children were excited fit to burst. Oloo was downcast for he had enjoyed having his sister around much to the annoyance of his wives, but he was the first to admit the untenability of her position.

Eventually all was ready. It was not much for it is folly to weigh oneself down either mentally or physically when moving from one life to another. They carried their sleeping skins, a meal of *ugali* cooked in sour milk to eat on the way, and as the only reminder of the old life, a pot of ghee. Now, ghee is a rich man's food for it is made from boiled butter-fat. The two women decided that since the children had known nothing but plenty, their hearts would become faint if they had to eat the bitter herbs of the poor without so much as a drop of oil to ease it down, as in all their lives they had eaten those herbs always cooked in milk and laced with ghee. So they carried the pot of ghee to help ease their way into the new life. Like the children of Israel, they left the flesh-pots of Egypt for uncertainties of Caanan.

It had taken Maria about twelve hours from dusk to dawn to reach Aluor; but with the children to slow their pace, for they had to stop every two hours to rest, they did not reach it until well after dusk. They walked in a single file with Maria in the lead, the two children alternating in the middle and Akoko in the rear. The children were the future and the future had to be protected. To keep them distracted Akoko told them stories of the heroes of old and the history of the tribe and Maria told them the adventures of the Baby Jesus or whatever stories she could remember from the Old Testament. Daniel and the lions, Elias, the man who went to heaven on a 'bicycle of fire', (translate chariot of fire); the great friendship of Daudi and Jonathan. When it came to telling a story, Maria was unequalled even by Akoko. She made happenings of long ago appear like things of yesterday and she spiced everything with such wit that even the most mundane story became alive.

"Daudi was a boy who was handsome of face and brave of heart. Because he was the last born, his job was to look after sheep. One day a lion came and grabbed a little lamb. Daudi ran after the lion and hit him on the rump. The lion was so surprised that the lamb dropped out of his mouth and ran bleating to its mother. The lion got so angry that he turned on Daudi. Daudi gripped his beard and plunged his sword into the lion's heart. So brave and good was he that God chose him to be King. You must be brave for to be a coward is an insult to God and man.

Jonathan was the son of the King and would have been King if God had not chosen Daudi in his stead but he was not bitter for he could see why; Daudi had a soul as pure as spring water and as brave as a lion. Jonathan loved him with all his heart. One day, the old King wanted to kill Daudi, but Jonathan warned him just in the nick of time. My children we should try to be friends to our friends like Jonathan was to Daudi. If you have a worthy friend (a rare thing) never spare yourself for him."

Eventually they trudged weary and footsore into the little lonely hut; spread out their sleeping skins with the light of the moon and fell into an exhausted slumber, secure in the knowledge that what is good never comes easy and what is good is worth every single struggle.

Outside the moon gleamed and the stars glittered in the inky sky. The African night resounded with the songs of the crickets and the croaking of frogs. The fireflies flitted here and there giving themselves completely to the joys of their short lives. There were mysterious shufflings and scratchings — busy sounds of the night animals in search of food and companionship — their concerns fixed only on the requirements of the moment.

Chapter 4

The children were enrolled in both the catechism and the reading class. Like his father before him, Owuor was a steady slogger — a non quitter. His cousin Awiti was a fast but unsteady learner. She could mesmerise the class with her powers of recall, then sit through another class and learn absolutely nothing for she could open a window in her mind and escape, to go and play in the warm inviting sun, her feet sinking in the soft green grass and her eyes following the multi-coloured butterfly, that warbling bird or that variegated leaf. She had a powerful imagination which was at once her strength and her weakness.

The children's day began early in the morning when the church bell tolled to awaken the faithful to the *Angelus* which they said with their elders. Then they helped weed the patches of the garden nearest to the hut, washed themselves and were off to school, the boy proudly wearing his first and only garment, a long *khaki* shirt that covered all, so long as no wind came to blow it up; the girl wearing a simple green tunic also her first and only garment which she could have guarded with her life if necessary.

The first hour was spent chanting the catechism or learning prayers which at the end of the year everybody was supposed to be able to say in Latin and vernacular as were the responses to the Mass. Of course some of them were better at it than others. Awiti was very good at memorising prayers both in Latin and vernacular while Owuor was formidable in catechism. There was a break after catechism for about thirty minutes after which the children regrouped in two classes. Class A was junior reading class and Class B was senior reading class. The only other subject taught was numbers. Here again, Awiti excelled in reading and Owuor took to numbers like a duck to water. Numbers were a trial to her not because she could not do them but because her nature simply did not allow her to apply herself to anything as boring as endless additions and subtractions. If her young mind could have formulated the question, she would have asked the teacher, "to what end?"

They went in the middle of the day to a frugal meal of *ugali* and herbs. Later as their elders became more settled there would be occasional chicken and very rarely, fish for this was far from the great lake. Meat was unheard of for an animal was only slaughtered ceremoniously during a funeral or a betrothal. Back home, meat had been plentiful for there had been enough animals to slaughter just for food and no other reason, but here they were only poor orphans and widows. On the whole they bore it very well mainly because the two women formed such a solid wall of love around their children. They were made to believe that everything was possible for those who persisted and were strong enough to ignore the mere taste of food or an empty feeling in the stomach.

Meanwhile, their grandmother was working harder than before to form some sort of a base for her grandchildren. She had never begged for food and she was not about to begin, not when there were larger tracks of land untilled. After her catechism in the morning she would spend the day out in the fields bent over this or that crop. She was tireless and unsparing of herself. The only help she had was that of her daughter Maria who tried to make her take it easy but to no avail. The two women became some sort of a fixture on the green sloping countryside, and the locals, not as motivated as they were, made endless jokes about their iron backs and caked feet.

Oloo, not one to sit by and see his sister suffer sent his twin sons, both now married with children, but as ebullient as ever, to take two cows and four goats to his sister — so that his grand nephew and niece need not suffer from lack of milk and ghee.

They arrived whistling and calling out for all they were worth and asking all and sundry where their aunt Akoko might be found. Eventually they found someone who knew Maria's house. They tethered the cows and spent the next few days building a cow pen and knowing their aunt, they made it sizeable for if anyone could wrest wealth from the soil, she could. After seeing the crops in the field, they built a couple of granaries as well.

At harvest time, Akoko received a bountiful harvest, kept enough for food and bartered the rest. Her cattle pen was well on its way to filling and she was well on her way to making a second fortune at the age of fifty-four. At Eastertime, the traditional time for renewal and baptism, Akoko was baptised Veronica, after the woman who had wiped Kristo's face on his way to Calvary and on whose kerchief he left an imprint of his face. In commemoration, she wore a kerchief on her head. The girl received the name Elizabeth and the boy became Petro.

Soon after, Maria decided to go back to her matrimonial home. She offered no explanations and her mother, looking in her eyes, let her go without demanding one. There are many longings and fears which can never be put fully into words.

The children however noticed that their grandmother devoted herself more to saying her rosary after her daughter's departure and that on some evenings she would kneel for a long period before the tabernacle in the church. In truth she did these things whenever she felt her soul was trembling on the edge of the abyss of fear of the future or longing for a past which could never be retrieved.

Akoko was the soul of discretion and never once complained about having to raise two children in so isolated a spot as she was doing, but she eventually caught the eye of the catechist whose duty it was to decide exactly where one should stay within the mission or the surrounding lands. First he had formed the habit of dropping in to check on her and her children. Soon he started talking to her especially when he realised that not only did she never repeat anything she heard to anyone, but also never went to anyone's house, or stood gossiping with other women. Her routine was simple; she was either in the church, in the fields or in her hut. Finally he began asking her advice on various matters, for the mission contained a motley collection of human beings, there for different reasons: some had come for food and clothing and security; others came to learn the new religion and some just dropped by before they thought of where else to go or what else to do.

Eventually he decided on his own initiative to build a house for her within a stone's throw of the church and they finally moved nearer human habitation and she uttered a heartfelt sigh of relief. Now that the children were so near, they became fully absorbed in the life of the church. Awiti became a dedicated sacristan assisting the nuns in arranging the altar and keeping the church clean; and Owuor became an ever present and enthusiastic altar boy. The priest, a Dutchman, took such a liking to this ever smiling and dogged lad that he started to teach him Latin and English. Naturally because his Latin was way ahead of his English, his pupil reflected his language skills and shortcomings, so he could chant '*Pater noster qui es in coelis*' in no time at all but could hardly do the same for 'Our Father who art in heaven'.

The year came and went and it was Easter again. This was even a greater favourite of the mission people than Christmas. On Good Friday, the church would be stripped bare and the large crucifix would be covered. No Mass was said. Saturday night, the Easter vigil would be kept in total darkness to commemorate the time Kristo spent in the dark of the tomb. At the stroke of midnight the candles would be lit in their dozens to celebrate the risen Messiah. The lights would be switched on (powered by a generator) and the whole place would be thrown into brilliant light. Then *Alleluias* would sound from the mouths of the faithful to welcome the risen Lord. The procession of priest and altar boys, candles aloft, incense swirling upwards would move slowly to the altar and the Mass would begin.

It was inevitable that Owuor, whose soul was a mixture of cool clear waters and burning embers, would at some point feel a call to the priesthood. The thought first crossed his mind when he was fourteen. It was a dilemna. If he was steeped in church ceremonial and dogma, wasn't he even more steeped in the richness of his heritage? His grandmother had made sure that he understood fully what being the grandson of Owuor Kembo meant; son of a chief;

grandson of a chief and a great chief. The only surviving male in the house of Owuor Kembo — his grandfather. He knew that his grandmother had set her determined heart on his wresting back the chief's stool now in the hands of the council of *Jodongo*. He also knew that his grand uncle Oloo would provide the means with which he would get back his birthright. He knew all these things. He would have loved to fight it out with his uncle Otieno if only to pay back some of what his grandmother had suffered. It was his duty. But there was this quiet, insistent, constant voice at the back of his mind that urged him towards a completely different life.

He agonised over it and it was constantly on the tip of his tongue to tell his grandmother who had hitherto understood all things; but whenever he looked into her beautiful face, so full of love, now beginning to get lined and wrinkled after years of toil in the sun and constant worry for his well being, words just failed him. One moment he would prepare to sacrifice his call to the priesthood for his grandmother, the next he would be filled with a longing for God so powerful, he could taste it. He was torn. Eventually he mentioned it to his cousin Awiti who was closer to him than a sister. She was only twelve but she understood the implication immediately.

"But you are going to be chief as soon as you are old enough!" she exclaimed.

"I know," he replied gloomily.

"Grandmother won't like this."

"I know."

"It is your duty to be chief."

"I know!" came the refrain again.

"Don't tell her yet. Maybe you will change your mind. Wait at least until mother is here — you know grandmother has a terrible temper — you might need protection." She might only be twelve, but when it came to intuition she was a woman all through. Owuor was man enough to know good advice when he saw it. Not that he felt he could change his mind, but a wait could do no harm and if he had a true call to priesthood, it should withstand the test if time. So he kept quiet and bided his time.

Chapter 5

Maria Nyabera arrived on the doorstep one evening three months after that Easter. She looked thin and quite haggard. The children ran to her in welcome. Her mother moved forward, saw her face and hesitated a little, somewhat arrested by the expression in her eyes, then she reached for her child anyhow. It is a fact of life that once a mother, always a mother until the day of death, even if the child is seventy. Sometimes it is pure joy but sometimes it means incredible pain and of all these pains, there is no pain like the knowledge that the child suffers and cannot be helped. Maria smiled with her mouth and in her voice there was a forced gaiety as she marshalled all her considerable story telling powers to entertain the children. She avoided her mother's eyes studiously throughout. Eventually it was bedtime and Owuor left to sleep in a friend's *simba* for he was too old to sleep with the womenfolk. Awiti brought her pallet and fell asleep by the hearth. The mother and the daughter were alone.

"My child." It was a bare murmur.

"Yes mother."

"What made you suffer like this?" She had been gone close to two years. She had meant to resist, to say nothing, as she had said nothing when going but before she knew what was happening, sob upon agonising sob broke from her throat and the story, the longing, the backtracking, the failure came pouring from her mouth.

She had just heard that the man's wife had died from someone who had just arrived at the mission from the village. She had tried to resist but she could not help herself and had hoped that some sort of licit union could be formed out of their previous relationship. They had lived together as man and wife for a while with her trying to bring him around to her way of thinking. A child had been born, a boy, and she had redoubled her efforts for his sake. It was soon clear, however, that the man was set in his ways and he had no intention of changing. He started courting a girl to be his second wife. Then the baby became ill as all the others had done before him and eventually died.

"Mother, I have sinned against God and I have failed you — I who led you to this place."

"My child, you have sinned yes, but you have failed no one, least of all me. To tumble and fall is human; so human that God, almost despairing of our ever really understanding him, made himself human for our sake — that we may touch him, and hear him and know him. Go to the church and talk to him there. Have you not understood these things? Do you not comprehend the depths of his love and mercy?" Nyabera stumbled out and spent the night kneeling before the tabernacle. The priest coming in the church in the morning found her there. She staggered to her feet.

"Bless me father for I have sinned. It is two years now since my last confession. I wish to confess." He went to his side of the screen and she to hers. After the absolution she came out to start her penance. She felt as if a load had been lifted off her shoulders.

Time heals all wounds. In time Maria saw that while she had been out looking for a son, she had one all along who loved her like a mother — the boy Owuor. For the first time she noticed his loving gaze, his helpful ways, his consistent attention to her. She had differed many times with her own daughter, but never once had she ever had to exchange words with her nephew. Owuor, a sensitive boy, seeing the agony his aunt was in, went out of his way to comfort her. His reading was by now excellent and he read to her frequently especially from psalms.

Out of the depths I have cried
unto thee O Lord
Lord hear my voice, be attentive
to my supplication
If thou, Lord, should mark iniquities
Who shall stand?

She liked that particular one so much that she asked him to read it again and again. Eventually she forgave herself — the last step in self acceptance.

One day when Maria and her nephew Owuor happened to be alone he broached the subject of his vocation.

"Maria, I think God is calling me to priesthood." he said quietly. She was taken entirely by surprise.

"What?"

"I think God is calling me to priesthood."

"Have you spoken to your grandmother?"

"No, I thought I'd speak to you first. Actually it was Awiti's idea. Besides I was afraid that I might cause her pain."

"You are so young — maybe you should wait a little."

"Waiting will not make me change my mind. I know that I have no choice in the matter but I hate to do this to her."

"Then I will speak to her about it; better still, you come with me and we will talk to her together."

As usual they found Akoko busy weeding her sorghum patch. They simply brought down their hoes and joined in the work. Nothing was said for quite a spell then Akoko who well knew that at such an hour, her grandson was usually occupied elsewhere asked:

"What brings Owuor here at this hour—it can't be for love of weeding. He has had something on his mind for a long time and has been as jumpy as an ant with its tail in hot embers. Speak up young man."

Owuor looked at his grandmother in confusion. Naturally he had thought that his secret was well kept. The confusion became respectful admiration. He should have known that nothing could escape this astute woman.

"Grandmother, you know that I have worked closely with the priest and I feel that I would like to enter the priesthood. I want to be a priest." His grandmother was nothing if not surprising, so he should not have been flabbergasted by her reaction but he was.

"I wondered when you would get the courage to come out with it. You would not be my grandson if you were a coward. You have concluded quite wrongly that I will stand in your way. It is true that I have had hopes that you might one day sit in the chief's stool that your father and your grandfather once occupied; but things have changed and people are turning to different things. I had also hoped that you would marry and provide many sons to ensure the continuity of the house of Owuor Kembo; but no I will not stand in your way. However, from now henceforth you shall fully take your grandfather's name so that as long as you live his name shall be heard among the people. You will not be Owuor Sino, but Owuor Kembo. That is all my boy. Do whatever the spirit bids you."

Owuor could only say weakly; "Oh grandmother!" The two women smiled at each other over his head.

And so it was that Peter Owuor Kembo aged fifteen — formely Petro Owuor Sino found himself a Seminarian at St Paul's Seminary Rakwaro. His worldly possessions were few, his academic knowledge haphazard; but he had faith in God and therefore in himself and he had love in his heart and the solid love of three women behind him. Finally he had unbounded hope in the future. So what if this hope was rosily coloured by his youthful enthusiasm? One wise man once said that it was better to have loved and lost than never to have loved at all. In the same vein, it is better to have been buoyed up by hope, the horizons limitless before one, than to have lived in the grey world of timid fearfulness. The course of the world is changed by those who dare to dream. Some dream of wealth and others dream of fame; Owuor dreamt of a life expended in service. He who had never really known his father or the joys of a father-son relationship, now dreamt of being the spiritual father of many.

And so he entered the rigors and splendour of life in the seminary. Sometimes when things were particularly tough, he would wonder whether mere blood and flesh would survive it, but it never entered in his mind to leave. If he had learned anything at all at his grandmother's knee, it was that a job once begun had to be completed. He was no quitter. He would survive. He would see it through. One day he would be Father Peter. Maybe one day a bishop. He was happy to serve Christ anywhere and in any way.

Chapter 6

After Owuor left for the seminary, it was decided that his cousin should join the newly founded primary school in which English, Mathematics, Geography, Nature Study and History albeit with a heavy colonial slant were taught, as opposed to the previous school where only religion, reading and simple arithmetic were taught. A certificate was issued on passing a tough examination at the end of the course — and this was a carte blanche to literally any job available to an African in those days. Awiti was enrolled in the school — one of the only two girls. The other thirty-two were boys. She was almost thirteen and on the threshold of puberty.

The drop-out rate was so high that by the end of the second year the other girl who was almost sixteen dropped out to get married. Five boys also dropped out for various reasons including lack of three shillings levied per year. At a time when most families simply had no cash and lived entirely on a barter system this was frequently too hefty a sum to raise. Almost all the students were adults and while it made good sense to learn religion for one year, it made absolutely no sense to prolong the agony for eight years to get a piece of paper that was supposed to enable one to work for the white man — and who in his right mind would want that? The accepted form of wealth was cattle — a man who had them was wealthy and one who did not have at least a few was regarded as the lowest form of life. Maybe for such and their children, pursuit of the white man's education held some attraction — but there was the insurmountable problem of the levy for if those rich in cattle could not easily raise that elusive three shillings how much more the son of a man who had nothing? In any case it was considered better to try to lift the yoke of poverty by tilling the land rather than lying about in some classroom.

If it was hard for a boy to get an education — it was well nigh impossible for a girl. The purpose of female existence was marriage and child bearing — and by the same token to bring wealth to her family with the bride price. In fact a poor man with absolutely nothing to his name except some daughters, had a guaranteed wealth if they could hang on long enough to come of age. If education was not necessary for boys, it was superfluous for girls. However, for Awiti several factors came together in her favour. The most important was the pioneering and daring spirit of her grandmother and mother. Secondly, she was the future of those two aging women. Now that her cousin and only close male relative was in the seminary she was the only connection they had to the continuity of the family, something that the African, like the Chinese, holds dear to his heart. She was the centre of their world and nothing was too good for her though they struggled not to show it or to spoil her in any external way. Therefore money was found for her education year in year out until she reached the top class at nineteen. By this time the class was down to eleven, she herself and ten boys. What is more, she held her position very well even in a subject she disliked as much as Mathematics, for as she grew older her earlier flightiness left her. She developed her grandmother's steely determination, which was not surprising because her grandmother was her confidante and mentor. But it was not easy and everybody looked at her askance. A girl! To be so clever, to show it openly, to receive commendation after commendation! It was too much! She should be ashamed or at least try to hide her brilliance, otherwise, they prophesied darkly, no man would marry her. That of course was supposed to be a catastrophe.

Out of the eleven who sat for the examination only five passed and Awiti was the best of them. The certificates were awarded three months later and all the villagers came to see for themselves.

"Elizabeth Awiti Okumu," called the head teacher. No PhD holder ever had such a sweet sense of victory as this barefoot African girl, who without even knowing it, was the proto-type of others yet to come. With the certificate came the invitation to a newly opened Teacher Training College. It was unbelievable! She had not even thought of the future. What was she to do?

"Grandmother! Mother! Look!"

"What is it my child? Asked the ever serene Akoko now a grizzled old lady but still possessing the sweetest smile that ever lit a woman's face. Maria on the other hand felt her heart thumping away in her chest, her mouth tasted bitter and she felt nauseated. All the fears of her childhood were coming back. There was a vice-like band around her head and she thought she would faint. In her head one thought went round and round, beating its wings like a trapped bird. "My child — not you, not you!" She would have given it a voice if her throat was not in a spasm. If anything happened to this child! If she was taken away from her she knew she would die. Her little baby, who had defied all odds to live to the very threshold of adulthood! "A sword shall pierce thy soul! A sword shall pierce thy soul!" and suddenly she realised she had spoken loudly and everyone turned around to stare.

"Control yourself," hissed Akoko as Awiti stared at her mother in shock. She hadn't even divulged the contents of the letter yet! What could her mother be talking about? Eventually the presentation was over. The teacher seeing commotion at the back commended Awiti for her good work, but wisely refrained from mentioning the invitation. The poor girl had suffered long enough at the hands of the boys and the villagers.

When the three got back to their simple grass thatched hut, the old woman reprimanded her middle-aged daughter as she had never done before. The young girl had meanwhile been dispatched to fetch water. She was glad to go for she was afraid of her mother.

"My child, I am terribly ashamed of you. You are no longer young yet you have never been anything but selfish with the selfishness of a child. You feel that other people may suffer, but as for you, it is your right to be happy. You shake like a reed in the wind because you have never forgiven God for not giving you as many children as other women whom you consider less worthy. And you feel that God owes it to you to make sure that your only child lives and prospers. Learn my child that God owes nobody anything. He gives to all men both wicked and good from his great bounty according to his wisdom and mercy. You are no longer a child yet you understand nothing. Don't you know that from the height of heaven and the vastness of his eternity he sees you as you shall be a hundred seasons hence when no one on earth will have any memory of you and your bloodline will have mingled and petered out like a well in the dry season?

You are not wise, my child, learn wisdom. Put your child in his hands who can both plant and bring fruition. Try to be happy for Awiti when she tells us the news whatever it is. Don't you see the world is changing and that she is acquiring what will make the difference as to whether she survives or perishes?" Maria eventually subsided and her racing heart stilled within her but when she heard her daughter's footsteps on the threshold the band tightened around her again and she started breathing fast—like a woman in labour. She struggled to control herself.

"Come in, Awiti, and read for us the letter the teacher gave you." said Akoko, her voice even. She watched her granddaughter who had been balancing the pot beautifully on her head, but looking somewhat unsure as to whether she should enter or go back with the pot. She brought the pot down to her knee, stooped and entered the house, the pot held at waist level — all in one sweeping graceful motion. She poured the water into the big mother pot which was used as a water reservoir, and brought out the envelope and proceeded to translate.

"This letter comes from a head teacher of a school called a college, where they teach teachers how to teach children. He says he is happy to offer me a place in his college so that I can also learn how to be a teacher. He says that this takes two years. He says that though they do not charge school fees, I will be expected to arrive with at least three frocks and a pair of shoes plus other small things such as soap and a towel. He says I should write to him as soon as possible to tell him whether I accept or not. The school will open in September, seven months from now." She wanted to add "I am so happy!" but thought better of it. There was complete silence for so long that she felt her skin prickle in apprehension. Eventually her grandmother spoke formally.

"I see. We have heard you, my child, but this is a serious matter. Your mother and I have to think about it carefully." For the first time in many years, she felt the need of the kind of support that a good and strong man could give. She missed her husband Chief Owuor Kembo and his level headed approach to life in general and sticky problems in particular.

Chapter 7

The new priest, Father Thomas offered to drive Awiti in his landrover to the teacher training college which was the first of its kind in the region. She was wearing a sky blue cotton frock with a white border at the hem and a brand new wooden box, shining with a yellowy varnish. It contained two spare frocks and toilet articles — a very sparse collection but she was proud of it. Her mood alternated between euphoria and gut chilling fear. She was twenty and completely out of her depth, but was she not the granddaughter of Akoko whose straight back had never been known to bend under any pressure? She would conduct herself accordingly.

There were six other girls and twenty-eight men. The dormitories were completely out of bounds and anyone found hovering near the dormitory of the other sex could be expelled summarily. The exeat days were different for the men and women so that it was easier for the students to meet someone on the outside than on the inside, but anyone suspected of maintaining such a liaison would also be in danger of expulsion. The two years were meant to be incident free and the authorities keenly felt the trust that the parents, especially the girls' parents had placed in them. They tried their best, but such was the nature of the challenge that it was not humanly impossible that once in a while some desperate lothario did not try to meet a girl on the outside during the girl's exeat. Usually it was with the girl's tacit approval otherwise one would be in big trouble. However, such was the strength of the moral climate of the day that a boy never dreamt of doing more than talk and make sheep's eyes at the girl of his dreams and the girl never dreamt of anything more than a handshake and talk. If the boy was very special, you might allow him to hold your hand a little longer than the brief millisecond of a handshake. Anything beyond that was unthinkable; sex outside marriage was out of the question and premarital pregnancy was simply the stuff of nightmares, not the reality of everyday. No one could have dreamt that within fifteen short years, the swinging sixties would erode the morals of the whole world bringing in its wake, a wave of single mothers and a horde of elderly women trying to contend with numerous grandchildren left by daughters gone to pursue an education or rebuild lives shattered by premature pregnancy.

Awiti who was now known by her christian name was on the whole quite unimpressed by the many overtures in her direction. She was a very good looking girl with her grandmother's wide set eyes, long neck, trim figure and her mother's height and grace. Her skin, which was medium dark, had a fine even texture. Her nose sat on her face as if the Creator had really thought hard before placing it carefully in place. Her lips so frequently firm and unsmiling, seemed to hold back a tantalizing secret about which one would give an arm and a leg to know. The men were fascinated, more so when they discovered she would not even flirt, was indifferent and apparently cold. They tried everything. She would be walking calmly to the shops during an exeat, and this hulk of a man would drop out of a tree and start walking lackadaisically by her side as if a man turned ape was something quite ordinary; or she would be reading in her room at night and a love lorn note would come flying into the room wrapped around a stone. It never seemed to occur to the desperate senders that such a missile could cause actual bodily harm to the subject of their passion or her innocent roommate or that they faced imminent expulsion if found out, for they had to be quite near the building to ensure accuracy. She would never tell on any one of them but she had to limit herself severely to only going out in the company of other girls, and keeping her window shut at night.

She knew nothing about men, having been brought up by women. Her cousin only came home rarely and because of the nature of his vocation was not into girl chasing. The village boys had been so over-awed by her prowess at school that they only thought of her as an object of derision not of desire. She was therefore quite disturbed by the boorish behaviour of some of the men, but she decided to take it in her stride. Eventually all the other girls were secretly paired either on the outside or in the inside but Elizabeth remained alone. Towards the end of the course it was discovered that she had a brother studying for priesthood, this, coupled with the brilliance of her performance led to bitter taunts. She was variously referred to as 'the nun' 'Virgin Mary' and 'church mouse' or other insulting names. She hung on grimly, now shunned by both men and women, for a non-conformist is always someone to fear.

One day she was out on exeat by herself, for now no one bothered her at all, when she met a soldier just discharged from the army which was now being disbanded after the Second World War. He was in military fatigues consisting of a colourless tunic and long shorts otherwise known as *kaptulas*. On his muscular slightly bandy legs were spirals of leggings which ended atop a pair of brilliant black boots. His skin was lighter than that of most people from the area so she thought he must be from further west. He was very handsome but in those days when relationships across the boundaries of religion, race or tribe were highly frowned upon, she decided not to tempt fate and was just about to move when he fell in step with a military swagger. What daring! She looked at him coldly — the kind of look which is meant to wither the insides of a man into a pile of ashes, but he kept on walking and smiling.

"Why is it that you are always alone?" he asked in perfect English and she recognised the accent — a St Maryan! What a surprise, and a military man! She had always thought they were a bunch of illiterates.

"What is that to you?" she did not mean to sound defensive, it just came out that way. Had he been watching all this time?

"All the others come out in pairs or meet someone out here, but you are always alone. I've watched you."

"Why?" she tried to sound defiant. She also edged away, imperceptibly she hoped.

"Please don't run away. I won't harm you. I have waited to meet you for the last six weeks. During the last exeat, courage deserted me! It is easier to fight Germans and their allies than to get the courage to talk to a girl. I was supposed to report to a civilian job two weeks ago but I couldn't go without speaking to you. So you see, you should not run away." He had switched to a combination of English and Vernacular — a common manner of speech in an emerging bi-lingual and tri-lingual African. In spite of his coloration, he spoke the local dialect perfectly.

"Where are you from?" How could she even show interest in this forward stranger? But she could not help herself. He took that as a heaven-sent opportunity to introduce himself fully.

"My name is Mark Anthony Oloo Sigu. I am from Seme. My village is very near that famous rock which rests upon another — *Kit Mikai*. In fact there are more rocks than anything else in that place, but we manage. I went to school in St Mary's Yala. I was conscripted into the army while job hunting in Nairobi. I've fought in many places about which I'll tell you some other time, if you let me. I was discharged from the army as a sergeant about two months ago. I came to this town which is not far from my village about six weeks ago to stay with my uncle. Then I saw you. What is your name?"

"Elizabeth Awiti." she answered, then wondered at herself in amazement. 'What could be wrong with me? Maybe I have cerebral malaria!' She surreptitiously felt her forehead. It was cool. Besides she felt quite wonderful and alive in every part of her being. Strange malaria.

"I am very pleased to meet you, Elizabeth." He offered her his hand and since she had been standing there like a fool listening to him, she decided that the least she could do was to shake it and then take off before having a fit or something. His handshake was brief, cool and correct. He did not let his fingers linger unpleasantly in her palm as some men did. At least the man had manners.

"May I see you during the next exeat?"

"No. Besides, I thought you were supposed to

report to some job?"

"Er, yes, I forgot. I will go if you allow me to write to you and if you promise to write back!"

"Oh, OK!" she said and then literally fled.

Chapter 8

He wrote three times before she got nerve enough to write back and that was because his letters were far from sentimental; they were full of fun and good humoured news.

"Yesterday, I was out for a walk in the evening. It was dark and my mind was elsewhere. I know you won't believe it but I was stone sober, anyway I tripped and fell into this pool and awakened a family of frogs and you couldn't believe the noise they made. The bull frog especially outdid himself. He must have thought me a rival!

I am a clerk in charge of a warehouse. It is very tame after the army. Not that I was brave. I remember I spent more time shooting into the air to scare off imaginary enemies and to reassure myself than I did actually killing anyone."

He could not get leave at all for the first six months so he knew that those letters were his life-line. With the intuition of one in love he knew how to put all of himself into his letters and yet show total restraint. He did not want to blow his chances with one stupid word. Gradually she relaxed and started writing him longer letters telling him things about herself.

"I have a grandmother, a mother and a cousin who is studying to be a priest. My grandfather and father and my cousin's father who is my uncle are all long dead. The two women have brought us up. I wish you could meet them. My grandmother is a real character, but she has been sickly of late. I am very worried about her. I owe her so much. My mother is very kind hearted and quite strong though she has always been in the shadow of her mother who is a woman of iron. I like to think that I am like my grandmother but I know that if any of the things that have happened to her were to happen to me, I would die."

Their courtship went on in this gentle off-hand manner, but at the end of six months they knew each other pretty well; at least she knew she liked him and he, who was impetuous knew that he was in love and wanted to get married. Meanwhile she sat for her examination and got her teacher's certificate. She was posted back to her old school and she was grateful for a chance to be near her mother and ailing grandmother. She was twenty-two and all the girls she had grown up with were married with children. She was an object of curiosity, a woman who worked at anything apart from tilling the land and rearing children was a hitherto unknown phenomenon. Her salary which was a mere fifty shillings a month, was a fortune in their eyes. The power of money in this new world was beginning to sink into people's mentality. Their envy was palpable, and she was taunted at every turn.

Akoko, now a very old lady nearing eighty was not at all well. She was weak and got breathless at the slightest exertion. Her ankles were constantly swollen and every once in a while her heart would do a strange dance within her rib cage — almost like the flutter of a bird trying to break free. Her eyes were dimmed with cataracts but her hearing was surprisingly good, and wonder of wonders her spirit was still bright and strong within that broken body. She had lived her life in one, long passionate giving of herself and now it was twilight and the end was near — so near that sometimes she felt it to be a mere heartbeat away with only her soft fluttering breath between this life and the next. She was a woman who had probably always known what she wanted and what was needed of her and she had lived her life accordingly. Though she was very wise, one could hardly say that she had been born in the wrong era; that had she lived in a different era, she would have been a great intellectual, a pioneer and a leader of humanity. In truth, such clarity of vision and strength of person are a discomfiture to all men of all ages and she would therefore never have really fitted in that, this or any other century; for human beings prefer to be left alone to muddle along in confusion — it is more comfortable than to suffer the pain of self knowledge.

Her thoughts now frequently dwelt on her late husband, dead these thirty years. He had been an extraordinary man; even though she had never appreciated just how extraordinary he was when he lived. He had been a man with no complexity and as often happens with those whose souls have perfect simplicity he had lived an extraordinary life without in any way appearing to do anything that appeared out of the ordinary. What monumental courage he must have had and how that courage had influenced and formed his young bride! What might she not have given to have him beside her as she walked these last faltering steps of her life? But to each, an allotted life span is given and against this, there is no appeal.

Yet she hung on, her strong will holding her yearning soul to a body it longed to leave. She just hung on determinedly and waited.

Mark wrote and said he was coming to see Elizabeth during his leave in two weeks' time. He said that he had important matters to discuss and would therefore go first to his home to collect his uncle and his brother to accompany him. Would she arrange to have a few male relatives to come to receive them? It was very important that she did so. Her heart did a flip-flop and her knees felt quite weak. Really! What a man! However there was no time to waste so she called her mother and grandmother and told them about Mark. Akoko's eyes gleamed.

"And why, child have you not told us about this man before? Two weeks indeed!"

"Where does he come from and what are the names of his parents?" this from Maria.

"He comes from Seme, but I don't know the names of his parents."

"What do you mean you don't know! How can you even consider having friendship with a man whose roots and antecedents you don't know? What is the world coming to!" She lamented. Akoko drew on her fast dwindling powers to bring back reason and order.

"Accept it Maria, the world is changing. All is not lost, however. We must listen to the suit according to *Chik* for we are still the children of Ramogi. You shall therefore leave for Sakwa at cockcrow tomorrow and fetch your brother-in-law — this girl's uncle. I shall also send word to Yimbo to my nephews, the twins Opiyo and Odongo. Those two rascals must be old men now. Finally I shall get Father Thomas to send for Owuor at the Seminary. He is the closest thing to a brother the girl has and he must be there. These Seme people must not think that because we are widows and Christians and sojourners in this place, we do not know how things are done." She patted her granddaughter's hand with calm affection. "It is going to be all right. You will see. So long as there is no consanguinity and he is no thief or witch there is nothing to worry about. In any case what is a witch except one who is driven by his shortcomings to harm others? Besides I believe in God. Do not worry, all will be well." And Elizabeth thought to herself, "What will I do without her when she is gone? She is the steady rock of our lives." She looked at the simple hut in which she had grown up. It was round and grass thatched. There was a kind of enclosed veranda at the entrance, and then there was the main room which was semicircular and the sleeping room which was also semicircular. Outside were four granaries and a small cooking hut. Three granaries were empty, a testimony to the declining strength of her grandmother. Beside the granaries was a cattle pen which was generally full at night when the herds came in from grazing. It was still quite a respectable herd of cattle usually attended by hired men. Most other women would not have bothered, seeing that the only son was headed for priesthood; but Akoko had to instill in her daughter and granddaughter that work was a discipline and poverty was an enemy to be fought. "God has no time for the lazy, but the devil has," was a favourite saying of hers.

It was a simple house in which she had led a simple life. But she had been surrounded by love and caring. She had lived among strangers but had never lacked the sense of continuity. It had been a good life.

The preparations were made and excitement was in the air. *Kong'o* was brewed in two large pots; a young bull was selected for slaughter and many cockerels were to meet a sticky end on that day (though they went about the business of intimidating the hens completely oblivious of the fact). Sorghum was ground in large quantities and arrangements were made for fresh tilapia to be brought from the lake, a long distance away. No effort would be spared, for a betrothal was a time to show largesse and for her only granddaughter, Akoko would outdo herself one last time.

The day finally arrived and it was a day as full of beauty as the day in which Owuor Kembo of Sakwa, in full battle regalia and a leopard skin loin piece had come to pay suit to the great chief Odero Gogni of Yimbo for the hand of his daughter Akoko Obanda. Yet some things were different. A stone's throw away was the church with its tall steeple bearing a cross at the top — a symbol of the new and different way of life, yet in some ways reminiscent of the reverence once paid to *Were* — the god of the eye of the rising sun who had guided the people. Further along was the school — the place of learning without which one was as a blind man in a strange house. All round was evidence of the rule of the white people who were good administrators but often unjust and unheeding to the pleas and aspirations of their black subjects. Indeed in the Central Province and in Nairobi especially among the Kikuyu, there were rumours of mass uprising against the colonial powers

Oloo the son of Sigu, otherwise known as Mark Anthony, arrived with his entourage of six including his uncle, at mid-morning. Aware of the importance and the impact of presence and carriage he arrived in his military fatigues, a colobus monkey headdress and a spear in his hand. He was after all a soldier. It was an intriguing combination of the old and the new. Anyone else might have looked odd but Oloo looked dashing. His complexion was deceptively light and it drew questioning glances from his hosts and hostesses. Had their daughter decided to marry a *ja-mwa* — a foreigner? Apart from Akoko who must have left her mother's womb with a broad outlook, all of them were strictly parochial and marriage to even a Luhya from across the border was considered a catastrophe. It was therefore a relief when the suitors broke into pure Luo with the dialect of the middle region of Ramogi. Their daughter was a prize, a beacon, a source of pride for the entire clan. They simply could not bear giving her away to a stranger.

"Brothers, we greet you and bring you many greetings from the people of Seme. My nephew Oloo son of my late brother Sigu came to me and said: "Father, I have found a girl and I want to get married. Now I am a reasonable man and I know the ways of *Chik* so I asked him, 'Son, one does not just find a girl in the air. One sends a *jawan'gyo* to go and spy a girl and find out her antecedents and character. Is she a thief or a witch? Is she lazy or shiftless? Might there be consanguinity between you and her? Who is her mother and father?' I tell you my brothers, that I was flabbergasted to hear that none of these things had ever crossed his mind. He knew that her mother's name was Maria and her grandmother's name was Akoko and that was all. You will therefore forgive us brothers because we do not know you and you do not know us. We only came because we had faith in our son who has always been a reasonable man. We therefore wish to introduce ourselves before we go on. I am Semo Rakula of Seme, our village is near that strange rock-upon-a-rock, *Kit-Mikai*. We are the descendants of that great warrior, Nyagudi Kogambi. Oloo and these young men are my sons and nephew. Oloo is a man of learning and what is more a soldier who has fought for the white man in distant lands. Now he is a clerk with a big *kambi* (company) in Nakuru, where he gets a good salary. So should this suit be acceptable to all you need have no fear that your daughter will starve. I tell you these things because there are things a *jawan'gyo* would have found out for you. Thank you brothers." A pot of *kong'o* was moved near him and he drew a long refreshing draught. Some things never change— a spokesman always needs to irrigate his throat.

"Brothers, people of Seme. My name is Oyange Silwal. The girl Awiti is the only child of my late brother Okumu. We are from Sakwa from the village of Gombe. The girl has grown up in Gem because her mother being a widow and having converted to Christianity decided to settle here which is a good thing because now she is like a light for the rest of us. She is highly educated and a teacher of children. So your son will be bringing a light to your home — an educated woman. He is indeed a very lucky man." At this the suitors shifted uncomfortably because they knew it was a preamble to some horrific demand for bride price. On observing this Oyange smiled secretly to himself. It was nothing of the sort, but it never did any harm to let suitors stew in their own juice a little. In fact he was very angry with Akoko and Maria for insisting that the bride price be a mere token. He himself would have set it twice the normal amount if not more. Who ever saw such a beauty, such learning? It was a waste. He had almost stormed off until Akoko reminded him how he had neglected his duty in raising his brother's child. Did he want to compound that by refusing to do this, his last duty to her? He was a superstitious man so he dared not leave after that.

Semo spoke again; "Brothers, people of Sakwa. We are happy to know you and hope that soon we shall not just be friends but relatives as well. We have heard what you have said. We wish to know what bride price would please you."

"For this jewel there can be no price. Therefore we have decided to give her to you free except for a token bull, two cows and six goats with which to furnish the requirements of *Chik*. The bull shall come to me in lieu of her father. The two cows and goats will be taken to Yimbo to the house of Oloo her grandmother's brother who in all ways was a father to the girl and her cousin and always provided for them." The aspiring suitors stared in disbelief. Held in readiness back in Seme were twenty four head of cattle, double the normal bride price which was the least they expected to be asked. Oloo had instructed his uncle to ask for a grace period of six months in which he would have looked for whatever else they would have demanded. And now this! They couldn't possibly give away such a girl for free. They must have something hidden up their sleeves. But they hadn't. He was just an incredibly lucky man and it was beginning to dawn on him.

Eventually everything was concluded and as conversation, food and *kong'o* flowed, Akoko asked her grandson-in-law to come and sit next to her. They talked at length and she was seen smiling and nodding her grey head frequently. At one point she burst into a wheezy breathless laughter and everybody's eyes turned towards them with interest. She was full of joy. She had lost one son to the white man's war; and by the grace of God she had gained another from the white man's army. Like Anna and Simeon of old she could now die in peace for her eyes had also seen the promise.

That night she died quietly in her pallet in the corner. She did not struggle and therefore her daughter Maria who always slept with one ear cocked in case her mother called out for her, did not awaken. Her soul simply slipped out of a body that had finally accepted to let go. It was that dark hour just before dawn when death, shrouded in darkness, most prefers to make his rounds. She died as she had lived: well; and that is all she would have wanted, life being, after all just a transient, if powerful dream.

Chapter 9

The funeral Mass was celebrated by two priests and six deacons one of whom was her grandson Peter Owuor Kembo. Her daughter Maria and her granddaughter sat in the front next to the simple coffin. Their eyes were red and swollen with weeping and still full of disbelief. She had looked so well, so chirpy, so like her old self; she had looked worse at other times but had not died — how could she die now when it had appeared as if she had rallied out of the worst? Like all who have heavily depended on a person, they were almost angry with her for leaving them. They still needed her so much. How could she just die like that and leave them? Maria who had nursed her mother throughout her last illness and had an inkling just how seriously ill she was and how much of her apparent improvement was due to strength of will not of body, found it a little easier than Elizabeth to accept Akoko's death. Besides she had buried so many others starting with her brother Obura, then her father Owuor Kembo, then her younger brother, then a husband and six children. She had in fact been surrounded by death in most of her adult life. It was there, just waiting, never satisfied, a true glutton. In this life there was one thing one could always count on and that was death. In a way, the only escape was to flow with the current of death as her mother had done and in that way to avoid a painful wrenching, but her mother had been no ordinary person at all. She Maria, had to step into her place somehow to the best of her ability.

Elizabeth was a different kettle of fish altogether.

With the impunity of the young, she had no comprehension of the dying process whatsoever. How could she when her whole being tingled with vibrant life? She had loved her grandmother desperately and tried to identify herself with all her aspirations. She had admired her unreservedly. Her cup of joy had run over when she saw the evident approval with which the old lady had looked at the man of her choice; and grandmother had been a very good judge of character, so she was confident that she had chosen well; but how could she just die like that? There was the wedding to be arranged, great grandchildren to be enjoyed! How could she die? She wept in confusion, anger and grief. How could she enjoy life, marriage and children without her beloved grandmother? The joy she would have felt had first to be reflected in her grandmother's eyes before it congealed into a reality for her. She was devastated and in a dangerous mood.

"Eternal rest grant her O Lord," intoned Father Thomas. "And may perpetual light shine upon her."

"May our departed sister Veronica rest in the peace of Christ."

"Amen," responded the gathered faithful.

They buried her in the 'limbo', the hallowed burial ground which the church had prepared. This was a break with the requirement of *Chik*, which had demanded that a married woman be buried in her husband's ancestral home to the left of the entrance to her house; but then Akoko had left that home never to return, over fifteen years before. She had left with body and spirit and there was no reason to return that body. Her dejected family went back to their hut to try and pick up the pieces again. Elizabeth took a pot and went to the river for there is always some peace to be found in routine however mechanical it is. She sat on a rock, her feet dangling in the water within the reach of any wandering leech but she did not care. She watched a dragon fly doing its acrobatics near the surface of the water. It went round and round in a dizzying whirl and then suddenly dived towards the water almost hitting it, then zoomed upwards in a beautiful arc without even getting a single claw wet. A praying mantis sat on a blade of elephant grass regarding all this unnecessary activity in prayerful contemplation; and in the nearby tree a dove cooed to its mate. "*Kech ka-aya! Kech ka-aya!*" which meant "I am hungry! I am hungry!"

Her thoughts, which were scattered and inconsequential, fluttered in and out of her mind without any order or direction. She saw herself as a little girl walking in between her mother in front and her grandmother in the rear with her cousin beside her on that epic journey to the mission. Even when it had turned dark, she had sensed no fear. She tried to recall her father's face but could not. She wondered what became of Owuor's mother. How could a mother totally forget her child? She then wondered what had become of all her classmates back in college. All in all she kept the one dark overwhelming thought just below the surface but eventually it burst through and she saw once again the clods of black soil falling on the rough hewn box with a terrible finality. A painful sob pushed its way past her tight throat and clenched jaw and burst through her resisting lips.

Her cousin Peter and Mark, her betrothed, found her there heaving and shaking from head to toe, completely out of control. Mark sat next to her and put his arm round her and murmured something about being sorry and coming as soon as he could. For a minute she sat there, unmoving and then awareness seemed to hit her suddenly. She jumped as if stung and screamed at him:

"Go away! Go away! I don't want to see you ever again!"

And with that she ran up the hill, her empty pot forgotten by the river. Mark stared at her open mouthed in disbelief. What on earth had he done?

"Leave her alone," said Peter kindly. He liked Mark already and knew that his cousin would be in good hands. "She is not herself. She loved grandmother a great deal. So did I as a matter of fact. She was both father and mother to me. She gave her life for us. Come, I will show you around the village. It will give me a chance to meet the people again. I am out of touch. The seminary is very demanding." He had grown into the full promise of his youth. Of medium height, he had an arresting face, not handsome but full of character with piercing eyes and a very square jaw. He had a beautiful well modulated voice and he had inherited Akoko's powerful vocal cords — but in bass. He was a joy to listen to at High Mass. Around him was a sense of purpose and a serenity, rarely found in one so young. Like his grandmother, he knew what he wanted, had counted the cost and would pay it without flinching for the rest of his life. In another year or two, he would be ordained to the priesthood and his only regret would be that she would not be there to watch him prostrated upon the ground taking his orders from his bishop.

Meanwhile Elizabeth had arrived at the hut, chest heaving and looking wild. Her mother took one look at her and remembered herself at fourteen, struck dumb at her brother's death, guided her inside, sat her down and started talking to her even as her own mother had done so long ago. She realised that this was a different manifestation of the same problem — the inability to accept the finality of death.

"She was the most beautiful girl in the whole village and the eldest daughter of the great chief Odero Gogni and the apple of his eye. Twelve suitors came trudging up the path to the *simba* to ask for his daughter's hand but he refused them all. Some were too old and had other wives, some had questionable characters and backgrounds; some he didn't just like. His daughter had to have the best.

One day a young man in full battle dress, handsome and full of *nyadhi*, that is full of style and presence, came up the path. He was a young chief and single and his name was Owuor Kembo..." She continued narrating the story of Akoko's life and eventually the girl quietened down and stopped shaking. She actually began to pay attention as the story unfolded and when the part came about the journey to Kisumu to appeal to the white DC, she exclaimed in disbelief and began asking questions. Her mother smiled and answered them. Eventually she concluded saying:

"Life does not always turn out exactly as we want it or as we expect it to. Once in a while it may give you a blow from which you think you cannot recover, but if you still have breath in you, always reel back and continue fighting for as your grandmother used to say, yesterday is not today and today is not tomorrow. Each day rises fresh from the hands of God bringing with it what it will."

Elizabeth left for the river to go and retrieve her forgotten pot in a better frame of mind. On the way, she met Peter and Mark and sheepishly went over to shake Mark's hand. He looked as if he had been given a reprieve from a death sentence.

"Er, I am sorry. I was not feeling well earlier."

"I understand. May we accompany you to the river?"

"Yes."

He followed her and patient Peter went with him. After all somebody had to chaperon the two to prevent village talk especially as she was still in mourning. Besides the girl's change of heart was nothing if not miraculous. "Grandmother must be watching over all of us from her place," he thought whimsically.

Chapter 10

After the period of mourning was over the wedding was postponed and then postponed again to give Peter now in Rome, time to complete his studies and get ordained. They were determined that one of his first priestly duties would be to marry them. These were the days when patience was still considered a virtue and the 'Come we stay and see whether we like it' kind of marriage had not been invented. Whether Christian or traditional a girl left home for her husband's on a given date and was considered married henceforth and not a day before.

Eventually Peter returned and was ordained as a priest — a Mill Hill-father. As he lay prostrate on the ground before his bishop, he thought of how he had longed for this day to come; of how much his grandmother would have loved to see him in his priestly robes; of the father he had never really known and the mother who for all intents and purposes had forgotten his existence — though that old scar no longer rankled as it had done in his youth. Others looking at him thought 'What sacrifice, what courage!' He felt only fortunate that God should call even one such as him. What could he have ever done to deserve it?

There were few priests and the parish to which he was sent was very large and the work exhausting. He had to celebrate Mass in various outflung places, attend to the sick and the dying, listen to confessions, administer baptisms and generally make himself available to any troubled soul whatever the hour; but he was a happy man and became beloved of the people as his stocky figure in its familiar black cassock went in and out among them. It is possible that with time a priest may take his calling for granted — treating his work as just another job; not so with Father Peter. This was especially obvious whenever he celebrated Mass particularly at the moment of consecration; his normally smiling face would be drawn with concentration and his gestures would assume a fluid grace as he lifted the circular host and declared: 'This is my Body which will be given up for you.' He did not just say it; he lived it, and he would continue to live it for the rest of his long life.

As soon as he settled down a little, he went back to the parish, Aluor in order to marry Elizabeth and Mark. The wedding was simple but the place was packed to the brim. The bride was dressed in a simple white poplin dress — with the tiniest of lace trimming. She had on a simple veil and white shoes — this time she had splurged on leather — after all how many times in her life does a girl wed? In spite of the austerity she was as radiant a bride as any that had ever walked up the aisle to begin a marriage that would last forty six years. Maybe if she stopped to consider the sheer length of time that the marriage might last, she might have faltered. After all to wake up and see the same face three hundred and sixty five times for forty-six years was not a joke; but the Church taught that she would receive actual graces to enable her to continue loving this one man and to withstand whatever vicissitudes might come their way. She chose to believe this with unshakeable faith.

And so Mark said:

"I, Mark Sigu do take you Elizabeth to be my lawful wedded wife, to have and to hold, to love and to cherish, in sickness and in health till death do us part." And likewise Elizabeth; then Father Peter declared them man and wife. The crowd clapped quite spontaneously. They had come to accept her with time, as part of themselves and were quite proud of her though they were sad that a man from the rocky wasteland of Seme would have carried her right from under their noses. All their acrimony and hatred were forgotten.

Mark took his bride off to Nakuru with him and they started their married life, in his modest bachelor pad which consisted of one room, a kitchenette and shared bathroom facilities, but they did not mind at all — it was home and they were happy. He was promoted to the front office of the Farmers Association he worked for and she started teaching at a nearby primary school.

One morning she woke up with a fearful attack of nausea and dizziness. She dashed out and threw up helplessly in the toilet. Mark came after her in alarm.

"What is it?"

"Don't know", she gasped.

"I'd better take you to the dispensary." He hurriedly made breakfast as she rested in a chair. After a cup of tea she felt better — so much better that she assured him that everything was OK. Since it was school holiday time she thought a little rest at home might do the trick so she sent him off to work. That evening he brought her some anti-malarial tablets which she obligingly swallowed. The following morning was chaos; not only was she throwing up but she had also fearful abdominal cramps. He called a neighbour and they rushed her to hospital. She was admitted immediately in a state of shock and dehydration. Not only had she vomited out everything, but had also started haemorrhaging violently. After hearing the story and examining her the doctor was furious. He started calling them all manner of names in his scant Swahili, until Mark stiffly informed him that he could understand English and would the man care to explain himself in a more understandable way? The doctor was Italian but his English was an improvement on his Swahili. Evidently what she had experienced the day before was a normal symptom of pregnancy but giving her anti-malarials was criminal for they were known to cause abortion in early pregnancy which is what was happening to her. Was he trying to kill his wife? If Mark had been less stricken he would have flattened the man with one blow — white man or no white man, but he had no energy even to continue standing so he sat down on a bench in a state of shocked disbelief.

They discharged Elizabeth after five days. She lost the pregnancy on the second day of her admission but had stayed on for observation for further evidence of chloroquin poisoning — but she had none. Mark dared not look at her — he felt so guilty but surprisingly she wasn't angry with him.

"How could you have known if even I didn't know? Don't worry, God will give us another." She did not even bother telling him that they had been twins. The poor man had suffered enough.

Such an experience is, however, very hard to shake off and now they were consciously trying to get another baby and as sometimes happens in such cases nothing happened. She remained confoundingly slim for the remainder of that year; and the next. It was too much. She forgot her earlier good intentions and one day actually accused him of having deliberately given her chloroquin to make her sterile. He was so angry that he stood up and lifted his hand as if to strike. He was actually foaming at the mouth. Then he turned on his heels and left the house. She tried to keep up her anger. After all she had been the wronged one, but when he had not come by late that night and on the following day, her anger turned to alarm and raw fear. Where could he be? Had he been in an accident? Had he committed suicide? Had he left her? If he had she had only herself to blame.

But that evening, he came home smelling like a brewery. He offered no explanation and she asked none; however family life continued somewhat uneasily for they were both still too young to give way to each other.

When the third year of marriage came and went with no visible offspring to show for it, Mark's mother arrived to demand an explanation. A woman with an education was an object of suspicion — who knows what she had been up to before her marriage? To Mark's credit, he told her in no uncertain terms whose business she was not allowed to mind.

"But – but – she's only a wife and I am your mother!"

"Yes. She is my wife, but you will soon be a stranger if you don't leave us alone. I'll put you on the bus this evening. You should go back and look after your husband." The old woman was beside herself with fury but Mark had the determination of a mule, so she went.

This incident went a long way to thaw things out between them and before long Elizabeth started having attacks of nausea again. This development was greeted with such enthusiasm by the two hopeful parents that they could barely blurt it out to the doctor who agreed she was pregnant. They went home walking on air.

"It will be a boy and he'll be a soldier like his father!" exclaimed Mark.

"Nonsense. She will be a girl and I will call her Veronica after my grandmother. I'll make sure that she gets a really good education and I will send her to the University at Makerere," said Elizabeth sweetly.

"Oh, OK. Whatever you say." He was too happy to quarrel. A child! That's all he wanted and he would work his boots off if need be to provide for them. It was time he went for some in-service training and improve his chances of promotion.

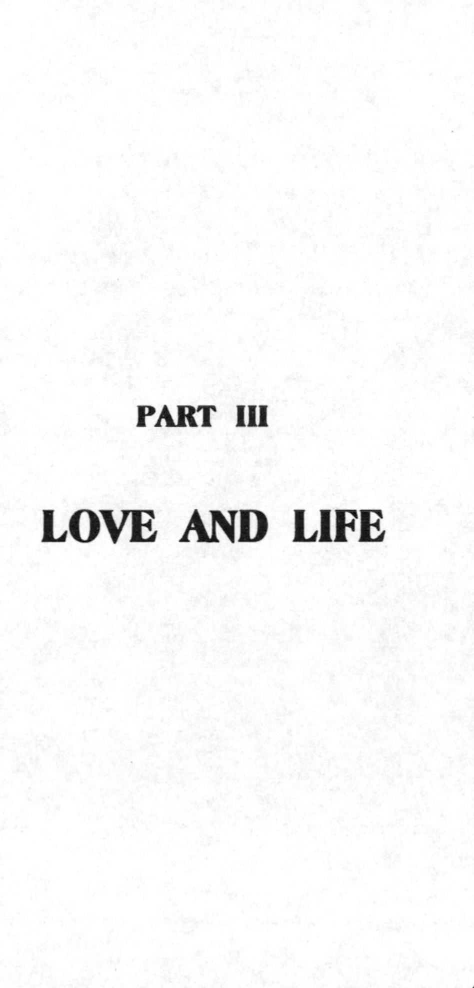

PART III

LOVE AND LIFE

Chapter 1

Veronica and her sister Rebecca arrived within minutes of each other at the general hospital. Veronica was smaller than Rebecca but was more vociferous. Apart from the difference in size, their personalities were completely different from the first day. Rebecca was plump, pretty and contented. She smiled at everyone including the flies on the wall. Her sister was skinny and avid. In spite of polishing off her own feed and most of her sister's she remained confoundingly lean. It was mystifying, so when the twins were three months old they were taken to the doctor to clarify the matter, but nothing wrong could be found with either. At five months, Vera sat up on her own while her sister remained content to lie on her back for another two months—by which time Vera was crawling all over the house. Becky decided that this was too much and tried to imitate her sister. She succeeded fairly well except that her progression was backwards. She just couldn't get the hang of crawling forwards. Eventually she did but by then Vera was cruising around with the support of stools, tables or whatever she could find. At ten months she walked away on her own two feet, arms held up high in the air to balance herself. It was clear that the young lady was in a hurry to go places. At thirteen months Becky also made her first faltering step and her parents uttered a sigh of relief.

Becky seemed to draw love from one and all from a very early age. She was soft, cuddly and pretty, and just plain irresistible. People wanted to touch her, to hold her and she was quite accommodating.

Vera did not want to be held, and the big flashing

eyes on her skinny face were restless and tempestuous. Even adults were a little afraid of her. She however had one saving grace; her capacity for love. Hers was and would remain a passionate nature. She took nothing for granted. She was completely loyal and from an early age her sister was the object of her love and protection. It was her business to see to it that Becky was happy and had everything she needed. She was willing and ready to do battle with anyone who crossed Becky's path and she was a fearless fighter although her tears were ready to fall at the slightest provocation. Once when she was about five, she almost tore a playmate apart before anyone realised what was happening because she was screaming at the top of her lungs while pummelling him. The boy remained mute and shocked and did not or could not utter a sound. He only remembered to snivel a little when they pulled the screaming Vera off him.

When the girls were two, Mark got his long awaited promotion and moved to a slightly bigger house which had an extra bedroom. It was just in the nick of time for Elizabeth was pregnant again and sleeping arrangements were becoming tricky. Their joy was however tempered by the fact that owing to the state of emergency, the country was becoming more and more dangerous even for ordinary people. Between the white johnies on one side and the Mau Mau freedom fighters on the other, death could arrive without warning. It was therefore decided that as soon as the baby was born, Elizabeth would move back to her old teaching job at Aluor where it was much safer, being far from the central region which was the enclave of the freedom fighters.

Aoro, a bouncing boy and the apple of his father's

eye was born in the middle of a long dry season — thus his name. When he was two weeks old he was whisked off to Aluor with his sisters. When she heard about it, their paternal grandmother was furious.

"How can you allow that woman to take off with my grandchildren? Is this why they refused to take a bride price for her? So that they could treat us like dirt?"

"Mother nobody is trying to treat anyone else like dirt. It is just that there is no suitable school for her to teach in around here. She can bring the children over during the holidays."

"Huff!" snorted his mother. Mark was almost sorry he had stopped by to see his mother on his way back to Nakuru.

Things became very bad and lorries carrying the dead, purportedly Mau Mau were a common sight. There was suspicion everywhere — white against black and black against white. The Kikuyu especially suffered greatly — and could be shot, maimed, killed or translocated at a moment's notice. They returned atrocity for atrocity and blood flowed — both black and white. Mark was very lonely without his wife and children. He particularly missed little Vera's constant chatter which he had found so irritating before. She had been tireless and irrepressible, but now he would have given anything to hear her say:

"Father, why is mother's stomach so big?"

"Uh-uh; don't know. Ask her."

"Mother! Father wants to know why your stomach is so big?" The little terror knew how to twist everything.

"There is a baby inside there waiting to be born." Her eyes would then grow as big as saucers.

"A baby!"

"Yes. Soon you will have a brother or a sister."

"Oh. I have a sister already."

"Well soon there will be another one."

"How can the baby see if he is in there?"

"He sleeps most of the time. Now go out and play with your sister. You ask too many questions."

How he missed them all, but there was nothing to be done except stick it out. He however became so lonely that he started to spend a lot of time drinking with his friends whenever it was safe to do so.

One thing led to another and before he knew what had hit him, he was involved with a girl. The girl was pretty, very pretty and what's more, accommodating, but apart from that nothing more could be said for her — except maybe that she had the personality of a leech and could cling closer than a vine. He was like a sick man. In no time at all she moved in with him and in another two months declared herself pregnant. That brought him to his senses with a jolt. He felt like a man who had been hooked on drugs and was trying to throw off the habit.

"What do you mean you are pregnant?" he asked shaking his head to try and clear the cobwebs.

"Well when you live with a man, you can get pregnant you know. I am pregnant." She pouted prettily. That usually brought results, but not this time.

"Nonsense; your boyfriends are numerous. I must have been sick to let you into my house. Get out. Get out now before something terrible happens to you. I am a married man with children and the woman I am married to is thrice the woman you are. Just get out now!" His voice was cold and threatening. He moved slowly towards her and as she was not pregnant anyway, she decided to count the mission lost, so she grabbed her things and fled. After she left he lay in bed for hours just thinking. He remembered how beautiful his wife was and what lovely children he had. He wept for himself and for them. He could not understand his action as he had never been a promiscuous man even before marriage.

Late that night, he made two resolutions: one for life and the other to be carried out the very next day.

True enough the next day he was seen jumping into a bus heading west. He had asked for emergency leave to go home to his wife.

It had been six months and the girls had grown and the boy was sitting up and taking notice. They rushed to him and surrounded him with the warmth of their love; but their mother held off a little.

"You've remembered us at last," she observed quietly.

"Yes. I am sorry. Er-er I was kind of busy but here I am now." He felt like the dirt in the street.

"Did you receive my letters? The girls had a bad attack of malaria. I thought Becky would die." He had received that letter but had read it in the haze of his infatuation. This was getting worse than he had feared.

"I got it, but there was no way I could get away. I am sorry," he added lamely.

"Why didn't you at least write to console us?" He kept quiet, but he knew he would rather die than tell her what had actually happened. Fortunately for him Elizabeth was not vindictive and did not hold grudges for long. She only said:

"We are all going back together. We are a family

and it is clear that you need someone to remind you of your duty all the time." He was only too willing to oblige, after all things could have been much worse. He would move house as soon as possible in case the neighbours started blabbing.

She eventually heard the rumours but chose to say nothing about it though he held his breath for days. She was learning the first cardinal rule of marriage: not everything has to be blurted out.

Chapter 2

The whole country was jubilant. Freedom! Independence! *Uhuru* was in the very air. Few really understood what it entailed but who cared? Let the white man go. We'd muddle along with our affairs. After all they are ours. The revered old man Jomo Kenyatta was at the helm and to assist him was the firebrand Jaramogi Oginga Odinga. The cabinet consisted of young, quite well educated Africans whose enthusiasm covered a multitude of sins especially lack of experience; but they would learn on the job. The sky was the limit for them mainly because the people they would lead had a few unusual characteristics though no one realised it then. The two most important of these were an amazing capacity for work and great resilience.

The people worked tirelessly and Kenyatta made the need to work, especially on the land, a clarion call. He ended almost all his speeches with a plea of *turudi mashambani* — let us return to the land. He exhorted his people to forget and to forgive and the people listened. They seemed to know instinctively that it was better to channel energy into work rather than into hate. Besides, the emergency years from 1952 to 1959 had been seven years of misery and bloodshed and nobody wanted to see such things again.

People wanted to live in peace; to educate their children; to have a friendly rivalry with their neighbours; to see who could reap more of the fruits of *Uhuru* for Kenyans have a taste for the good things of life. Finally each Kenyan loved his own skin dearly and though politicians would try to incite them to violence in later years, this basic love of self would see the people through such difficult times as would have set the peoples of other African nations at each others' throats without compunction.

The whites left in droves fearing for their lives. The nature of Kenyans had not become evident in those days. For those who stayed this would become a haven of peace unequalled anywhere in the continent, not even in South Africa to which some fled. There were many places to be filled and few Africans with enough education to fill them. Promotions were rapid even for those with only a modicum of ability. Mark Sigu, a man of considerable energy, benefitted. He joined a correspondence school and worked hard. In 1967 he became a manager and he moved to a much larger house which was just as well for he had quite a large family made more so by his wife's propensity to having twins. There was Vera and Becky — now aged twelve; Aoro aged ten; Anthony jnr otherwise known as Tony aged eight; a set of twin boys naturally named Opiyo and Odongo aged five and the baby — Mary who was barely one: seven in all. He himself was forty three and his wife thirty seven. She was so busy with the children that she had no time to study further, but she still taught at school.

All in all the Sigu family was a happy one. There was money, but not too much, and plenty of love — simple and unpretentious. Mark gathered his family protectively under his wing and when he realised that no love was lost between his wife and his mother he quietly made a resolution to resettle his family elsewhere. He did things for Elizabeth that would never have even crossed the mind of a full blooded African man — with a low opinion of women bred into him. She was constantly overworked in spite of the house help they had. Seven children at home and forty children in a classroom are a lot of work; so Mark took to helping her around the house — especially in taking the children off her hands. His friends derided this for a while but when he proved adamant, they gave him up as a lost cause.

The children grew so fast and in fact were a measure with which to gauge the passing of time. Vera was a brilliant student and carried off trophy after trophy in her school. She had a tremendous amount of energy and was into every activity from debate to sports. She was not beautiful at least not in the exquisite way her sister was, but she had a strong and arresting face, a lithe and graceful body. If it were not for the fact that she was open and friendly and never put anyone down, it would have been quite easy to dislike her, but Vera was ever ready to help and assist and so was quite popular in spite of her brilliance and force of personality. When she was fourteen and in the top class of her primary school, they made her the school captain — a position which had only been held by boys before. Her father was quite beside himself.

Becky was a different kettle of fish altogether. There was no denying the fact that she was a beauty and would always be one. She had large limpid eyes, a perfect face and a soft fine skin. It was not that Becky was lazy, or even stupid; she just did not know the meaning of exerting herself. She got whatever she wanted without creating any waves or getting into any unpleasant situation for she was very fastidious and utterly selfish. Her school work was satisfactory, for poor work was very likely to bring down the ceiling around one's head at home. But

Becky had a problem. She disliked her sister with a violence which was alien to a child and worse she hid it well behind that beautiful face. Maybe if she had brought it out, it might have helped but she kept it just beneath her consciousness. Vera loved her and accompanied her everywhere, showed her off to all for she had no capacity for meanness or envy; so no one at home ever suspected. Of necessity, they shared a room and the way in which Becky kept her things strictly to herself and her side of the room spotlessly clean might have alerted their mother were it not for Vera's all concealing love. In any case all parents make mistakes; Mark and Elizabeth were no exception.

When they sat for their final primary school examination, Vera as was expected had an almost perfect score and with it she won a place at a top National School for girls. Becky only did well enough to get a place in the district school. Their parents were elated until Vera brought them down by declaring that she was not going to school at all. Her parents exchanged a perplexed look. What was this? Was the child ill or something?

"Are you feeling well?" asked her mother solicitously.

"I am all right, but I am not going." Tears stood out in her eyes and her mother knew her well enough to know that a torrent was on its way. So she said:

"It's all right. We can talk about it later." Mark shifted on his feet uneasily. He was at a loss but was wise enough to let Elizabeth lead.

"No, mother," Vera bit her lip in determination and tear drops hung dangerously on the edge of her lower lid. "I want to talk about it now." This was supposed to be a happy ocassion. To have two daughters admitted to high school was not a small thing. What could be wrong?

"All right. Why don't you want to go?"

"I want to go to Becky's school!" she blurted out.

"Huh?" Mark couldn't believe his ears; but then now at least it made some sense. They tried argument, coercion, enticement to no avail. Becky herself looked on all this and then smiled quietly to herself and left the room. Vera was nothing if not determined. She would go to school only if she went with her sister since her sister could not come with her. Her father for the first time in his life felt like beating her into submission, but he knew it would only make her more determined. Later that night as they lay in bed discussing the matter, his wife said the only sensible thing that had been said that day.

"You know, Vera is the sort of person to make a success of her life wherever she happens to be. It is not only children in National Schools who pass examinations. Besides she can then look after her sister. I never feel quite safe about that child."

And so the young ladies put their things together and became boarders at Riverside High School — and a new phase of their lives started.

Chapter 3

Aoro Sigu was a throwback to his great uncle Obura. He was swift and bright; confident and curious. He would have liked to be a good boy but his nature simply did not allow it. With his brother Tony and occasionally the twins, life was made to yield one adventure after another, but adventure has its price especially when a boy arrives home wet, shivering and half drowned to face a stern father and a disbelieving mother.

"And what have you been up to?" This was father, his hand reaching for the shelf where he kept his main implement of discipline — a supple switch. Tony kept mum — he was a sterling guy to have for a brother, but not the twins; they saw the move towards the switch and their lips started to tremble.

"They m-made us d-do it." said Odongo, shaking.

"Yes! We didn't want to, but they made us!" said Opiyo gathering courage. It does no harm to stretch the truth a little especially if your backside is in danger of a conflagration. He forgot that he and his twin had begged on their bended knees to be allowed to go along and having arrived at the river had pleaded to be taught how to swim. When your little brother looks at you with such hero-worship, who on earth can say no? So everybody stripped down to the bare essentials — which was nothing — better to keep all one's clothes dry or mother might ask questions. The lesson was given without incident, if without much success. Aoro gave the order and everyone trooped back to the river bank.

The two older boys then brought out their home-made fishing lines and got engrossed in the little fish that flitted to and fro in the water. The twins watched this for a while but soon got bored especially as no fish looked particularly interested in the bits of worm being waved at them; soon they wandered off on their own and left the two anglers to their work. Time came to a standstill. Then the silence was suddenly broken by a frightened gulpy scream, followed by yell after yell. The brothers dropped their lines and ran up the river towards the sound. They rounded the bend just in time to see Odongo's head disappearing under water. On the bank stood Opiyo — perfectly still except for his mouth which continued to emit yells fit to wake the dead. There was no time to think — Aoro and Tony dived in to rescue their drowning brother. They got hold of him and dragged him towards the bank — and since the two had never heard of lifesavers, they nearly killed the poor blighter in the process.

Once safely on terra firma, it was by sheer luck that they put him on his side from which position he rolled gently on his face and thus vomited out the water without choking on it. His guardian angel must have been working overtime, otherwise he would have died. Aoro and Tony were too shocked to do anything but go straight home. In any case the aftershock had set in and they were shaking badly. They hoped that if they survived the switch they might get some dry clothes and some food to eat. When you are a fast growing boy food is never far from your mind because your body seems to process it almost faster than you can eat it.

So the twins blabbed out the story, carefully doctored to absolve them of all blame. Aoro and Tony looked at them with loathing and then looked at each other with quick understanding: the twins would be banned forthwith from all their activities.

Meanwhile, their father was apopletic. He knew vaguely that there was a river — but he had thought it was a long way out of town. And how under heaven, had his offspring found it anyway? He thought of the near drowning and his face darkened with anger. Elizabeth took one hasty look at him and decided to take over.

"You boys go to your room at once. When I come in there, Aoro, I expect to find you and your brothers bathed and ready for bed. The twins will have their dinner. You two will not. Off with you." The bigger boys groaned with one voice; better the switch than death by starvation.

Late that night two famished boys sneaked into the kitchen to grab some food. Elizabeth heard them rummaging about and smiled to herself.

"It looks as if you two have become thieves as well." The boys froze. This long day was turning into a real nightmare, not only would they starve to death, but they would do so with their backsides on fire.

Elizabeth walked into the kitchen, reached into a cupboard and produced a plate of *chapatis*. She then got two plates and spooned cold *dengu* (green gram) soup into them. The boys looked uncertainly at her, saw the smile in her eyes and fell to without further ado.

"I hope next time you go out with your brothers, you will be more watchful. He could have drowned you know."

"Yes mother!" But as soon as they got back to their room with their full stomachs peacefully going about the business of digestion, the two brothers looked at each other and then at the twins intertwined in their sleep.

"We'll never take these two useless puppies with us again."

"Never," concurred Tony—a man of few words. It became the pre-occupation of their lives to dodge the twins and their parents' vigilance for the rest of the school holidays. Aoro was the leader and Tony his determined and fearless shadow. Aoro's temerity was well balanced by Tony's calm courage. The younger boy had no sense of physical fear and did not know the meaning of giving up. His brother was endowed with brains and physical agility. Tony was short and squat and while lacking Aoro's almost mad genius, he was no fool and he had determination. Aoro maintained a brilliant record at school without trying. Tony maintained a brilliant record without appearing to try.

One night, Tony woke up with a pain in his right loin that got worse by the minute. After struggling for about an hour he woke his brother.

"Aoro, I think I am sick." he whispered.

"Um," mumbled Aoro sleepily then rolled over and fell promptly asleep again. Tony bit his lip to keep from screaming. He got up, staggered and fell on his knees. He clutched his stomach and let out an involuntary yell. This time his brother shot up, switched on the light took one look at his brother's agonised face and dashed out of the room.

"Father! Mother! Come quickly. Tony is dying." He burst into their room throwing his manners completely to the wind. Elizabeth was already on her way across the room. Like all mothers she slept without sleeping and Tony's scream had brought her to consciousness and to her feet before Aoro started out of his room. Mark struggled to wake up and saw his wife streaking out of the room.

"What the heck is going on?" he asked the empty room. There was of course no answer, but the panicked sound from the boys' room was enough to direct him.

Tony was writhing on the floor; clearly the boy was very sick. Mark rushed to the neighbours to ask for transport. Those were the days before people learned to barricade themselves behind their doors for fear of thugs masquerading as people in distress. The neighbour, who owned a VW rushed the sick boy, held on his mother's lap in the front seat with his father in the back, to the general hospital. Doctors who stare death in the face on a daily basis are never in as much a hurry as relatives would like them to be, but eventually the boy was seen and a diagnosis of acute appendicitis was made. He was scheduled for an emergency operation, but since there was one apparently more serious case before him, it wasn't until the early hours of the morning that they took him to theatre, where an ugly inflamed appendix was incised and removed.

Back at home Aoro was climbing walls with fear and worry. His sisters with the death like slumber of the young had managed to sleep throughout the whole commotion. At dawn he decided enough was enough so he went to their room and shook them awake.

"What is it, you ugly boy?" asked Becky sweetly. Vera looked at him and got out of bed hurriedly.

"What is it?" she asked alarmed.

"Tony's sick. He was rushed to hospital at night and they haven't come back." He could not add the unspeakable — the fear that his brother was dying or dead.

"Why didn't you wake us you idiot?" asked Vera

annoyed that such a thing could happen without her knowing it; so she took it out on her brother. Becky continued to lie in bed. Few things bored her as much as sickness, suffering and death. She simply could not identify with them. At sixteen she was a breath taking beauty and had a horde of admirers and aspiring boyfriends none of whom she had yet shown an interest in. She did not believe in wasting time. Besides her sister was always with her and she knew her parents would not take kindly to such goings on. She stretched luxuriously in bed, enjoying the feel of her young lithe body. Aoro, tired of being called names retired back to his room. Vera looked questioningly at her sister, then went to the kitchen to make breakfast. She was beginning to have her doubts about that young lady.

At around eight in the morning their weary parents trooped in. Nobody dared ask the question, but their round fearful eyes were eloquent enough.

"He had an operation. He is going to be all right. We can all go and see him at lunch time today." Their sigh of relief was heartfelt and unanimous.

Chapter 4

Aoro could not get over his brother's operation. He examined the incision carefully and noted the way in which the stitches had left tiny dots on either side of the healed scar. He was simply fascinated.

A fortnight later, he caught a hapless frog napping under a stone and decided to do an operation. He called Tony to hold down the struggling amphibian and then nicked its belly with an old blade. The frog passed out or did whatever it is frogs do when in shock — anyway it stopped struggling. Aoro then sewed the wound together with a needle he had taken from his mother's sewing basket and a piece of sisal string — the bleeding stopped and the patient suddenly came to life, broke loose and hopped off madly. The surgeon looked quite impressed with himself. His love affair with medicine had begun.

Before that long holiday was over Father Peter came to visit his nephews and nieces. He was a great favourite with all the children but seemed to strike it off especially with Tony who became quite loquacious in his presence. Aoro was a little jealous of their relationship because the two seemed to communicate at a different level altogether. When Uncle Peter was around he felt that Tony did not entirely belong to him — he had a great need of people and a possessive nature and Tony was the person he loved most in this world.

Tony was especially interested in the mystery of the Mass and asked endless questions about things that Aoro, with his restless nature had never even noticed.

His curiosity was insatiable and his brother looked at him as if he was in the grip of some ailment.

Yet Tony had such a lovable personality, and so loyal that one could always find it in one's heart to forgive him anything. Besides, when not being monopolised by Tony, Uncle Peter was great company and was full of stories and fun and was game for practically any game the boys wanted to play. Vera loved him for his intelligence — she had a great deal of respect for intelligence. Even disdainful Becky thawed a little in his presence. One twin or other was always perched on his shoulder and even baby Mary who disliked most people would toddle towards him out of her own volition.

So when Uncle Peter announced one night that he would soon be ordained a bishop everybody was delighted and insisted that they wanted to come to the ceremony.

"Soon you will be a cardinal and then you can choose the Pope or be Pope yourself," declared Tony with proprietary pride. He seemed to know a lot about these matters and his parents looked at him with interest. Could they be having a budding vocation in their midst? His mother, mission bred as she was and still a firm Catholic after all these years, was all for it. Mark had his doubts. It wasn't that he was not a good Catholic; it was just that he did not believe as fervently as his wife did, though he thought that religion on the whole was a good thing. Like many other quite decent people his religion had become a convenient and unquestioning habit. Although he had four sons, he would have been reluctant to give one up, especially a clever and determined fellow like Tony. Like so many he had a notion at the back of his mind, never quite given voice, that only those who were a bit daft could possibly want to be priests. Yet he liked and respected

Father Peter and liked a good sermon as much as any one else. Such are the contradictions of human nature.

All the same Mark felt very lucky in his children. Vera had set an unbeatable record at school; Becky was not doing too badly though her preoccupation with herself caused her mother a lot of concern. Was there also a bit of cooling in the girls' relationship with each other? He hoped not. Aoro had always managed to maintain a continuous lead in his class until the time of his final examination that last November. His mother however felt that he did not apply himself as diligently as he should and could have. Tony was a good steady lad — no worry there unless the Church grabbed him. The twins Opiyo and Odongo who were identical in appearance were still unsteady and had not found their niche. They were nine and apart from the tendency especially of the younger to tell fibs, were not doing too badly. The baby now five, was no longer a baby but an active little girl — a bit spoilt by having so many older sisters and brothers at her beck and call, not to mention a doting father.

Father Peter eventually left the family and travelled to Aluor to spend a little time with his cousin Maria, who was now seventy. Her relatives had been giving her a hard time wanting her to go back to her ancestral village. She was very attached to the mission but she was lonely, so the twins Opiyo and Odongo were dispatched to go and live with her and to attend the school which their mother had gone to so long ago. It was felt that it would be an opportunity for them to learn self sufficiency, to find their feet, as well as to keep their aging grandmother company.

Naturally they were not keen to leave home, but they had their family's toughness, and were keen to tackle the challenge that living away from the shadow of their bigger all knowing brothers presented. Besides grandmother was unfailingly kind and they would have each other for company.

When the results eventually came Aoro had performed so well that he was invited to one of the best schools in the country. He walked on air for days and felt like crowing especially when he remembered his mother's scathing remarks about his character in general and his laziness in particular. She took it in good grace and congratulated him warmly. Which parent would not enjoy being proved so pleasantly wrong?

Tony who still had two years to go was downcast. He would miss his brother terribly. The twins had already gone to their grandmother's while Vera and Becky would soon be back in boarding school. That left only him and his sister Mary—who could hardly be considered company. He was forlorn — his brother had been his close companion for all the twelve years of his life and he loved him with all the strength of his tenacious mind.

The only advantage for Tony was that his uncle's ordination to the bishopric would take place when all the others were away in school so only he and maybe his little sister would be able to go. He really wanted to see that ceremony. Meanwhile he threw himself into his studies with determination. In all the world, there was now only one school he wished to attend and that was Aoro's. Nothing would be left to chance, he would get there if it killed him.

Aoro eventually left for school. He too was sorry to leave home, but he was also eager to start a new life free from parental vigilance; and also to test his razor sharp mind against those of his classmates. It would be exciting. The excitement however lasted only up to the school gate. The place was too cold, the food too bad, the discipline too harsh. Within his first week, he had gotten on the wrong side of both the House Captain (for failing to make his bed on time among other faults) and of the Head Prefect. The latter was a true achievement for the Head Prefect was a lofty soul who ordinarily did not deign to notice a mere Form One boy — a low form of life indeed, but Aoro got his attention all right, for one misdemeanor after another.

Things went from bad to worse. It was clear that the boy had a problem with discipline. So he was suspended and ordered to come back with his father.

When he walked into the house, his parents thought that it was half term. Tony was all over him and he tried to bluster his way through.

"Is something wrong?" Was there anything that ever escaped that woman's scrutiny? Elizabeth's eyes were focused disconcertingly upon him.

"Er - no. Of course not."

"But that is the fourth time you have told us what a dirty sort the Head Boy is and the fifth time you've told us what a mean character the House Captain is. Are you having a problem at school?"

"Er - yes, but it is because those two are always picking on me and telling on me to the teachers."

"May I see the letter?" asked the mother.

"What letter?" stammered the boy — wishing he were elsewhere.

"Please don't waste my time." He reluctantly produced the crumpled envelope from his back pocket. He had been greatly tempted to open it but he still had a strong desire to live and a crime like that would have worsened an already terrible situation.

When Mark got home that evening he met a grim Elizabeth and a trembling son.

"Your son needs to be taken to an approved school, look at this," she handed him the letter. He read it quietly; then read it again in case his eyes were playing tricks on him. He said nothing. After dinner, he called his family together.

"I have always done my best to provide for you, my children. Of all the things I provide, the most important is education and so far I have been pleased with your efforts. However, I cannot force anyone to go to school, especially if such a person is a man almost as tall as I am. When one is young, his parents are bound by duty to provide for him. When he becomes a man, and Aoro here is obviously a man — since he is tall and has a deep voice and a moustache — it's his duty to provide for himself." The man in question hung his head in shame.

"Aoro, school is not necessary for a bright, strong fellow like you. School is only for those fools who still want to learn. Today I will give you food. Tomorrow you go out and earn it. I will also allow you to stay in this house for one month after which I expect you to move out and look for a place of your own." Mark stood up and left the room — his dumbfounded family staring after him. He had never troubled his head with vague theories about the supposed fragility of growing minds, and if he had he would have pointed out the fact that he had yet to father a fragile child. He woke up his son at dawn and ordered him out.

"But father! I have not had breakfast!"

"Since when did you see breakfast walking in here by itself? Go out and earn yours." He reached for his belt. Aoro grabbed his shirt and took to his heels. He would take his chances out in the streets. Out there he learned for the first time that everything cost money and that he hadn't the foggiest idea about how to earn it. When he got home that evening, he was famished but nobody offered him any tea. At dinner, no place was set for him and his father sat sternly at the head of the table, his face hewn out of granite. Aoro slunk into his room and sat groaning on his bed. The whole situation was getting out of hand.

Late that night Tony watched him quietly as he got out of bed and headed for the kitchen. It gave a funny sense of *déjà vu*. He had lived through that scene in different circumstances not so long ago. This time however, he knew that there would be no success. He had seen Elizabeth lock the kitchen with a resolute expression on her face.

The following morning, Aoro did not have to be awoken. It is impossible to sleep on an empty stomach. That night even the porridge at school would have looked good to eat. Anything at all looks good if death by starvation is imminent. He waited for his father in the sitting room feeling a great affinity to the proverbial prodigal son, wondering whether using that rogue's flowery language might help his case: "Father I have sinned before you and God;" but he knew his father well enough to realise that such language would cause his immediate banishment back to the pig-pen. Besides his father might just take him up on his offer and make him into a house-servant. When Mark emerged from his room, Aoro stood up respectfully, his hands held at his back.

This man held his future in his hands.

"What are you still doing here?"

"Father! I am very sorry, please forgive me. I promise never to do any of those things again. I will work hard. You know how hard I can work. I'll never make you ashamed of me again. Father! Father..." this last as Mark made as if to turn away.

"Yes young man?" he turned and enquired calmly of his son. Aoro was actually sweating and was fast becoming incoherent. He had not eaten for thirty six hours. Suddenly, he keeled over and passed out. His mother who had been watching secretly from the kitchen rushed out to her son. Mark walked into the bathroom and returned with a basinful of water which he unceremoniously threw on the face of his eldest son and heir. The boy came to and shook his head. He looked at his father and his father looked at him — an unequal tussle of wills. And Aoro recognised for the first time that here was a man to be respected and feared, not just vaguely loved and hoodwinked at every opportunity. He lowered his eyes and waited for his sentence.

Chapter 5

Mark had the devoted love of his wife and the affection of all his children. He was not a hard man to love for he was fair and just; was firm but understanding and evidently loved them all; but between him and his youngest child grew the tenderest of attachments. This last one had come unexpectedly and had threatened miscarriage after miscarriage needing frequent hospitalisation of the mother and constant worry on the part of the father. The doctors said that she had high blood pressure and that the pregnancy might have to be terminated before time to prevent severe damage or death of the mother. Terminated! He was after all a man who valued human life; yet he loved his wife.

"We will try to hold back for as long as possible to give the baby a fighting chance; but you must realise this is a very serious condition and we might lose both mother and child." Mark just stared dumbly at the man.

"I suggest that you take her to the National Hospital where there are better facilities than we have here." The man waited for a while and getting no response, decided to go and write a referral note. At the time, the pregnancy was only six and a half months and the baby would have died if she had been born then — aborted the doctors called it; because according to them, it was only considered a miscarriage if the pregnancy was seven months or more with the possibility of a viable baby being salvaged. Viable meant that the chance of survival, in those days, was about twenty-five percent. Three out of four such babies died and the ones who survived had a high proportion of brain damage, mental retardation and blindness. Mark's head reeled under the onslaught. His wife would die for a baby who had practically no chances at all.

Elizabeth insisted on being told what was wrong. When she was sure that she had fully grasped what was being said, she took matters in her own hands. She was not the grand-daughter of Akoko for nothing.

"Of course we will go to that hospital. If they do admit me, Mark you can go back to the children and only come to visit me over the weekends or whenever you can. Don't worry — my grandmother promised me that I would live a long life. And the baby will be quite all right. I will call her Nyabera—the good one — after my mother. You just wait and see."

"How do you know it is a girl?" asked the mystified Mark. Women were strange, but his wife was the strangest of them all.

"You think I have carried six children without learning a thing or two?" she asked smiling. He himself was only too glad to have the decision taken off his hands.

Elizabeth stayed in the hospital for another one and a half months, then it became imperative to induce labour to save both mother and child.

"If we leave it there any longer, the stress might kill it. We will give you an injection to start labour tomorrow."

"Would you call my husband please?" was all she said. Courage by any other name smells just as sweet. Anyone who has had induction of labour will tell you that natural labour is much easier. The pain is insistent and unremitting, building up to a crescendo of continuous agony; but Elizabeth survived it and so did the baby who was such a skinny, wizened little thing, that its mother took one look at it and asked for water. The puzzled nurses brought her a cupful in which she dipped her fingers, touched the baby's forehead and whispered:

"I baptise you, Mary, in the name of the Father, the Son and the Holy Spirit." Though there are other worlds, Mary however, had no intention of leaving this one just yet. Once she was out of the stressful environment of the womb, she never looked back. After two weeks, she had gained a pound and a half and looked more like a human baby than a monkey. Her mother's blood pressure remained rock steady and Mark took his wife and his little daughter, held firmly in his arms, back home.

He could therefore not be blamed if he had a weak spot for this little one grabbed out of the jaws of death. He would come into the house and ask, "Where is Baby?" until the day his wife reminded him that there were six other children in the house as well as little Mary.

All his children had gone to public schools, but when it was Mary's turn, only a private school could do; and now that he had a car, and her little legs could not carry her to school, she had to be driven there. Only the fact that her mother kept her head prevented the young lady from being completely spoilt. Still she had to smile sometimes just watching father and daughter. However the other children grumbled a little.

"What does she have to do to be punished — commit murder?" asked Becky scathingly. She liked to be the centre of attention — and Mary threatened this.

"Go easy on her," said Vera who had an in-built

sense of security that nothing could ruffle.

"But you know that he does anything she asks him to do. It's not fair."

"Grow up," replied Vera shortly. She was seventeen and so tired had she become of her sister's poutings and preenings and extreme selfishness that she made a promise to herself to go very far away from her as soon as she could. This would be very soon because the two were going to sit for their Ordinary Level examinations in a matter of two months. Vera had already applied for a place at the school she had missed out on four years ago when love for her sister had clouded her judgement.

That year, 1972, would also see young Tony sitting for his Certificate of Primary Education to try for a place at the school where Aoro was. He had worked incessantly hard and had his head buried in a book most of the time. He was short and stocky, with a driving determination that would take him far at whatever he chose to do. There was nothing errant or flighty about him. At thirteen he already knew what he wanted out of life and had accepted that hard work was the price.

Anyone who has had to live with someone faced with a major examination knows that the atmosphere is constantly charged and can be sparked off by literally anything. In 1972, the Sigus had three such candidates — Vera, Becky and Tony: it was lucky that Tony was a self possessed fellow; but Vera, realising by the minute the magnitude of the sacrifice she had made for her uncaring sister, was tense in her determination to recapture that lost chance. Becky who was now well aware of the importance of doing well at school, not for her parents' sake, but for her own, was close to a nervous breakdown as she drove herself to work at a pace she was unaccustomed to; again, Vera had ceased to take her side automatically and now tended to bite her head off at the slightest provocation.

So it was that as Becky tried to take out her frustrations on her little sister Mary, Vera became more and more scathing until one night the whole thing blew up and the two started screaming accusations and counter-accusations.

"You hate me! You never liked me! You only came to my school to spy on me because you are jealous of me you ugly witch, you pretender!" This was too much for Vera.

"I sacrificed a golden chance to be with you stupid girl and you return it with nothing but insults!" Tears welled in her eyes and she dashed them away angrily with her fist; then she grabbed her sister just as their mother burst into the room. Elizabeth managed to cool down tempers somewhat and took Vera aside as the more reasonable one.

"Leave your sister alone! I expected better of you Vera, I really did." Vera sniffed angrily, madder now at the uncontrollable dams that were in her eyes. When would she ever learn not to take everything so to heart?

A semblance of normality was restored, but the relationship between the twins had received a blow from which it would never fully recover.

Chapter 6

Eventually the exam results were published. Vera got a first division pass with distinctions in Mathematics, Biology, Physics, Geography and English and credits in Chemistry and Literature. She also managed a pass in Needlework which pleased her immensely because she had feared that she would fail the confounded subject. She hated to fail and had therefore suffered the needle pricks gladly.

Becky managed a second division pass with which she was well pleased as were her parents. Tony whose calm assurance had began to show signs of cracking surpassed his wildest dreams by obtaining a perfect score of thirty-six points. He held himself tightly and then let out a lusty yell.

"Watch out guys, here I come!" he shouted. Elizabeth, who had a particularly soft spot for this son smiled at him.

"You worked for it. I'm sure Aoro is dying to know. You must write and tell him."

"That's a great idea!" he ran on ahead. His joy simply could not be contained by a sedate pace.

Becky wanted to look for a job immediately. It would mean freedom and she craved freedom. Mark would not hear of it. His breathtaking eighteen year old daughter? Out in the streets full of predatory men, by herself? Never.

"That cannot be young lady. You are going right back to your old school to study for your Advanced Level Certificate in History, Literature and Geography just like they have told you to."

"But father! All I want to be is an air-hostess.

Why should I go back to school? That's for Vera who wants to be a professor."

"An air-hostess?" Mark could not believe his ears. "Over my dead body!"

Becky looked at his face and retreated to her room. She remembered the story of Aoro and his near starvation. She would bid her time; no use in antagonising the old geezer.

Vera enthusiastically took on Mathematics, Physics and Chemistry. This time she said good-bye to her sister and left without a backward glance. Tony left to join Aoro and his mother's heart went with him. Soon the house echoed with emptiness for even little Mary was away at school throughout the day. The children were growing up and the going away movement was becoming an exodus. Elizabeth wished that the twin boys were with her to fill the house with noise and good cheer.

One day a telegram arrived from Aluor. Now letters from that place were few and far between. They mainly consisted of notes from the twins asking for this, that or the other. A telegram rarely ever carried good news and Mark's hands shook a little as he tore it open.

"COME" it declared. "YOUR MOTHER IS VERY ILL." It must be Maria! He rushed out of his office and went to get his wife. She was in the middle of a lesson and one of the teachers had to call her out. One look at Mark's face was enough. He had never been much good at hiding things behind a blank mask and Elizabeth could read him like a book.

"What is wrong?" He said nothing, just quietly handed her the telegram.

"Mother ill! But she was so well when we went

to see her last month! Oh my God! We must go at once!"

"Yes dear. I've already spoken to the headmaster — so just get into the car and we'll go right home." Firm, decisive Elizabeth was standing there looking confused and unsure of her next action. When they got home, she walked into the sitting room and again just stood there. She had the most oppressive premonition of doom pressing in on her from all sides and she simply could not make any sensible move. So Mark took over, packed a few things for her, made arrangements with the neighbours to collect little Mary, put his wife in the car and drove off.

Most children have a father and a mother and Elizabeth had been no exception apart from the fact that her father had been a woman — her grandmother Akoko. Now her mother was ill, probably dying and she experienced a completely different pain from the one she had experienced at her grandmother's death. There is a bond that exists between mother and child that is completely primeval in nature and only comes to the surface of the conscious mind in all its primitive force when either mother or child is in some sort of peril — not surprising considering that as a child lies in its mother's womb, the first sound it hears is her heartbeat and the first human voice it recognises is hers. For the next many months, the child's most satisfying experience will be to lie next to her heart, nursing at the breast — so that the powerful connection is not severed with the cutting of the cord.

Maria Nyabera had been a good mother to Elizabeth and her cousin Peter and in her own generous way, had given unstintingly of herself to them and to her own mother. Elizabeth remembered how tenderly she had looked after Akoko when she became old and ailing and she hoped with a sick despairing dread that she would get the same chance to show her mother how much she cared in spite of the distance between them.

"I have failed her." These were the first words she had spoken since their departure from Nakuru and now they were approaching the outskirts of Kericho town. Mark cautioned himself to tread carefully for he remembered only too clearly how she had almost broken off their engagement at her grandmother's death, blaming him for God alone knew what.

"How have you failed, dear?" he asked cautiously.

"Don't keep on calling me dear! You know very well I should have visited her more frequently — instead of just staying with you, who are young and healthy and don't need me!"

Mark knew better than to point out that not more than two months had ever passed without Elizabeth dashing west to see her mother; or the great sacrifice that they had both made in giving up two of their children to her. He knew her well enough to know that she would only bite off his head and he liked it well enough where it was — firmly attached to his body. He was lucky for he had many brothers staying at home with his own mother so he didn't have to constantly worry on that score. He really understood her predicament.

"You don't understand anything at all!" the lady declared as if reading his mind. "You don't know how torn I've often felt, how I long to divide myself in two, so that I can be in both places at once!"

Mark said nothing but thought to himself that marriage was a very useful thing: there was always someone to vent one's fury on however and especially unjustifiably. Elizabeth kept on alternating between long silences and irrational self accusatory statements until they were a few miles from Aluor. She then kept completely quiet. It was dark by then but when they approached the hut they found a crowd of people gathered there and both their hearts sank. She must be dead!

The twins rushed out into their parents arms, and the people surrounded them; but Elizabeth had no eyes for anyone — she just walked into the hut. She had to see that beloved face one last time.

"She is not here. Father Thomas took her to the hospital at Maseno." So she was not dead yet, thank God. It must have been eight o'clock, but she simply turned on her heels and went out to the car again despite the protests of the villagers. This night would not pass without her seeing her mother. Mark and the twins followed her out. They knew that argument was of no use.

When they finally reached Maseno at about nine o'clock, they had to plead to be allowed in. They found Maria, who had suffered a massive stroke, still in a coma. The clinical officer on duty held out no hope but suggested they return in the morning to confirm with the doctor. It was then decided that Elizabeth stay with her mother and Mark take the children home. He would return in the morning.

Elizabeth pulled up a stool and sat by her mother all that night listening to the changing patterns of her breathing; first it was stertorous but steady; then she went into periodic breathing with lapses so long that her daughter, afraid that she had stopped altogether, would squeeze her hand at which she would start breathing again. Once she actually opened her eyes and Elizabeth tried to talk to her but got no response. She would have bombarded the nurses with her questions but she was afraid they would throw her out.

At seven o'clock, just before the doctor came for his rounds Maria Nyabera, daughter of Chief Owuor Kembo and Akoko Obanda; and wife to Okumu Angolo breathed her last with her only daughter at her bed-side; but death is such a lonely and private matter that all others however loving, can only be observers. Elizabeth stood by that bed-side for a long time. It was a strange feeling to realise that one is an orphan even if one is forty-three and that the one person who has always loved one without question is no more.

Father Thomas who had had a soft spot for this ever smiling parishioner of his was very helpful. He helped transport the body, and assisted His Lordship Bishop Peter Kembo with the requiem Mass, then the funeral procession, with altar boys leading, proceeded to the burial ground where Maria was laid to rest beside her mother. It was the end of an era. The year was nineteen hundred and seventy three, almost a hundred seasons after the girl-child, Akoko Obanda had arrived wailing into the world — the first daughter of the great Chief Odero Gogni, by his second wife Akech. She it was who had been the source of this river which at one point had trickled to a mere rivulet in danger of petering out, but which once again in her grand-daughter Elizabeth, and in her seven children was gathering momentum.

The dead have no use for the living who have eventually to tear themselves away so that the business of life might somehow continue. Elizabeth gathered her children and they left the fresh mound of red soil by itself in the hot afternoon sun. There were things to do — the hut had to be closed, a few cherished things taken, but most given away. The children had to go back to their various schools and she herselfback to her house. There was nothing but memories to hold her to this place — her adoptive home to which she had come as a very little girl.

Chapter 7

The twins were torn between being glad to be home again and missing their grandmother to whom they had grown very attached. Opiyo appeared to have benefitted most from the two year sojourn with his grandmother. He was now a steady eyed independent lad who could be counted upon to do his bit. Odongo on the other hand had not made up his mind whether to be fish or fowl. In fact he was amphibian with frequent changes of disposition. One moment he would be a calm adult and the next a squirming baby. How could two people look exactly alike and be so different, Elizabeth wondered? Opiyo was turning out very much like his brother Tony, while Odongo had Aoro's quicksilver personality without the strength and the determination; but then again one can't expect to have all winners. As it was, the Sigus were lucky in their children.

That following year there was a record five candidates in the house and tension once again reigned supreme. Vera and Becky were doing their Advanced Level Examination, Aoro his Ordinary Level, and the twins Opiyo and Odongo their Certificate of Primary Education. Books and papers were all over the place and tempers were short. Vera at nineteen had undergone a metamorphosis from a gawky thin faced teenager into a striking young woman and the boys, who had previously had eyes only for Becky started to take notice. Becky of course noticed this and was jealous. Vera herself was unaware since all the neighbourhood boys were afraid of Mark, who had been known to throw ardent admirers bodily across the fence. He had not been a soldier for nothing—and no young pup was allowed to nose around his precious girls. Naturally he had quite forgotten what he himself had been like a quarter of a century before. Short is the human memory.

One particularly persistent young man called Tommy Muhambe however kept coming back until Vera who was not only unaware, but was totally lacking in feminine wiles, became aware of him. He was in University studying Veterinary Medicine and was twenty one. More important he was madly in love — with that passion which only first love can arouse. One Sunday, he actually asked her to go to the movies with him. She was quite impressed by his temerity because the thought of Mark was usually enough to cool off the most ardent of young men. She thought of the tomes waiting for her and the triple A's she wanted to score in Maths, Physics and Chemistry and decided one movie wouldn't kill her. So she broached the subject after dinner that night while her open mouthed siblings waited for the sky to cave in at such audacity.

"Father, Tommy asked me to the movies next Saturday. May I go? I would really like to." She looked at him levelly but not antagonistically — one adult to another. Mark could not ignore that gentle challenge. He would have loved to steal a quick look at Elizabeth — for guidance and inspiration — but obviously could not.

"Who is this Tommy?" he asked to buy time. He knew Tommy very well. He was Mike Muhambe's son at the University — a nice enough young man were it not for the fact that he was Luhya and was eyeing his eldest daughter. Vera was not given to making unreasonable demands or causing trouble for trouble's sake, therefore she could not be denied off-hand. She would simply come up with any number of convincing arguments. Even the tendency to spill tears seemed to have waned as she approached adulthood.

"He is the Muhambe's son who does Vet Medicine at the university. I thought you knew him." The other children hung on to her every word filled with excited admiration. Becky would have fainted first before facing up to her father. Aoro remembered only too clearly what a tussle with Mark could lead to.

"Yes, I know him," conceded Mark rallying his scattered senses. "However your mother and I have to think and talk about this because it is very important, not only for you but for your brothers and sisters as well." What he meant was that much as he trusted Vera, he was afraid that lifting of barriers may still be premature for the rest.

"That's OK father," answered the young lady. She then left the room and her brothers and sisters stared after her with approval. That was one champion sister!

Mark and Elizabeth held an emergency conference that night—at least it was emergency for Mark who had hoped for a respite of at least another two years. It is disconcerting to realise that your little girl has grown up and has developed an interest in someone other than yourself.

"What shall we do?" began Mark characteristically.

"About what?"

"You know very well what I mean. This business of going to the movies with that — that good for nothing son of Muhambe."

"Tommy is not a good for nothing; please don't exaggerate. He is a nice, polite, hard working young man. That aside, what could you possibly do — lock her up?" asked Elizabeth.

"Whose side are you on?"

"I am not on any one's side. Be reasonable and realise that at least it is Vera and Tommy — who are two very responsible youngsters. At her age, you have no choice but to say yes — and pray."

"Are you crazy? What if she became pregnant or something?"

"Mark Sigu; have you ever heard of the word friendship? It is possible for two people to be friends without it leading to anything else. I know that sometimes an apparently intelligent person can make mistakes, but again one can only hope. Accept the fact that you have daughters and that men are going to show interest."

So it came to pass that Vera and Tommy went to the movies on the following Saturday and found that they had a lot to talk about. Vera wanted to know what life at campus was like and Tommy was only too willing to talk. Thus begun a long lasting friendship.

Becky wasted no time in putting in her demand, but for her it was a matter of being equal to her sister. She had no time for the gawky youths who hung around her and she treated them with amused contempt.

Aoro who was seventeen and at an awkward age with a large number of pimples on his face decided that things could wait. He was too busy with his books anyway. He was determined to get distinctions in Chemistry, Biology and possibly Physics and Maths. His aim was of course to excel in subjects that might one day facilitate his entrance into medical school.

The year drew to a close, the examinations were duly done and the tired students dispersed for their Christmas holidays. Vera got a job teaching at a nearby *harambee* school and the boys decided to go and visit some of their uncles in Seme and also spend some time with their Uncle Peter, bishop of the diocese of Kisumu.

Becky stayed at home because she couldn't find a job to her liking. She was not interested in teaching in the *harambee* schools because 'it was boring' as she put it. So she stayed at home and concentrated on making herself beautiful.

The twins' results were out first and predictably Opiyo had passed with flying colours while his twin brother failed — the first member of the family to do so. He didn't look particularly concerned about it until his father informed him that he would have to repeat the class.

"No. I won't!"

"Suit yourself — go look for a job tomorrow. You know the rules in this house: you only stay here as long as you are going to school. Once you've had enough of schooling as you apparently have, you go out and work like everyone else."

"Why can't you get me a school? I know boys who had worse scores and are in High School, why not me?"

"Since when did you see me doing any such thing? You are welcome to go and stay with those families, but if you want my help you have to go to school and show me that you deserve it."

The O-Level results were next in line and Aoro who had eventually settled down to some real hard work — so great had his ambition become — lifted six distinctions in Maths, Chemistry, Physics,

Biology, Geography, English and Kiswahili — attaining a perfect aggregate of six points, one of the best in the country. He was beside himself with joy and would have loved to practise some more surgery on a frog, but no amphibian was forthcoming—once bitten twice shy.

Lastly the Advanced Level results were announced and Vera had achieved A's in Maths and Physics and a B in Chemistry. She had decided at the last minute to choose Electrical Engineering instead of Architecture—which was merely academic—; she had qualified for both. Becky got one weak principle in English Literature, and flunked in the rest of her subjects. She had seemed pre-occupied of late and did not seem to pay as much attention to the results as would have been expected.

One morning Vera woke up to find an empty bed. Becky was not an early riser — a problem on which her mother had dwelt at graphic length without any evident improvement. Vera sat up and saw a note propped on a stool in such a way that she could not have missed it.

"Dear Vera," it began sweetly enough. "I am leaving home to go and stay with some friends of mine in Nairobi. I am determined to become an air-hostess — and they can give me the connections that I need. Please tell Mum and Dad not to worry. You always know what to say to them while I have always felt like an outsider. I am sure no one will miss me anyway. Hope you make professor. Your sister Becky."

Vera sat still for a very long time, remembering what it had been like when they had been little girls with no animosity between them. She knew in her heart that she had failed her sister, recognising —

without pride, her superiority to her sister in everything but looks. She should have had a heart big enough to forgive and to reconcile, but she had been too proud and who knows maybe a little jealous of her sister's exquisite beauty. She sighed and stood up. Her parents had to be told and somehow convinced to let Becky follow her own star.

Chapter 8

Campus life was exhilarating. For the first time there were no parents or teachers to watch your every move. The lecturers gave their lectures in the lecture theatres or halls and left it at that. There were hall-wardens in the halls of residence — but they were not very much in evidence. Vera for one never even met her hall's warden. Freedom was in the very air and naturally went into people's heads. The women's halls of residence, 'the Box' as it was known, was the hunting ground for all and sundry, and big cars were very evident especially on Saturdays when well dressed, well-to-do men descended upon the place. It was thc thing to have a girl friend in campus. Only too naturally, the male students did not like it. In fact there were two categories of girls — the fast-moving 'Mercedes' types and the 'clipboards'. These latter were the ones who had boyfriends in campus and acquired that name because their boyfriends owned nothing to offer except their clipboards for holding lecture notes; these would be seen tucked firmly under their arms as they tried to fast talk some girl or other. It pays to have a good tongue in your head if you have no money in your pockets.

Vera had Tommy and it helped because with him in the background, she could say no to the happy hunters. Her course was so demanding in fact that she rarely had time for anything except the occasional movie and the one hour of Mass every Sunday that somehow she had never outgrown though she often wondered what it was she actually believed in — like many others before her, she was undergoing a crisis. It was no longer kosher to accept things just because Mum said so. That one, holy, apostolic and catholic Church, formerly the bedrock of existence, had many apparent faults — even to one not given to the kind of emotionalism that the fundamentalist bible wavers had to offer. She really had to sit down one day and find out if she really believed, but for now there was the exciting world of light and heavy currents to explore.

Tommy came by every Saturday to see her, and if money allowed, he would take her out. Judging from the complaints of his friends, he was a lucky man indeed. Vera understood that lack of money was not leprosy and that one could be just as happy eating a packet of chips on a bench at Uhuru Park as when eating an expensive meal at the Inter-Continental with a man whose eyes followed every pretty face that came by. He was very fond of Vera and immensely enjoyed her lively intelligent conversation. She had such an expressive face full of zest and laughter. Tommy was no fool and he knew that only a fool would let such a woman out of his grasp. Soon he would be out of campus and working and he wanted to settle down as soon as possible. He felt no strong need to sample the market first; but there was a problem and that problem was Vera. He had felt instinctively that she was one to go at her own pace and never to be pushed, and so he had hastened slowly. She had responded by treating him with the utmost friendliness and always greeted him with a warm smile; but she remained friendly and nothing else.

Was she just keeping him dangling? But no, that would be entirely against his concept of her unless he was mistaken and wiser men than him had made that mistake before. She was warm but never ardent.

While he was not promiscuous, on the contrary he was very reticent and would have rather died than be seen with some of the women his colleagues "collected" during boom-time — that one or two weekperiod of wealth after the allowances had been paid out; he felt that she should have been more responsive. What could it be that held her back always?

Eventually he decided that time was running out for him. He would be through with his four year Vet Medicine course in another few months. So he decided to approach the problem head on.

"Vera, will you marry me?"

"Oh, Tommy!" She should have seen this coming.

She was twenty-two and not a child any more. A man could not possibly keep on seeing you for three years without caring deeply. He was a good man and she was a fool not to say yes immediately. For one thing, she would be eternally grateful that he had never put any undue pressure on her — for she was quite unsure how she would have responded. She was instinctively monogamous; for her there could only be one man, and yet she felt that her life was full of unanswered questions and secret longings. How could she explain these to him without hurting his feelings?

He looked at the changing expressions on her face and the gradual clouding of her eyes — the sadness.

"Oh, Tommy," she repeated again helplessly.

"Does that mean yes, but that you are too overwhelmed by my proposal to make a coherent speech of acceptance?" he asked trying to ease things for her by making jest out of such a serious matter.

She laughed and the tears spilled out of her eyes for the first time in many years. He looked at her closely and then knew in his heart that he had lost her even though she herself did not know it. She wiped her eyes.

"You have been my best friend for three years. You have been good, faithful and loyal, and I know that these are rare things in many men. Why can't I say yes immediately and be done with it? You know I love you. I think you are a wonderful man. Yet I can't say yes; not just now anyway. I feel unfinished, as if I'm not completely formed; that I still have some growing up to do — which I am sure sounds like nonsense in this country where women marry in their teens and manage to have successful marriages. But you are right. We have been seeing too much of each other. Why don't you date other girls for a while and see how you like it. I can't go on monopolising you like this." She smiled at him to try and ease the hurt a little.

"And you?" he would kill the man who so much as looked at her. He felt terrible inside. Suddenly he couldn't take any more and lumbered up to his feet and literally staggered away. She looked after him sadly — she had definitely botched that up. Long after he left, she continued sitting in the same place, shoulders hunched and head bent — lost to the world.

When she finally got up from their favourite bench in the park, she knew that a phase had passed in her life: she would never be a carefree child again. Innocence has a tendency to disappear when one discovers in oneself the power to really hurt — good intentions not withstanding. In her loneliness and confusion, she suddenly thought of her sister Becky.

It was time she unearthed that lady—maybe things had thawed out a little between them; besides she needed family around her. Her attempts at locating her sister had so far met with total failure. She had either covered her tracks well or had had to settle for a job other than air- hostessing. Maybe she had gone into modelling, God knew she was beautiful enough.

So Vera jumped into a bus and once again headed for the airport. Her hopes sank lower and lower so that by the time the bus was hurtling down Jogoo Road at a characteristically Kenyan speed she had all but given up. When it eventually reached the Jomo Kenyatta Airport it was all she could do to get out of the bus and start asking around again. Travellers were milling around her, pushing or pulling their luggage; and for the first time she felt an urge to travel and see the world. Maybe that is what had so impelled her sister to a job with such possibilities. As she approached the booth with Kenya Airways written on it, who should walk straight into her but Becky looking breathtaking in uniform.

"Vera!"

"Becky!"

The awkward moment was interrupted by a child, who while running away from his irrate mother rocketted straight into them nearly throwing Vera off her feet. Becky grabbed her, steadied her and said to her;

"Let's get out of here. I am beat!"

"Are you sure?" asked Vera in disbelief. She had expected Becky to stare at her coldly and then walk away — but she actually looked glad to see her.

"Of course I am! Let's go to my place. How's the University coming along?"

"Oh OK. Lots of hard work though."

"You always loved that; don't tell me you have changed!" Vera laughed.

"I am really glad to see you Becky."

"Just that? No accusations? Things like why haven't you gone home to see your parents, etcetera. You *have* changed."

"So have you. And you are more beautiful than ever."

"Don't big heart me, Vera. I am still the same — I love the good things of life—comfort, expensive clothes, good looking men—the works. And talking of men, the reason I haven't gone home to see the old folks is my current boyfriend. You'll see when we get home. Do you have a boyfriend? Still seeing Tommy?"

"Yes and no. I think we broke up today."

"You think! You know something — you were always weird. If you want to break off with a man, make it clean. There is no point leaving one dangling around — they just annoy you. Ask me a few tricks on how to say no in such a way that even the dumbest man will understand and still think you are an angel. Why did you break up with Tommy? I thought he was exactly your type — good, hardworking, clean living — that sort of thing. You have someone else in mind?"

"No." This new fast talking Becky was fascinating.

"Listen, dummy. You don't drop a man unless you have a good reason to and the only two good reasons I know are either he is two-timing you, or you have found someone else." Her sister obviously had learnt nothing of the world. What kind of a place was that university anyway or was her sister with all her brilliance, just socially dumb?

"It was none of those Becky. Please give it a

break."

"Hey, I believe you actually loved the creep!"

"He is not a creep. And yes, I loved him but I could not convince myself that marrying him was what I wanted — at least not just yet," answered Vera and Becky sighed in sheer exasperation.

"I know he is an angel, but do you believe he will hang around waiting for you? If so, then he must be as weird as you are."

"You know something? I agree — you haven't changed that much after all."

"That's better," answered Becky as the taxi drew up in front of an expensive looking block of flats.

"This is where you live?" asked Vera in shock. "You must make a lot of money!"

"There are more ways than one to skin a cat," answered Becky ambiguously as she inserted a key into the lock.

Chapter 9

Becky's flat, from the carpet on the floor, to the pictures on the wall spelled one word — money. Vera stood dumbfounded in the doorway. She had thought that only ministers and directors of large companies could afford to live like that — but here was her twenty-two year old sister flopping into a large, overstuffed white sofa as if she had every right to sit in it. Recovering, Vera moved in tentatively and sat on the edge of a chair.

"This air-hostessing can't be bad!"

"Actually, my friend pays for the flat."

"Some friend — are there any more around?"

Becky just laughed and said:

"You know I was jealous of you all my life."

"You were?" asked Vera shocked by such a revelation.

"Are you surprised? You had everything — guts, drive, ambition and brains. You always seemed to know where you were going and what you wanted. And Mum and Dad thought the sun rose and set in your eyes. Every time you stood up to receive one more present, one more accolade, to give one more vote of thanks to some big shot on behalf of the student body — I would be consumed with jealousy. Do you know I never got one single, miserable present in school; do you? I lived for the day when I would be equal to you."

"But Becky! You were, are so beautiful. In all my life, I have yet to see anyone who looks anything like you! Boys started hanging around you practically in nursery school!"

"And you think it is enough? Would you trade

places with me?"

"That's not fair."

"Grow up. Nobody's fair in this world. Don't expect it. Answer my question."

Mercifully, at that moment, there was a knock and a big, sunburnt, blue eyed, yellow haired *mzungu* entered. He walked in, looked quizically at Vera and then went to Becky. He gave her a peck on the cheek and said:

"Hi honey. How was the flight?"

"OK John. Did you miss me?"

"Miss you! In this town full of pretty girls?" then he saw the look on Vera's face, laughed and hastened to add: "Of course I missed you. I even miss you when you go down-town to do some shopping. Who's your friend?"

"Not my friend. This is my sister Vera. Vera, this is John Courtney — he is a pilot and my fiancé, we intend to get married next month."

"Hi Vera. I've heard a lot about you."

"All good I hope," muttered Vera utterly shocked... She knew it could happen but now she verified the sad and dreaded possiblity. What a day!

"Your sister thinks that all that is good and beautiful is to be found in you —I was dying to meet you and I must say I am surprised to find only a woman of flesh and blood!" he said smiling at her. At least he had a sense of humour. His accent was strange and Vera couldn't place it.

"I must leave you girls to catch up on news about each other. Becky I'll be in the bedroom." He stood up and walked out of the room.

"Now you can see why I didn't want to go home."

"How can you possibly think of getting married without at least letting them know? Give them a chance. They are your parents and they care about you whatever you might think."

"But he is white! Remember father couldn't even stand Tommy who is only a Luhya from the neighbouring province. He will just shout at me."

"That might be so — he gave *me* a shock. You'd have to get used to people getting shocked and staring at you. So it is not surprising that your father might react the same way; but it is your duty to tell them."

"Why don't you tell them for me?"

"Forget it, once is enough. Dad nearly passed out — so mad was he. I never had to talk so fast or so hard in my life. He wanted to come after you immediately until I pointed out just how large a place Nairobi is. Still I would hate to go through that again. This, dear sister, is your ball game."

Becky got up and stood looking out of the window at the street below.

"Why is it that I've never really felt a part of them?"

"Because you were always too pre-occupied with yourself to notice how much they really cared. It does help to tear your eyes off the mirror once in a while to really look at other people you know."

"Hey! You are really angry with me."

"Look Becky. You are an adult. Surely you can face your own father and mother and tell them that this is the man you have chosen. They won't kill you. They can't tie you down. They may or may not give their blessing, but at least they will know that you are safe and happy. I don't have a child, but if I did, I'd hate to be permanently guessing about her whereabouts and welfare. Besides I think they are damned good parents — if you ask me. If they say no, it is only because they are thinking of your own good. Have you stopped to think how difficult it is going to be for you — and your children? Where will you live? Where does he come from anyway?"

"He is Canadian. We might live in Canada or here in Kenya — we have not decided. He really likes the country and its people, you know. He is a nice man—too nice for his own good. The fact that someone is white does not mean that he is automatically bad and looks down on Africans."

"I didn't suggest that at all! But you have to care deeply about each other to survive the ostracism, the loneliness that a mixed marriage brings with it. Other people won't understand at all; and some will think that you only married him for his money; others will hold their breath to see how soon he discards you for another pretty face."

"Might you be one of them?"

"I will take that as a joke. In fact I like him, I think he really loves you; but I have known you all your life and I don't trust your reasons for entering this marriage. To put it plainly do you love him?"

"How sweet of you. Whatever I say, you'll never believe I love him. Of course I like money and all it can buy, but there have been richer men — who are not only black but have offered me even more than he can. Why am I defending myself to you anyway? I am not that bad and you are not that good."

"No I am not good. I am sorry if it sounded that way. Do what you think fit. We are both grown up now — I was just giving you my point of view. Please forget it. May I say good-bye to John? I really must leave now."

Becky looked at her sister for a long time, with a strange expression in her eyes — half longing, half defiant. She then left the room and was away for more than the few minutes it would have taken to get her fiancé. When they eventually came out, John said:

"I hear you've been trying to convince Becky to go home and break the news, eh? It might interest you to know that I've been saying the same thing since we decided to get married; but Becky thinks that her family will think that I am an ogre. Now am I that bad Vera?" He really was a nice guy.

"Of course not!" Vera said laughing. "Do go home. It is the thing to do in this society. Otherwise nobody will believe that your intentions are good no matter what your colour. Our father's fierce all right. He is an ex-soldier you know; but all he has ever wanted was the best for his children. I think you will survive."

After Vera took her leave, John said to Becky:

"That's a very fine young woman you have for a sister — I can see why you talk non-stop about her. You must really love her."

"I don't! I mean I don't talk non-stop about her! And of course I love her. She fought more battles for me than you'll ever know and she is the most loyal of sisters!"

"See!" declared John triumphantly. Becky looked daggers at him and then just laughed.

"Anyway I think she is right," he continued. "There is enough stacked against us as it is without my starting my marriage by antagonising your father. I'll even take a cow or two if necessary. Isn't that what a real man does when he marries a real woman of the clan?"

"Go to hell!"

"Your sweet temper is in real evidence today, but

what I mean is, I don't want to be treated like some roguish *mzungu* out to take advantage of someone's innocent daughter. I'd like to get married properly, have children who will know their double heritage properly and a father-in-law who at least respects me. Get it?"

"You really are beginning to sound exactly like sweet Vera. I have always had a chip on my shoulder where that young lady is concerned, she is everything I would have liked to be if anyone had asked me."

"To me, you are perfect just the way you are — when shall we go?"

"Where?"

"To see your parents of course. I thought that was what we were talking about?"

"Oh, OK. Since you are so determined, I will call them tonight and make the arrangements. Happy now?"

"Seventh heaven," he said grinning.

And so it was that Becky returned home after an absence of almost three years.

Chapter 10

In the 'Box', the women's hall of residence, no one was consulted before being assigned a room mate and one could end up with a real creep. In the first year, there was one room to be shared between two people. In the second and third years, one moved into a semi-divided room which guaranteed at least some privacy. Vera was very lucky in the room-mate she drew in her second year. She was a commerce student called Mary-Anne Ngugi — a nice human being by any standard. She had a boyfriend whose name was Matthew Saisi who was studying Design. He was very friendly and had in fact hit it off with Tommy very well. Their shared room was therefore like an island in the midst of the tumultuous sea that was the 'Box'. Mary-Anne was a Nairobian whose parents lived in Buru Buru. Being an only daughter in a family of six, her parents treated her like something special and constantly brought her food from home. Most of this found its way to Vera, whom Mary-Anne treated like the sister she had never had. Vera had maintained the great appetite of her childhood — but as always remained enviably slim. So when Vera came in that night weeping, Mary-Anne was very solicitous of her. She put her in bed and just held her in her arms until she calmed down, then she made a cup of cocoa just the way Vera liked it — dark brown and sweet, with no milk.

"Want to talk?"

"Tommy and I broke up today. Then I went to look for my sister — I felt so lonely."

"A sister?"

"Yes, my twin sister."

"You have a sister in this town?"

"Yes!"

"How come she never comes to see you?"

"Are you going to listen!"

"Sorry, I was surprised, that's all. You broke up with Tommy!" The expression on her face was so comical that Vera just laughed.

"I might as well let you tell the story Mary-Anne."

"Sorry, but you can't throw such shockers my way and expect me to think sensibly. Please tell me."

"Tommy asked me to marry him and I said no."

"What was his crime?"

"Nothing. It's got nothing to do with him at all. I just did not feel right about it, that's all."

"There are many questions I could and should ask, but I will ask only one — how did he take it?"

"You know Tommy, he tried to take it with good humour and then suddenly he couldn't take any more and he left."

"Do you realise that you might live to regret this? Boys like Tommy simply don't grow off trees you know. Some girl is going to snap him up faster than fast. All the same it is not for me to censure you — an adult woman. Think about it; you may see things differently tomorrow. Tell me about your sister. Your twin sister, if you please!"

"Yes, Becky; she is the most beautiful woman I have ever met. I mean she is perfect. You know the way most of us however pretty could always do with a little more of this or a little less of that? But not Becky. I loved her absolutely when we were children. Everybody did; but you know there is something about a really beautiful person that eventually makes them repellent. They take a lot of things for granted. I suppose they learn early that they don't have to try as hard as other people; after all everybody tries to please them. When we were teenagers, I gradually realised how selfish and difficult she was. We quarrelled and things were never the same again. After Sixth Form, she ran away from home and became an air-hostess. What she wanted was what mattered to her — not how anybody else felt. My father was against it. Naturally he wanted her into teaching, nursing or some such occupation. But an air hostess! Exposed to all sorts of people of questionable character! Never. That did not deter her and I personally thought it a good thing that she was determined on at least one score. Anyway yesterday I managed to track her down and would you believe it, she is living with a *mzungu* pilot whom she intends to marry soon — in secret!"

"What do you have against him?"

"Nothing. As a matter of fact I rather liked him. He is obviously madly in love but I have doubts about my sister."

"Are you sure you are not jealous of her? She can't be that bad."

"Yes, I must have been a little jealous, she was of me also of course. We were so different that I suppose some jealousy was inevitable. She had the beauty and I had the brains. But so many people exclaiming about one's beauty can get to anybody's head and it went to hers. Though you might just be right, I also had a feeling that she has become a little warmer, less centred on herself, so I may be mistaken."

"Do you have any brothers or other sisters."

"Oh yes. Four brothers and one little sister. The

oldest boy, Aoro is coming to the medical school in September. He is a mad genius, but a very nice human being—that is if you can get him to sit down for a few minutes. Tony has gone to a seminary—for as long as I can remember, he has wanted to be a priest."

"You are going to have a priest in the family?"

"Er-actually Tony will be the second. My uncle Peter is the bishop of the diocese of Kisumu."

"A priest and a bishop! You must be proud. If it was me, I would brag about it all the time!" Mary-Anne looked quite amazed. "I must say you don't look very religious though you do go to Mass."

"How does a religious person look?" asked Vera beginning to feel drowsy.

"Oh come on. You know what I mean. I'd better let you sleep. You've had a very long day." Mary-Anne retreated to her side and Vera fell promptly asleep, but was soon in the grip of a nightmare she had had recurrently in childhood. Ordinarily she had no fear of wide open spaces and in fact enjoyed her visits to the country; but in this dream she was walking, compulsively and she could not stop. Above her was the wide blue sky, dotted with wispy white clouds. The blue looked deep, infinite and terrible—causing a constriction in her throat and a feeling of suffocation in her chest. Around her was an endless sea of savannah country with only an occasional shrub to break the monotony. This would have been bad enough had she not known that she was walking, hurtling now, towards the horizon which at first appeared a great distance away but which she was now approaching at a dizzying speed against which she was helpless; she reached the edge, which fell off into a bottomless abyss and she was gripped by pure atavistic terror as she hung there, suspended. She woke up in a cold sweat, her heart pounding. It was still dark. She checked her watch, it was only four o'clock, so she switched on her bedside lamp and pulled out John Steinbeck's *East of Eden.* She was reading it for the second time and found the book as inspiring as ever. The calm compassionate wisdom of Lee, the chinese servant; the suppressed anger in the otherwise big hearted Cal; the cold and distant idealism of his brother Aron, and the uncomprehending love of their father Adam, were all feelings she could identify with. Said Steinbeck in connection with one of his characters who had just died, 'Each of us should live in such a way that when we die people will say of us — what shall we do now that he is gone?' Vera wondered whether that could be said of her. "I am sure if I died only Mum and Dad would really miss me or even know that I had ever existed. I am only existing, not really living."

Eventually she noticed the morning light filtering in through a chink in the curtain. She got up wearily, grabbed her towel and made for the bathroom. Mary-Anne was still fast asleep. It was Sunday so there was no point waking her up.

When she got back, she found Mary-Anne seated on her bed, brown legs dangling on the side, her chin cupped in both her hands. She was deep in thought and looked startled to see her.

"Hey! I thought you were still asleep!"

"I've been awake for hours."

"I should have checked. I was thinking about you just before you came in but I assumed you were still asleep so I didn't want to disturb you." Mary-Anne smiled broadly, her pretty face dimpling. She was most disarming, always bubbling over with happiness. Vera looked at her and felt weary, depressed and ancient. What was wrong with her anyway? Couldn't she part company with a boy without feeling so horrible?

"To judge from the look on your face, I am sure they must be some very nice thoughts. What are they?"

"Well I was thinking that- er- that you might want to come to a recollection with me next Saturday — down at Park View College."

"I've never been there — I thought they trained secretaries or something?"

"Yes they do, among other things. Will you come?"

"What's a recollection anyway?"

"Well, it's just that: a session where you turn out the external and turn into the inner you, to see how that neglected part of you is doing. Someone directs the thoughts of the group to some chosen topics for the day — well it's hard to explain. Why don't you come and see for yourself? I am sure you'll like it."

"What sort of people go there?"

"All sorts, this one is being held for young single professional women or female university students."

What did it matter? It sounded interesting anyway and Mary-Anne had been really good to her.

"Oh OK. I'll come if only to make you happy."

"You are the one who'll be even happier."

The two girls then got ready and went down to St Paul's University Chapel for Mass. Usually Mass at St Paul's was fun and the priest, who was also a professor and had a PhD in Philosophy, had a thorough grasp of current affairs and student psychology and was therefore very popular with the students. The church was usually packed to the brim. This Sunday was no exception and he held his audience in thrall until the very last words — "The Mass is ended. Go in peace to love the Lord and to serve one another." In her state of heightening awareness, Vera found these words poignant. To love God? How? Wasn't that for people like Tony and uncle Peter who seemed to identify almost instinctively with spiritual things — almost as if they understood a secret language of their own? And this business about serving others... How? In which way? Which others?

She supposed that she was a good Catholic, at least better than most. She rarely ever missed Mass and believed in most things that the Church taught. She had last gone to confession in her mid teens. Thereafter, she had just felt that she could not let anyone probe her soul — she would manage by herself somehow. She was aware that the Church disapproved of artificial birth control, but here again while submitting to popular belief that there was a population explosion, she was unaware of the actual reasoning behind the teaching of the Church. Being intelligent as well as honest she suddenly perceived that in real truth she knew next to nothing about the faith to which she had submitted for twenty three years. She retained a vague memory of her catechism, but on the whole her faith was an amorphous mass of popular morality, misconceptions, intuitions about the Church being the right one without any concrete facts to back any of these things up. Her knowledge of Scripture was sketchy — mainly the parables that she heard during Mass, a sprinkling from the Epistles, something about Peter being the rock upon which the Church was built, and other disconnected facts of that nature. How did an intelligent, thinking person waste all the Sundays of her life paying homage to a faith about which she knew so little? Was it her fault, or had she been an unlucky victim who had simply fallen through the net while others were held in place until they reached understanding? Why was she having these crazy thoughts anyway? She was young, and she had her whole life to enjoy. She would postpone the questions for now and think of more pleasant things. The University Players were staging the play *Our Husband has Gone Mad Again*. She would attend that and try to forget Tony, Becky, the Church and everything that could not be solved by the application of solid scientific principles.

She did go to the play, and she enjoyed it. The week came and she busied herself with her lectures and assignments. The end of year exam was just a month away and examination fever had started to grip the campus as people hysterically tried to read three books at a go, unearth long forgotten notes and exam papers and keep up with their lectures all at the same time. This was the time when depressives jumped out of windows, gobbled up bottlefuls of valium or used other ways to escape the intolerable tension. Vera however had long formed the habit of staying on top of her work throughout the year and never letting it swamp her. She also believed firmly in taking time to rest, read a novel or do something different right at the peak of the tension, in spite of her demanding course. So when Mary-Anne who was also another believer in the therapeutic value of occasional rest, reminded her, that Friday evening, that the recollection started at nine and that they would have to leave at eight thirty on Saturday morning, she merely nodded her assent and went on with her work.

On Saturday morning, they walked to the University bus stop and boarded a *matatu* van headed for Kangemi. The music was deafening, but at that hour and in that direction, at least the van was only half full — a fact for which they were very grateful. Usually the *matatu* would be packed with people, bodies jammed together, touts hurling insults and gyrating dangerously at the door to the beat of the blaring music. Sometimes they raced the van, grabbed a rail and swung themselves in like large monkeys and one momentarily closed one's eyes in anticipation of the sound of wheels crunching over a fallen body — and sometimes, though rarely, this did happen; rarely because the touts were masters of their art.

They arrived a little late, for the *matatu* kept stopping to solicit even disinterested by-standers to get into their van named Apollo II — the rocket which took the first man to the moon. Between stops, the *matatu* hurtled down Waiyaki Way at speeds approaching the supersonic — in defiance of a sticker stuck on the windscreen just next to the driver entitled: A *Speed Song* and which ran something like—

80 K.P.H. – Guide me Oh Thou Great Jehova
100 K.P.H. – God will Take Care of You
120 K.P.H. – Nearer My God to Thee
140 K.P.H. – This World is not My Home
160 K.P.H. – Lord I am Coming Home
Over 180 K.P.H. – Sweet Memories

The girls were almost becoming 'sweet memories' when the *matatu* screeched to a halt and deposited them at the gate of Parkview College. It sped off down the road to Sodom, which was the name of the slum just before Kangemi and Mary-Anne, a little shaken, led the way into the compound.

"I think we'll take a bus back to campus."

"You can say that again," agreed Vera.

The two girls went into a stone building rather bare-looking on the outside. They were met by a young woman who said something briefly to Mary-Anne, she nodded then opened a door, and another into a small chapel in which several people were already gathered. The room was in semi-darkness except for a pool of light from a desk lamp which fell on a book from which a priest in a white cassock was reading. Mary-Anne bowed to one knee, hitting the floor with a light thud. Vera, not used to such a complete genuflection, just bent a knee and then slid into a pew next to her friend.

"A chapel!" she thought, looking around at the unusual decorations on the ceiling and on the altar. A beautiful statue of the Virgin, resplendent in a crown stood in one corner. A candle flickered near the tabernacle and two others on the altar. There was a smell of incense in the air. It was a while before Vera could collect her wits enough to listen to what the priest was reading and saying, but even before then she felt the peaceful stillness of the place steal into her soul like a fragrance — something that just came and against which one had no resistance.

"It makes me very sad to see a Catholic, a child of God, called by Baptism to be another Christ — calming his conscience with a purely formal piety, with a religiosity that leads him to pray now and again, and only if he thinks it worthwhile," read the priest and Vera thought to herself, "What! Is the guy reading my mind or something?"

"He goes to Mass on holidays of obligation," went on the priest relentlessly, "Though not all of them, while he cares punctiliously for the welfare of his stomach." Her mind turned in on itself and she could see the outlining of something hazy, forming itself, trying to push itself to the surface of her consciousness, but it was still too amoebic to be grasped.

Later, they said the Rosary, a prayer which she had spent her childhood trying to dodge but which now came automatically to her lips bringing unspeakable consolation. Later still someone gave a talk on *Work as a means of sanctification*, but she didn't understand it. Work to her was something you did, enjoyed, hopefully earned money from, but which she could not connect with anything other than material well-being.

They walked out of the chapel and Mary-Anne introduced her to a collection of people of every hue, colour, and accent. They all shook her hand enthusiastically.

"Did you like it?" asked Mary-Anne as they waited for a bus.

"Well, I didn't know you were taking me to church. You sounded so mysterious!"

"Not mysterious. It was just hard to explain. A recollection is an experience which one has to go through to understand. In fact several experiences. Each time you have a different problem, a different experience, a different level of participation, of understanding. I am sure some of it did not make any sense to you."

"You are right. To try to live one's faith better, to let it permeate one's entire life — that makes sense. Otherwise going to church becomes a mere circus as it has for me; but that bit about work as a means of achieving holiness puzzles me."

"It is a matter of linking different thought processes. You have put the one half of it very well — faith permeating one's life. That's good. I like it. But what does one's entire life consist of? What does your life consist of, Vera?"

"Well I have my lectures, my assignments, my work actually," she replied beginning to vaguely see.

"Yes! So your faith has to permeate your work — the activity which occupies your day and which you will be engaged in, all your life. What else do you have to offer an all loving, benevolent God? You are not a nun, or a recluse, who can pray all day and thus be constantly in the presence of God. So your work becomes your prayer."

"But how?"

"Do it well and offer it to God. Eventually it becomes a habit. I used to be quite restless. I still am. So when I sit down to read and I get the itch to jump up and come around to gossip a little, I remind myself that what I am doing is all I have to offer my God and if I do it badly or halfway, I will have botched up my sacrifice, rather like Cain who preferred to eat meat — and give God the vegetables." Vera laughed at that.

"You are funny. I never heard that explanation before. I often wondered what God had against those carrots and *sukumawiki*. How do you know so much any way?"

"I read and read some more. I think it is a shame to have a degree in commerce, yet in matters of faith which is such an intrinsic part of the human person, have only kindergarten level knowledge."

"Well my friend, that describes me to a T." Vera's

face clouded again.

"Don't worry. It is a disease that is easy to treat. I'll lend you a couple of books this evening to start you off. You are not the kind of person who needs anything more than just that—a point of departure."

"Tell me Mary, who are those people anyway?"

"Oh! They are a mixed group of people — just about anyone who is interested can come. The organisers are members of Opus Dei — which is Latin for God's work. It is an institution within the Catholic Church whose founder put forward the idea that the quest for perfection was possible even for ordinary lay people engaged in ordinary occupations."

"You really are amazing."

"I am not. It is just that I saw the futility of existing just for the sake of existing, earlier. Then an aunt of mine put me in contact with these people. The rest is, to put it in a nutshell, striving, struggling, working and reading; starting again and again hoping to make it more perfect each time.

Back in their room Mary-Anne gave Vera a battered copy of *The Faith Explained* and a little book called *The Way*. Vera started on a hungry search for enlightment and like everything she did, she went at it with passion and dedication. It would eventually change her life.

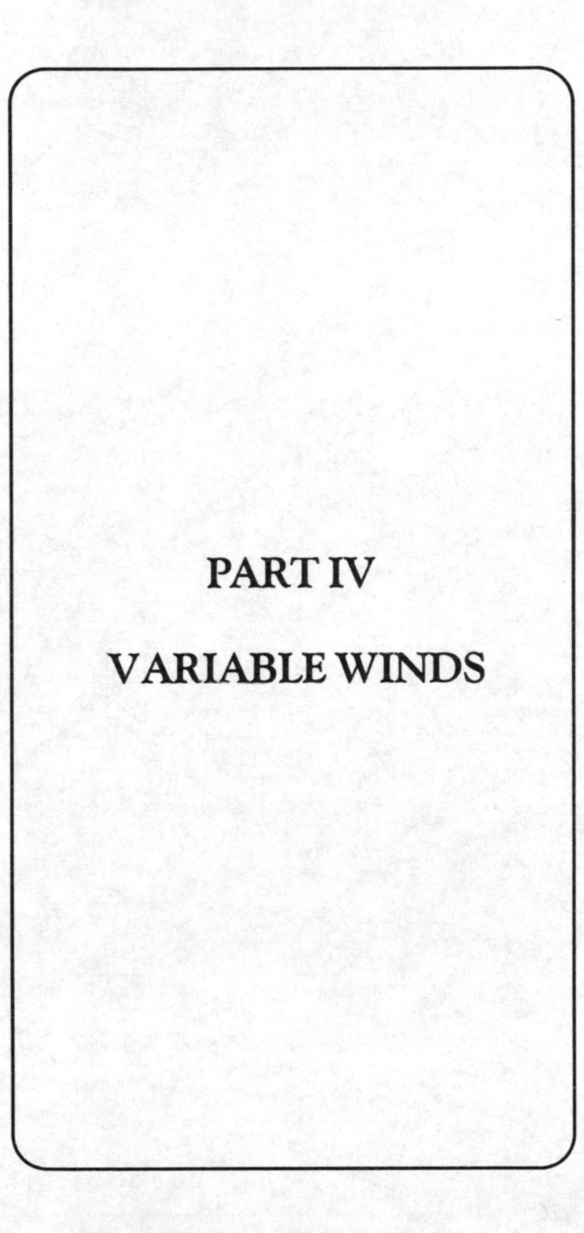

PART IV

VARIABLE WINDS

Chapter 1

Aoro Sigu grabbed his clipboard and descended to the first floor of the anatomy block, his heart pounding. The previously noisy mob of first year medical students were all strangely quiet for this was the day of initiation into the medical fraternity. They were going to meet their first 'patient'. The laboratory was a long building with two rows of metal tables on which lay long bundles completely swathed in white strips of clothing. There was a strange acrid smell in the air. They were asked to assign themselves to a table in groups of six and this they did without thinking. Had they known, they would have chosen their table-mates with more care — for they would have to work with the same group for one whole year. But the moment was too solemn and they were all too shaken to take much notice.

Aoro ranged himself with the others around table six. His group consisted of four other men and a girl whom he had only seen briefly upstairs in the lecture room. At close quarters, they could see that the covered form was clearly human. There was no mistaking it. The lecturer, Dr Gitonga gave a short introductory speech.

"You must remember always that the cadaver before you was once a human being with feelings and who deserved a decent burial but is here for your sakes so that you may learn the science of anatomy which is the cornerstone of medicine. The cadaver must therefore be treated with utmost respect and any part not under dissection must be properly covered. I repeat, expose only the part under dissection. Any question? "

There was silence, then a hand shot up. It was the same guy who had asked all the questions upstairs. There are always such people in each classroom or lecture theatre. They are professional question askers.

"Won't it rot?" Upstairs he had wanted to know why something was wriggling in the projected slide of the foot pad of a monkey. He wanted to know whether it was still alive.

"No it will not rot. The body has been preserved with formalin — a powerful chemical — notice the smell in the air. It will last more than the one year you will take to dissect it from head to toe," answered Dr Gitonga. "How do we go about it?" Asked the girl at Aoro's table. "You will follow the instructions in your *Cunningham's Manual of Anatomy*; and of course I will be here to help out any time you are stuck. Please begin."

Aoro looked at his team-mates. They looked back at him. Nobody made a move towards the kit of instruments placed carefully on the covered abdomen of the cadaver. Eventually the girl made as if to grab it but Aoro reached it a split second before she did.

"Hey man read from the manual!" he waved a scalpel at the four who appeared to have been turned into pillars of salt of the Mrs Lot variety.

"Don't you think we should introduce ourselves? If you say 'hey woman' to me I might just stick that sharp knife you are holding into your belly!" This wisecrack served to lessen the tension somewhat, and everyone relaxed a little.

"Good idea. My name is Aoro Sigu," he answered smiling at her.

"And I am Wandia Mugo," answered the girl

smiling back.

"I am Jeremy Kizingo."

"Kithinji Makau."

"Paul Omondi Rakula — doctor to be!" Everybody laughed at that and people at the other tables turned to stare at them. Were they maniacs or something? How could they laugh in the presence of sixteen dead bodies? Little did they know that the cadaver would become so much a part of their existence that they would barely remember to wash their hands before lunch after a morning of delving deep into human tissues. The jokes would of course grow crazier by the year. The last man at Aoro's table was called Simon Onyancha — a tall heavy set fellow from Kisii.

Except for Kithinji Makau who seemed to have trouble handling the cadaver, the other five soon formed a good team. One person would read from the manual, another would dissect and separate the tissues and the rest would try to identify the revealed structures. Anatomy was the science which firmly grounded the image of the human body into a doctor's head; it was the cornerstone of medicine. In reality it was just a test of one's power of recall — an invaluable tool for a doctor. To carry in one's head the names, distribution and function of hundreds of muscles, nerves, blood vessels, parts of the brain, the skeleton, and all the internal organs require a no mean feat of memorisation. However it soon became clear that two people were fighting for the top position in anatomy. They were both from table six — Aoro Sigu and that slip of a girl Wandia Mugo.

There were other subjects to be learned including Biochemistry and Physiology, but none caused as much tension and rivalry as anatomy. If you saw a medic mumbling to himself, it was not because he was at prayer; the poor guy was practising his anatomy. By the end of the third and last semester, the battle for supremacy in anatomy became palpable. People slept with their *Cunningham's Manuals* and their *Gray's Text Book of Anatomy.* Where two or three were gathered together, anatomy was the main subject. Finally the day came. The written papers were done and the day for practicals came. You could have cut the tension with a knife after everyone took his place in front of some displayed bit of human tissue or a slide under a microscope. Each time the bell rang one had to move to the next item, irrespective of whether one had managed to identify the previous one or not. The time was fixed.

Then came the oral examination — the bane of every medical student's existence. It is all very well to be dumbfounded before a microscope or a displayed nerve or muscle; but to make a fool of oneself in front of a panel of examiners turned everybody's insides into heaving molten lava. Added to this was the fact that the orals came last when the students were in a state of exhaustion and general collapse. It is not a miracle that the medical school contributed regularly to the congestion at Mathare Mental Hospital or worse to the number of suicides.

The results were eventually posted and as expected two names were at the top. Aoro looked at his name in disbelief. He had achieved a distinction with 77 points. But Wandia had beaten him with that one vital point — she had 78. He was male enough to feel deeply disappointed, but man enough to offer to buy her a drink at the cafeteria.

"It was touch and go between you and me, Sigu;

it could have gone either way," offered the young lady. "Besides you showed me dust in Physiology and Biochemistry."

"Very limited dust it was — and I really wanted Anatomy, not those others. Pride I suppose. This is the first time I've been beaten by a girl."

"Does it matter so much?"

"A little. I am human you know."

"Yet you are buying me a drink."

"It's the least I can do. A tough lady like you deserves dinner — at the Hilton."

"Is that how you see me? Tough, I mean?" She was a little disappointed — much to her surprise. What did she care about him? Like most of the male medical students he was arrogant and it should have given her great satisfaction to bring him down a peg or two; but it didn't. Aoro looked at her; really looked at her. Not just as a companion in demolishing the cadaver, but as another human being and a woman. She had a very light complexion, typical of the Kikuyu and lovely long black hair. Her face, though not beautiful in the way his sister Becky's was, was lively and expressive and was frequently lighted up by a warm smile from a rather wide mouth.

"Does it insult you — to be called tough? I meant it as a compliment. I think one has to be as tough as nails to survive this course."

"But soon we'll be dealing with real people, some in serious trouble. How do you combine toughness with a feeling for people?"

He looked at her with respect. In his quest for supremacy in anatomy, he had forgotten that the purpose was eventually to care for the sick and dying.

"I sure hope we'll manage," he answered soberly.

Later as they were leaving he said to her;

"May I write to you during the holidays? Three months is a long time. It would be nice to be in contact with someone who understands."

She hesitated. Beyond his prowess at anatomy she did not know him at all. Besides five years was a long time and she really did not want to be bogged down with a relationship so early in her medical school career.

"I will be moving from place to place. I won't stay in one place for long. All those relatives, you know," she answered evasively — and smiled to take the sting off her words. Aoro nodded politely and shook her hand in farewell. He watched her as she walked away. Somebody should have told her that he was the great grandson of Akoko daughter of the great Chief Odero, and that he did not know the meaning of the words 'giving up'. In other words the quest was on.

Chapter 2

Aoro walked out of the labour room theatre feeling like a punch drunk fighter. He had been on his feet for the last 24 hours with a thirty minute break for supper. There had been no time for lunch. The only times he had sat down were the brief minutes required to jot down patients' notes. Then there had been a brief lull after 2.30 p.m. and he had almost run into the call room to take a nap, but exactly forty five minutes later the phone rang. There was a case of severe fetal distress with poor progress of labour. Would he join the resident in theatre at once to assist with the case? He had dropped into bed fully clothed, so he simply dragged his body up and walked heavy-eyed and groggy-kneed out of the room. On his way out he passed the paediatric resident who had also been called in readiness to resuscitate the endangered baby. The residents relieved each other every twelve hours and so these two were much fresher than he was. Aoro mumbled a greeting at him.

The Obstetric resident was in his final year of training and was therefore quite fast. He had the abdomen open and the baby out in exactly ten minutes. The baby was covered in its own waste showing just how severely distressed it had been. He gave it to the nurse who rushed the limp form to the waiting paediatric resident for resuscitation. Aoro stared after it hoping it would survive.

"Retract man!" shouted the irritable resident at Aoro. "Are you asleep or something?" Aoro felt like retorting back — but the end was so near — so sweetly near. He didn't want anyone besmirching his clean record this late with some stupid remark like 'insubordinate', 'unco-operative' or something like that. So he pulled harder on the retractor to open the gaping incision further and kept his mouth shut. The resident started closing the womb. At least this guy was fast. Some were just foul mouthed but awkward in their surgery. By the time they finished it was almost three thirty and there were patients on the queue waiting to be attended to. He checked on the baby to see how it was doing. It was a big baby girl — too big for this first-time mother. He noticed with satisfaction that though the score had been only one out of ten at birth — showing that only the baby's heart had been beating — it had risen to eight at five minutes and a perfect ten at ten minutes. As they bundled it off to nursery for observation — he hoped fervently that she would be OK. He still had some human feeling in him. He started attending to the other patients.

Aoro was an intern and internship is a period which is marked in every doctor's mind like a splash of white paint on a dark background. The edges are clear but the middle is hazy for much as they survive it, they never quite know where the remarkable reserves of energy come from. Time to oneself becomes a coveted possession and sleep a jealously guarded mistress. Food was eaten if and when time allowed. One's social life was almost guaranteed to disappear unless one's mate was determined, understanding and forgiving. To work for thirty six continuous hours was commonplace. The number of nights a week that one slept depended on the number of interns available. A fully free weekend was a prize beyond compare. If the person you loved was also an intern in a different hospital in another province, then the relationship had to be iron bound to survive.

Wandia was an intern at Machakos General Hospital which was two hours away by public transport, which was all the two had. There was no guarantee that when you got your few precious hours and rushed over, you would find the other person free to spend even a little time with you. He might be in theatre or in a ward round with his consultant breathing fire and brimstone down his neck, or he may be held up doing a procedure on a patient. In the last year, Wandia and Aoro had had only one such coinciding free day. He lived in constant fear that some fast talking Kamba doctor would take his girl away.

But all things come to an end and the two had only two weeks to go before they were signed off from their respective hospitals. With that would automatically come the right to be registered as a medical practitioner in Kenya, freedom and a few other human rights, such as the right to ask a girl to marry you.

Aoro saw the four patients who were waiting. One was in advanced labour and was sent immediately to the delivery room. The rest were in early labour and he sent them to the first stage rooms. It was morning by then and time to prepare for the ward round. An intern has many nightmares, but the ward round is the most recurrent one. On bad days, there might not even have been time to rush down to one's room for a bath and breakfast. In walks the consultant — the representative of God in the ward — looking sharp in an expensive suit, excellent shirt and first class tie. He naturally does not need a white coat or a name tag, for everyone knows him and kowtows to him. Medically speaking, he has arrived. Next to him is the resident who has to bow his head a little (not as much as the intern) just in case his consultant thought him uppity. Finally in the pecking order, came the bedraggled, half starved, probably unwashed intern. It was his job to present each case, take most of the blame and do all the donkey-work — like collection of specimen, administration of intravenous drugs and collection of reports from different laboratories. He also had to assist his superiors, should they have to do a procedure. If an intern had a good helpful resident, he knew that fortune had smiled upon him. If his consultant was considerate as well, he took it as a singular sign of God's warm favour. If they were both bad — then it was no more than one could expect of internship.

"This is Helena Kituku, twenty nine year old female who has a bad obstetric history. She has one living child and has lost four pregnancies at about six months. She is now twenty eight weeks pregnant and was admitted with lower abdominal pain of four hours duration. A diagnosis of premature labour was made and we have started her on treatment and put her on bed rest to try and reverse the labour."

"Have you done a blood slide for malaria parasites?"

"A blood slide?" The case was so cut and dried that Aoro had not thought to investigate the patient for other causes of miscarriage.

"The name of this patient, doctor, sounds like it is from Kambaland. Wouldn't that suggest to you that a fever such as malaria might contribute to her state?"

Aoro knew that in this case, malaria was highly unlikely; but he was too tired to argue; besides, an intern never won in such arguments and if he did the consultant might not take it in good grace.

"It is a possibility. I will do a blood slide immediately after the ward round." The ward round went on in a more or less similar tone and by the time they had seen all the patients — over forty of them — including the newly delivered mothers on the floor of the post-natal ward — dubbed Kawangware because it bore a startling resemblance to that slum— teeming as it did with humanity, Aoro was ready to keel over. He sat down for a little while and drank a cup of tea, then he got up and started doing his procedures.

When he eventually left for lunch, he had been in that ward for thirty hours except for the half hour spent at supper the day before. It was not for nothing that interns were called house-men. 'Houseboys' would be even more apt. The sun shone warmly on his dark face as he walked towards the doctors' mess. A student nurse smiled at him — a smile as warm as the afternoon sun. He was a good-looking fellow even with the tired lines around his eyes and the deep furrows on his forehead which had not been there the year before when he had been a carefree student. He smiled absently at her. Even if his heart had not been elsewhere, he would have been too tired to be anything but absent minded. One of these days, he might feel alive again, but for now survival was paramount. Two weeks looked like eternity. But it would end. 'It had to end!', he thought, as he wolfed down his meal and then went to his little flat and stretched on the uncomfortable bed and set his alarm to ring in exactly one hour. He had to be back in the wards to complete his investigations by three o'clock — and that was pushing it because no specimens were ever collected after four o'clock. But he had to sleep a little or burst.

When the alarm rang, Aoro roused himself from his deathlike sleep and groaned as each bone and muscle protested against the insult. Surely one hour could not be over! He looked at the clock. It was only two-thirty. Damn! Even the clock had ganged up with the rest against him. He made as if to lie down again, then the door bell rang once more. So that was it! Who could it be? He didn't want company; didn't care for it, didn't need it. He needed sleep. Sleep!

"Is any one there?" called a female voice.

"Wandia!" He bounded across to the sitting room, exhaustion completely forgotten, and yanked open the door.

"Oh it so good to see you," he said ushering her in.

"It's good to see I have not been completely forgotten," she said. "I've not heard from you for a whole month. I thought I'd find a female firmly installed in my place."

"You know that is not possible. This internship business is bloody hell. The days and nights are a blur. You know I think about you all the time. In some strange way you are always here with me. I suppose that is why I don't write as much as I should. I am not much good at writing anyway. I prefer to talk and watch your face as you answer me." He smiled — the smile that caught her attention in the first place — a little crooked, and entirely disarming.

She sat in the ugly government issue chair and even her slight frame made it groan.

"My mum's ill. I am actually on my way to Murang'a but I thought I'd pass by and say hello."

"I am sorry. I hope it's not too serious."

"She has not been very well you know. She is diabetic and I hear her blood sugar's out of control and she has an ulcer on her foot that won't heal."

"Sounds bad."

"Yeah". she sighed and was lost in thoughts of her childhood, running barefoot in the red fertile volcanic soil, after her mother — going home after a hard days work in the *shamba*. She and her mother had always been very close and having been named after her maternal grandmother, her mother had never referred to her as anything but *Mami* with the tenderest inflection in her voice.

"Mother!" chirped little Wandia.

"Yes, *Mami* ?"

"When I grow up, I want to be a doctor. I want to make sick people well." Sickness and death were never far from her since the death of her father from liver failure two years before.

"Oh! I thought you wanted to be a teacher?" teased her mother.

"Well yes! That too." She admired her mother a great deal. It was no joke raising five children single handed — her husband having been sole bread winner. She had to work very hard on the five acre plot of land to keep food on the table, clothes on the back but most essential of all, get money for school fees.

"You must love her a great deal." What he meant was of course that she must care a great deal about him to have stopped by to see him during such a mission. Wandia sighed again.

"She means everything to me." She looked at him steadily for a little while. "So do you — though I am beginning to think it's a waste of time. When are you going to propose if at all? We've known each other for six years. Six years! What I don't have by now I'll never get. I am twenty six years old and you are looking at the finished product. And I am tired of being asked when I'll bring home the man from *Ruguru* — meaning the man from the west as my relatives refer to you."

"You do mean it, don't you? It is not brain fever due to overwork and lack of sleep, is it?" He said it half in jest, half in earnest.

"You really are too much," she said getting up.

"Come on! Do have a sense of humour. It isn't everyday a girl proposes to me. As a matter of fact this is the first time — so forgive me if I don't quite know what to say. But you know there's never been anyone else since I met you. To hell with it, since we are in the age of equality, why don't I just say that there's never been anyone else? The answer is — yes I'll marry you. Any day you want. Today, if we can get anyone to marry us."

"You are really a comedian, you know. What are you still doing here — an underpaid intern? You should be out there earning your millions with Bill Cosby and the rest." This was how their conversation always ended. Two strong wills pitted against each other. She wondered if she was taking on more than she could manage. But he had a power over her — which even he did not know. There was no one else. There could be no one else. Still she was piqued by him.

"Point taken. But I am dead serious. You can tell your mum that I'll be over to pay my courtesy call as soon as this internship business is over. My intentions towards her daughter have always been good even if I am not a son of Mumbi and Gikuyu —

the founders of your great tribe."

The alarm rang and cut him short.

"Yak! I've got to run, honey. I have gallonfuls of blood letting yet to be done. I'll just walk you to the bus stop and then get on with the job at hand." He grabbed his coat and opened the door. She understood. After all, she herself was an intern and at the mercy of the clock and the beck and call of others. It was one hell of a life and one hell of a courtship. Why couldn't she fall in love with an ordinary guy who worked ordinary hours? One doctor in the house was more than enough. She wondered if the marriage would survive the onslaught of medicine. Time would tell.

Chapter 3

Wandia's mother was one of those dogged Kikuyu women who did not know the meaning of giving up. Her love for her children was also characteristic for there are no mothers anywhere in the world who are more devoted to their offspring or more self sacrificing in that same cause.

"*Mami!*" she said, her creased face creasing even further as she smiled at her daughter. She had aged beyond her years due to worry and overwork and lately from the ravages of diabetes; but around her was a calm serene air — a spirit at peace with itself and the world. "I did not think they would let you come so easily!"

"My friends offered to cover for me for the next two or three days. And how are you mother?" she asked trying to sound matter of fact. It was all she could do to refrain from uncovering her leg.

"Very well. They look after me very well here. The foot is much better. In fact I should go home to attend to my coffee now, instead of sitting here doing nothing."

"You and your coffee! It isn't as if you still need so much money now that we are all grown up. You should take it easy. What started the foot anyway?"

"Oh — it was a tiny cut from a carelessly placed piece of barbed wire — nothing really. I don't know why it has festered so."

"But I told you mother. Any kind of wound however small will fester in a diabetic; so you should take more care of your feet. I told you!" Her voice rose — betraying her fear and anxiety.

"Yes you did, *Mami*. Don't worry. Everything is

in the hands of God. I shall be all right." The old lady was a saved Christian and believed firmly that God was in charge. Looking at her even the agnostic Wandia had to admit that may be faith did work wonders — else how had she managed to survive at all, let alone perform such an excellent job at rearing her children?

"Sister!" she called out to a nearby nurse. "This is my daughter. The one I told you about — you know, the doctor."

"How are you, doctor?"

"Fine, thank you sister. I'd like to have a look at that foot, if you don't mind."

"Sure." she removed the swathes of bandage from the foot. "It was much worse when she came. We were afraid we would have to amputate. But she has responded very well to treatment." True enough the foot was not as bad as she had feared. It was dry and the unhealed part was red and healthy. There wasn't the tell tale grey black sogginess characteristic of gangrene. Thank God! It was a load off her mind.

"So! When are we to see this man from *Ruguru*?"

"Oh mother!"

"Seriously daughter. You are a big girl now. You have finished school. You are working. What more do you want?"

"Don't you mind that he is not of our tribe?" asked Wandia full of wonder.

"Marriage is hard. Sometimes it is necessary to talk to a man in a language that he understands thoroughly. Apart from that, I don't see any other reason against marrying a man from wherever you wish."

"Oh, I think he understands English and Swahili very well. So I suppose I should be able to get the message across," answered Wandia laughing. "Actually he told me that he would like to call on us as soon as internship is over. So you'd better get well and go home."

"I shall do that! Just you wait and see how fast I'll get out of here." They talked about all sorts of things — Wandia's work and her mother's farming activities. She was now busy trying out all kinds of things on her little farm — she was especially delighted with zero grazing and her herd of Friesians.

"Would you believe I get up to a hundred and thirty litres of milk from that little herd? I feed them where they stand, no wandering around looking for food these days."

"How's your coffee doing?"

"Not so much money in that, nowadays. I have a mind to uproot those trees you know."

"Wait and see. Things might improve."

"Oh well, I am kind of attached to those trees. Without them, I would not have managed to give you children an education at all."

"You did a great job, mum. No doubt about it."

"With the help of God my child. Never forget that."

"If you say so mother," answered Wandia dutifully. But she had only one real religion — medicine. Everything else palled into insignificance before her great ambitions. She wanted to study pathology — one of the toughest, most demanding disciplines in medicine; then she wanted to become a lecturer at the medical school and thus become a teacher, as her mother had hoped. Thereafter she wanted to specialise in haematology — diseases of the blood fascinated her. She had it all mapped out. All she wanted from God was life. If she had life —

and being a doctor she was under no misapprehension as to how fast one could lose it; if she had life — all else would be hers.

She stood up.

"I have to go, mother. I'll spend the night at Esther's house and then see you tomorrow before I leave." Esther was her older sister — who taught at the local high school and lived in the compound with her husband who was the headmaster. It was long since the two sisters had been together, and she hadn't even seen the newest baby yet — a terrible, yet not intentional omission. The baby was named after Wandia's mother and therefore was someone special to her. So she looked into shop windows as she went — until she saw the perfect present, a frilly dress in pale pink and baby blue. The price would put a nice dent in her purse, but what the hell!

Esther was still in class, the older children in school and so Wandia had little Wangechi to herself. The six month old bundle of energy took to her aunt at once and was bouncing away and blowing bubbles to her heart's content when her mother walked in, at which point she defected — letting it be known at the top of her lungs just whom she preferred.

"OK! OK!"

The sisters laughed, hugged and then fell into the business of baby worship in earnest.

"She is a beauty, eh!"

"What do you expect — she takes after me," said the proud mother.

"What! These are my eyes. You look exactly like your auntie Wandia, don't you baby?"

The baby gurgled in whole hearted assent. "See? She agrees."

"This one laughs at anything. And you my dear are lost. How's work?"

"The worst part is almost over. I'll soon be freer and I won't neglect you again. By the way, how are Kamau and Tim? Haven't seen them since my graduation day."

"They are both OK. Kamau's wife is expecting another baby. He is a bank manager now. Timothy is still waiting for the beautiful ones to be born. Meanwhile he chases whatever else is available."

"He'd better be careful; I hear there is a disease called Aids waiting to pounce on any careless person these days."

"I have heard rumours also; but most say it is just Western propaganda. Anyway you doctors can do miracles these days. A mere VD cannot elude a cure for too long."

"Thanks for your touching faith. Michael drove over from Nairobi with his wife and sons to see me. I was so happy but I could only spare an hour for him — and even then he had to wait for half an hour before I could extricate myself from my patients."

"Ugh! I could never be a doctor. Though teaching has its miseries — especially the pay."

The other children arrived from school and Wandia was lost in hugs and demands for sweets and chocolate.

"Who was top of the class last term?"

"I was!" answered Mugo — the younger boy.

"A sweet for you. And who helped mummy the most?" There was only one contender for that prize — and Anne the oldest child stepped forward calmly. Even given the difference in years, her resemblance to her grandmother in both manner and demeanour was startling. Nothing in this world would ever really surprise her. She had been born wise.

"And what good have you done you rascal?"

asked Wandia of her older nephew who was about eight years old.

"Oh auntie!"

"Well?"

He gave her an impish smile.

"How would you know Mugo and Anne were good if I wasn't bad?" he asked brightly.

"OK! I suppose it is better to have some use than to have no use at all," answered Wandia in the face of such logic. "Here's your sweet."

"Children! Wash your hands for tea."

Just then Esther's husband — also named Michael, came in. He was a short spritely man with side bands and rather long wavy hair — very unusual. He pre-empted all possible questions by introducing himself to strangers as a full blooded Kikuyu with only a touch of fierce Maasai in the distant past. True enough he had a fiery temper and was quite respected if not feared by his students and teachers.

"How are you, *daktari* ?" he asked shaking Wandia's hand.

"Fine thank you, *mwalimu*," answered Wandia in the same spirit. *Daktari* was Kiswahili word for doctor and *mwalimu* for teacher. They took tea and Wandia lost herself in the joys of being among family again. She and her brothers and sisters had always been very close — a closeness born of not just blood ties, but of many hardships faced together. Nothing breeds generosity like the need to share equally when you know that by thus doing you will go hungry.

Later that night when the sisters were alone together again, Esther enquired about Aoro.

"Have you made up your mind about him?"

"Yes I have. And so has he."

"Do you think it will work?"

"Why not? He is a Kenyan. It isn't like we are from different ends of the globe." There was an edge to her voice.

"Please don't snap at me. I only want you to be happy you know."

"I am sorry."

"You must realise that little irritations become more glaring, when there is that basic difference. For example, few in-laws are endearing; but I can't imagine anything more annoying than their talking to their son, and your children, in a language you cannot understand. It makes you even more of an outsider than you are already."

"I don't think the Sigus are like that at all."

"I hope not, but you can never tell."

On that note they separated and went to bed.

Chapter 4

He tried to look impassive without much success. He had too expressive a face. The woman he loved sat next to him in the fast moving minibus and studied his face. In a rather uncomfortable way she reminded him of his mother, Elizabeth, who had all-seeing eyes. But it was not of his mother that he thought at this particular moment; rather it was Mark. The last battle of wills he and his father had had was a lifetime ago and he had been miserably worsted. Now he was twenty-seven and he intended to win; still he had the healthy fear one has of a tried and tested adversary.

He smiled at her and she smiled back, in calm understanding. The meeting with her family had gone so well. So well. They had welcomed him, made him feel at home, fed him; laughed with him and at him good humouredly. All had been there with their spouses and children. In spite of their hard start in life, or may be because of it, they had all done very well and the oldest brother in fact owned a company and was very wealthy — a tycoon, though one would never have guessed it by looking at his lean, brown, but friendly face — as handsome as a male model. Esther had done everything to make him feel at home and referred to him as *muthoni* — brother-in-law. Kamau was the picture of dependable respectability — a man who knew money. Timothy, who was a little older than Aoro, was a typical good time boy (you can't win them all — as Elizabeth would have said). He had a sleek looking sports car, and a stunning woman draped upon his arm, but his smile was open and friendly.

Now he was taking Wandia to his parents.

"Did I ever tell you how my father once tried to starve me to death?" he asked suddenly.

"No, but I am sure he had a damn good reason."

"Yah, I guess. I had been suspended from school for, well, infringement of a few rules and ruffling the head boy's feathers — they were rather sleek — I couldn't resist them," he smiled in remembrance. "The old boy never gave me even a chance to explain. He ordered me to look for work immediately and accommodation in a month. Actually I am grateful now, but was not then. I like medicine. And I will be a surgeon if it kills me. This would never have been possible if he hadn't been so tough on me then."

"You are still afraid of him," she observed quietly.

"What! No way! I am a man, I earn my salary, I live in my house. I am not afraid of him."

A little fear is not a bad thing, she thought to herself; especially for one such as you. Living with him would be like walking a tight-rope. It could be done, but it would require consummate skill.

Elizabeth stood at the window waiting. Mark was ostensibly resting in the bedroom of their farm house — more of a ranch than a farm in fact — one hundred acres of fine grazing land upon which they had built their retirement home. It was a few miles out of Nakuru — near Njoro. She remembered word by word the letter their son had written. He had preferred to write — rather than call.

My dear parents,

I hope you are well. You will be glad to hear that I have finished my internship successfully. I have now one month's leave and I will come home on Thursday the 28th to see you. I am bringing a girl with me — the girl I intend to marry. Her name is Wandia and she is a doctor. I am sure you will like her. No, love her.

I am your affectionate son,
Aoro.

The envelope had been addressed to Mark who opened it, read the letter and passed it to her.

"At least she is from the country," he said sounding a bit odd. She looked at him and then lowered her eyes to the letter. It was characteristically Aoro — brief and to the point. She felt kind of sorry for Mark. First there had been Becky who had left home unceremoniously only to return with a white man in tow. A very nice man but apparently not nice enough for Becky. He had found out that she was having an affair during his trips abroad and had sued for a divorce. Now she was living alone with the children, financially well off, but unhappy. It was one thing to enjoy the thrills of an affair, but a different thing altogether to have a carte blanche to do exactly as you pleased. John had been terribly hurt of course and Mark had been furious with her.

Then Tony had joined priesthood— Mark resisted it at first but recently, during Tony's ordination he had been full of pride for his son — whose face had shone with joy and youthful dedication.

Vera's case had been the hardest to accept. Mark thought of the world of Vera, and deferred to her in everything. Then she had arrived home one day and declared that she wanted to join the Catholic Prelature of Opus Dei as a non-marrying member. It didn't help that Mark had never heard of Opus Dei and could not understand why Vera could not marry. But he had eventually accepted because he loved her. Because she looked so happy, so radiant. Anything that could bring such joy and serenity could not be that bad. It was a pity though that she did not wear a veil or a habit. That way he could at least have bragged about her a little to his friends. His children were a source of great envy to his less lucky friends. Vera for one was a fully qualified electronics expert and had a lucrative job in the city with a large salary and all sorts of benefits. Women like that tended to marry the most amazing wimps and Mark had held his breath in fear. But in the end all Vera wanted was to dedicate her life and her work to God, and there was no turning her back.

So Elizabeth secretly hoped that Aoro would bring home a nice girl — naturally a Luo like himself — who would proceed to have many children — all a nice, ordinary black colour.

She had heard the farm-hand greeting them, and soon afterwards saw the pair walking through the gate and up to the house. The girl was brown and very slim with long black hair. Elizabeth noted her large earnest eyes as she looked at her son and in a typically Elizabeth manner made up her mind immediately about the girl. Her son had chosen well. She opened the door just as Aoro lifted his hand to knock.

"Welcome! This must be Wandia!" she ushered them inside and bustled around in welcome.

"Yes I am. How are you? You must be Aoro's mother — he resembles you a great deal."

"No. My mother used to say that he is a spitting image of her brother, my uncle Obura, who died in the First World War."

"Why are you talking about me as if I were not here. You didn't even shake my hand, mother!"

"Sorry son. How are you? You are thin! Don't they feed you there?"

"I no longer live in the mess. I have a house now. I cook for myself."

"Last time I checked there wasn't so much as an onion in that house," said Wandia laughing. "I wonder what he cooks. Even the cockroaches looked thin." Everybody burst out laughing just as Mark walked in. He was grey, but otherwise still very arresting. Aoro stood up.

"How are you father?"

"Very well, thank you. How are you?"

"Fine. This is my friend Wandia. My father."

"How are you Mr Sigu?" She was at her most correct. No point in antagonising the guy. It was his son she was interested in. There was a brief lull in the conversation and then Elizabeth said brightly:

"Why don't you help me get some tea, Wandia?"

"Yes, yes," she answered jumping to her feet with alacrity. They left the old lion and the young one to their duel.

"Well son, how have things been with you?"

"OK Father. I am a registered doctor now. I want to work for two years or so, to gain some experience — and then I'll go back to study surgery — that's always been my interest."

"Good. Very Good. How about this marriage business — don't you think it is too soon? I mean you've only worked for a year — do you really have anything to offer a wife?"

"I guess not. But then I doubt if a large house and a Mercedes Benz would make any difference to Wandia. She's not that kind of girl."

"You can never tell. She is a Kikuyu after all — they have a thing about money. In any case why don't you wait a little? I am sure there is a nice Luo girl somewhere who'd make a perfect wife for you."

"Father," Aoro struggled to control his voice. "Father, I don't know anything about the rest of the tribe, but I know Wandia. She is the one I have chosen. I love her — which is a feeling that I cannot just transfer from one girl to another at will. In any case I have done anatomy, and beneath the skin everyone is remarkably the same. Even the blood, which is supposed to be thicker than water is all just a combination of iron and protein in every instance. Some people are good. Others are bad — it's got very little to do with their blood or tribe. It's all in the heart. I am sure you know that father."

Mark was silent for so long that his son feared that he would simply get up and walk away.

"You are my eldest son and whatever you may think, I love you. I am very proud of you. I want you to be happy. Even though you are a doctor — and I suppose doctors know a lot, there are some things that are understood only by experience. I was only trying to forestall any possible misery which may arise in future. Things like the language to be spoken at home, the religion to be practised — and by the way to what faith does she belong?"

"Her mother who is a widow is a Protestant — of the saved variety. She is very dedicated to it. Her father was a non-practising Catholic. Wandia herself subscribes to no faith that I know of."

"What faith do you subscribe to yourself?"

"Me?" asked Aoro taken aback.

"Yes you."

"I am no Tony or Vera, but I suppose I am a Catholic."

"What I mean is that does it matter enough to you to make a difference if Wandia got saved and took along the children?"

"I hope we should be able to talk things over as adults, father. She is not an irrational person."

"No doubt about it son. It is clear you have made up your mind and I wish you the best. Have you raised the issue about the bride price with her family?"

"Yes, I did. Her mother informed me that the only thing she wanted was for me to live in peace with her daughter."

"Interesting." Mark was beginning to have second thoughts about things he had heard about the avaricious Kikuyu. Maybe he had been mistaken after all.

Meanwhile in the kitchen Elizabeth and Wandia were getting on like a house on fire. It was not suprising — their interests met at one focal point — Aoro. Elizabeth was more than willing to talk and Wandia was eager to hear.

"Aoro is a very lucky boy — no wonder the Luos say that it is better to be lucky than to be good. I would never have credited him with the brains to get a girl like you. Some empty head, pretty face perhaps, but not a woman with character."

"But you hardly know me Mrs Sigu," protested Wandia. "And I hope I am not that ugly!"

"There is knowing and knowing about. I believe you can know somebody instantly. The rest is just knowing things about them. As for beauty," she studied Wandia's face — the large deceptively sleepy eyes, the high cheekbones and the wide generous mouth. Not beautiful, but very attractive. She had a slight but excellent figure. "As for beauty, I couldn't have done better if I had chosen for my son."

"Oh thanks! I am flattered."

"He is a bit wild you know and not always steady, but there is something in him that if you can get to, then you will have a wonderful companion. I believe you two will be happy."

"I hope so! Sometimes I fear that our differences are too much. You know we used to be great rivals before we became friends. I beat him in anatomy and most men I know would have gone off in a huff. He took it as a challenge and pursued me relentlessly thereafter. I snubbed him, God alone knows how many times — I mean he was just a boy and I wanted a man — somebody older that I could feel safe with — a father figure — my father died early you know. Each time though, he would say something about being Akoko's grandson and never giving up!"

Elizabeth laughed heartily at that.

"Amazing. Akoko was my grandmother who was very well born according to the standards of those days. Her father was not just a chief — but a great chief. She was a lady of iron and wise, wiser than anyone I have ever known. Maybe you will get a child like her. My daughter Vera, who is named after her is so like her in so many ways. For her age she has a clarity of vision which baffles even me. If you are ever in trouble go and talk to her. She is only two or three years older than you are but her wisdom is beyond her years."

"What does she do?"

"She in an electronics expert. She is also a member of Opus Dei an institution of the Catholic Church."

"I am not religious so I doubt if she would have time for me."

"Vera has time for everybody. And you can discuss anything under the sun with her. She is the most open minded person I know and the only person I know who believes that each person is free to choose whatever he wants so long as he harms no one else, of course. But here I am going on about Vera while it is Aoro you want to know about. Let's take in the tea and take a look at his baby photos. I believe the two must have thrashed out their differences by now." The elderly woman and the young one made their way into the sitting-room, laden with that most ubiquitous and most pacific of drinks — tea.

Chapter 5

Everybody chipped in to make Aoro's and Wandia's wedding a resounding success. The groom looked handsome in a pale grey suit and the bride was positively radiant in cascades of white lace. Everyone involved felt as if he had a stake in the marriage and thus willed it to succeed.

The festivities went on late into the night and eventually everybody dropped off replete and footsore from food and dance. The couple crept off and drove home in Vera's car to collect their bags. Vera had arranged with a business colleague for the two to make use of a company cottage just off the coast of Malindi. There they spent an idyllic seven days but soon it was time to get back home. The mundane activities of everyday life awaited them. Wandia had to organise her transfer from Machakos to Nairobi and Aoro's bachelor pad had to be made more habitable. Wedding presents had to be opened and thank you notes dispatched.

Vera and Wandia who were as different as east from west, yet so similar in some ways, became fast friends. Each sensed an inner strength in the other and automatically responded to it. Becky remained unhappily aloof. Whatever thawing had occurred before was now firmly frozen over. Vera was concerned as to the kind of influence her life-style might have on her children who had inherited their mother's extraordinary beauty, went to exclusive schools, but somehow looked lost and confused; for Becky changed men as frequently as she changed clothes.

Vera was so incensed at one point that she forgot her strictly 'handsoff' policy and suggested to her sister that she send the children home to Mark and Elizabeth or to Canada to their father. Becky's answer was scathing and to the point. If Vera knew so much about children why didn't she get married and get some of her own? Vera was very quiet for a moment that seemed to last forever. Looking at the smooth planes of her face and the calm clear eyes, one would not have known that a fierce struggle for self control was going on inside.

"I am sorry if that is the way you see it," she said at last, her voice even. "But I was not thinking of either me or you, but of the children. For their sakes, I think we should be able to rise above our differences, whatever they are." She stood up and just as she did, Alicia, Becky's eldest child walked in and on seeing her aunt ran to her smiling.

"Auntie! Auntie! I didn't know you were here!" She gave her aunt a big hug and sat gazing at her. She was a truly lovely child having inherited the best of both worlds with big brown eyes, masses of wavy deep brown hair and her mother's lovely complexion but with a lighter tone. Unlike Becky though, there was humaneness in the sensitive mouth and receptive eyes.

"Well now you know. Where's your brother?"

"In his room," Jonny missed his father a lot and he tended to stay in his room since his departure. He was a quiet child with few friends. Vera noticed how Alicia had not said a single word to her mother. Becky had no time for her children and they in turn had learned to do without her — not without some deep hurts. But she loved her aunt Vera so much that she once asked her whether she could come and live with her. Vera's heart had contracted:

"No you can't."

"But why?"

"For many reasons, but mostly because you have a mummy that loves you. And daddy may come to see you once in a while. I am only your auntie you know."

"Oh." It was a small resigned sound.

Faced with the dilemma of Becky and her children she instinctively turned to Wandia. She was young yes, but she was a doctor and a damn smart girl to boot. Maybe she would have some ideas.

She found Wandia sitting in the balcony of their flat sunning herself in the warm evening sun. She had not been at work for a couple of days because she had a bad cold. She was pregnant and had confided to Vera that she was expecting twins. Vera was delighted and treated her like a priceless and breakable porcelain object—which had amused her hugely.

"People have triplets you know, and they survive," mused Wandia. And true enough she had been remarkably fit. Her appetite was great, morning sickness had not shown its miserable face and she continued working hard until now at eight months her obstetrician had decided that her cough was too severe and might rupture the membranes before time. In truth she herself was glad to rest a little. The babies seemed to alternate between playing football and handball with her internal organs and they were getting heavier by the minute. It would be nice to laze, if only for a few days.

"Hi elephant," greeted Vera — smiling at her.

"Hi! Don't count on my being elephant for much longer. The way I am coughing I may just send a baby flying out unceremoniously at any moment."

"I hope not!"

"It sure would be a relief. These relatives of yours

are giving my insides a thorough beating. Sometimes I feel as if it is Gor Mahia versus AFC football clubs vieing for some trophy at City Stadium. It is really awful."

"Sounds interesting," answered Vera laughing. She dragged a chair and sat looking at her sister-in-law.

"I need your advice."

"Sure."

"This business with my sister Becky. Since she and John broke up she has thrown all caution to the winds. It's almost as if she hates herself. Every time I see her she has a different man and she doesn't care who knows it and that includes her own children. The effect on the children is noticeable already. Johnny hardly talks and Alicia acts as if her mother is not there. I went there today and told her to send the children to Mum and Dad or to their father."

"And?"

"She insulted me."

"How old are the children?"

"Alicia's seven and Johnny is five."

"I am a bit surprised. It is unlike you to butt in, but I suppose you were pretty incensed. That aside, there is nothing much you can do. The law bends over backwards to allow children to stay with their mother. Besides how do you know that John would be interested? Children can really ground one. As for Mark and Elizabeth — forget it. They've done their job and done it pretty well. However, now that you bring the matter up, I must tell you that I have had some disquiet about Becky. I think she has lost a significant amount of weight. Have you noticed?"

"What are you suggesting?" asked Vera horror written all over her face.

"Well according to you she *is* promiscuous."

"What a terrible word."

"I know. But I think we have more cause for worry than you suspect."

"How terrible!" She was beginning to sound like a broken record. This was her sister. She did love her. Hell, they'd started life together from the first moment of conception. Besides, these terrible things only happened to other people. Not people you knew and loved.

"My friend, Aids is spreading faster than wildfire. Sexual behaviour and attitudes are very hard to change. For a long time people only feared pregnancy. Once that fear was supposedly banished and antibiotics became available to cure all manner of venereal disease — anything went. As for God — hasn't he been completely forgotten if he ever existed?"

"No," answered Vera with quiet conviction. "You can run away, but you cannot forget. The memory of Him is deep there within you."

"Oh!" Wandia looked into her subconscious but no such memory stirred. "I can feel nothing."

"Don't worry. There will be a day and a place."

"If you say so," Wandia gave Vera her stock answer.

They sat like that for a while, each lost in thought. Eventually Wandia dragged herself to her feet awkwardly using all manner of manoeuvres.

"Come in. I will make you a cup of tea. The Greeks had their ambrosia. We Kenyans have tea."

"You are crazy you know," laughed Vera and looked at her sister-in-law with gentle affection. Aoro was a lucky man indeed. "There is this saying that you don't have to be good, all you have to be is lucky. Aoro is one such lucky man. I suppose it is the law of fair distribution."

"Oh he is stabilising and he does have a lot of good intentions; furthermore life with him is always interesting. He does come up with some amazing things. I am also lucky that he has utmost respect for Mark and tries to emulate him in most things."

"Is that true?" Vera was amazed. In so far as she knew, Aoro had never had any use for a father he considered too harsh. But everybody changes and everybody grows up sooner or later.

"Quite true — though he himself does not see it like that. He thinks that he is charting a completely unexplored path to good husbandhood and fatherhood."

Vera had to make tea as Wandia went into a spasm of coughing that sent her reeling into a chair. When she brought her a cup, she found her half-lying, half-sitting and clutching her abdomen. The time had come.

Chapter 6

Wandia watched her son Daniel; she frequently watched him for many reasons. He was a beautiful child, chubby with a fine skin and a happy face. But on closer inspection it could be seen that his eyes, set rather far apart slanted upwards and outwards. Compared to his twin sister, Lisa, he was rather short and at the age of four he still drooled a little. Daniel had Down Syndrome and five years later Wandia still remembered the shock, the pain, the sheer disbelief she had experienced when she held her infant son in her arms for the first time. Aoro had tried to tell her; had promised the obstetrician that he could handle it. But words had failed him. The pain and the denial had been too great. The sense of failure was overwhelming; for he had failed; at least in his eyes. He should have been able to give her a perfect first child and he had not. The fact that Daniel had a completely perfect twin just made the contrast too glaring. She was only twenty eight. Statistically this was a problem that should occur in elderly mothers. It was confounded bad luck.

But one could not help but love Daniel. He was the happiest fellow alive. So he was slow, made more obvious by the speed of his sister's growth. Daniel simply copied whatever she did, slowly mastered it and good naturedly went on to something else. Lisa made it her business to ensure Daniel's safety and well-being. When she was first taken to kindergarten, she threw such a tantrum that Daniel, who could barely talk and was only partially potty trained, had to be brought along. In a way history was repeating itself.

Wandia and Aoro had also adopted Becky's two

children Alicia and Johnny, after Becky's death two years before. Becky had developed full blown Aids and at her death she had become a mere grotesque shadow of her former self. The lovely eyes were dimmed, the beautiful face was a death's head mask, the mouth excoriated to the quick, the limbs wasted and the skin was covered with unsightly blemishes. She would talk to no one and confided to none the fear and despair she must have felt; she sent everyone away with bitter words. Vera wrote to John when she saw her sister failing so rapidly, but he never wrote back and to date no one had seen or heard from him.

When it became clear that Becky would not come out of hospital alive, the family met and after much discussion it was decided that it would be least disruptive for the children if they went to live with the two doctors. It was a show of confidence that touched Wandia deeply. As it later transpired however, all they really needed was a home; for their mother had not only a hefty insurance, but left so large an estate that everyone was amazed. She had a string of maisonettes, two bungalows in Spring Valley and actually owned a block of offices and shops in Westlands; what is more her affairs were in spic and span order with everything clearly documented and legally tied up and her debts were easily cleared by the sale of one of her houses. She had appointed a firm of trustees to run her affairs on behalf of her children and for their benefit. Her sister Vera had been appointed guardian of the children and was allowed to choose which family member they would live with. This family member would draw money from the estate in amounts deemed sufficient to provide comfortably for the children. Her will clarified these issues and then went on to state:

"My sister Vera and I have had differences, but I have no doubt that she would have made an excellent mother — much better than I ever was. The children love her. So it is with confidence that I leave every aspect of their care in her capable hands with the assistance of whichever family members she chooses for I appreciate that the nature of her calling may not allow her to establish her own home. I want her to know that I love my children though my way of expressing it may not have satisfied her. I expressed it by making sure that they will never lack in the things I believe in. It is true that money cannot buy happiness or I would have been happy; but it can buy pretty well everything else. OK it cannot buy life either — for I am dying and will die in the slowest most painful way possible, but I am not sorry for the way I have lived; for I found out however late, that everything, everything has a price. This is the price of living the way I have lived. So be it; I will pay it."

Vera wept afresh when the will was read out. What could make anyone so bitter? They had had good loving parents and all her brothers and her other sister were happy warm-hearted people with ordinary faults, but not with such bitterness — the bitterness of gall — and that in someone so beautiful! She had been only thirty-three and until the last six months of her illness she had still been the loveliest person Vera had ever seen.

Vera was only too glad to put the children in Wandia's capable hands and the results were soon visible. Aoro suddenly faced with a household consisting of four children grew up in a hurry. He hit off especially with little Johnny who had never really had a good father figure to relate to. The men of the house consisting of Aoro, Johnny and Daniel as soon as he could walk, were often seen playing ball in the playground down below. Daniel was rarely off his bum, but the happy smile never left his face. He was not the brightest child alive, those honours went to Lisa and Johnny—when he finally came out of his shell. He was not even the most gifted — that honour went to Alicia out of whose hands beautiful things and beautiful music were already being created apparently quite effortlessly and who sáng like a bird. No, Daniel was none of these things; but no one could be unhappy in the presence of such thorough going happiness and sheer joy of living. His mother loved him almost desperately.

But today her keen eyes watched him frantically and they brimmed over with tears and she screamed silently at a God she did not believe in. Daniel had leukaemia. It had started with two episodes of nose bleeding, quite severe. Then he wouldn't brush his teeth and on examining his mouth his mother found that his gums were also soggy and bleeding. She summoned the maid.

"Does this child ever eat the mid morning snack of fruits I told you to be giving him?" asked Wandia in her bad Swahili.

"*Ndio Mama.*" answered the maid in her beautiful coastal accent Swahili, with a long drawn lilt on the vowels. On normal days, this contrast was cause for laughter, but this was not a normal day. Wandia, alarmed, lifted the heavy boy in her arms and laid him out on the sofa. She examined his neck and there were many little and not so little lumps on it. She found some more in his armpit and on his groin. On feeling his tummy, she found that the spleen was quite enlarged. She stood up trembling.

"What is it mummy?" asked Daniel in his slow husky way.

"Nothing baby. Nothing. You don't have to brush your teeth — you can do it tomorrow when you feel better."

"OK!" he answered smiling; brushing had become rather uncomfortable lately.

When Aoro finally got home, Wandia was beside herself. She was in early pregnancy and he sensed immediately that something was wrong from the unfriendly greeting he received.

"Where the hell have you been?"

He was a resident in surgery and that meant he kept all manner of weird hours. She knew it and rarely ever commented on it. She was usually too busy with her own studies anyway, to worry over much.

"Oh I decided to pop into the library to read a little. You know it is impossible to read in this house."

"Well I do it frequently enough. We have children and we cannot just forget they need us."

"OK. OK. Maybe I have a slow brain or something. I am sorry. Why are you so combative anyway?" Why was she fighting? She didn't know except that she was beside herself with worry.

"I think Daniel has leukaemia," she said her lips trembling.

"Oh!" It didn't occur to him to doubt her. Her prowess as a clinician was well known. He went on trying to console her, "But there are leukaemias and leukaemias." It was true. Some forms of leukaemia were deadly while others were comparatively easy to treat and even cure. Blood cancer was a common occurrence in people with Down Syndrome. It was just that they had thought that disaster could not strike twice.

"Are you telling me?" she asked bitterly.

"Please, honey..."

"Don't honey me. Go to hell." She turned on her heel and went to bed. Aoro ate his dinner alone, then went to look at his sleeping son. He felt the flesh around the child's neck and armpits and found the tell tale little lumps. He stood staring at the sleeping face for a long time; then went back to the sitting-room and called his sister Vera. He had to wait for a long time before someone answered the phone.

"Vera, would you come over tomorrow? Wandia is in a rather bad way and you know she is in early pregnancy. She kind of trusts you, you know."

"What's wrong?" asked Vera alarmed.

He felt like weeping.

"We suspect that Daniel has blood cancer."

"Cancer! He is only a baby!"

"This particular form tends to dog people with Down Syndrome and it can occur at any age."

"Maybe it is something else."

"I hope so," answered the beleaguered father without much hope.

"Don't worry too much please. I will come."

"Thanks sis." He hung up.

The next day, the two took their son to the most eminent specialist on blood diseases in the country. Vera came along. Wandia remained pointedly silent. The specialist listened to their story, examined the child and ordered immediate admission. Daniel took it all in good grace until the man with the needles came to draw blood. He wept pitiably. He had known nothing but love and comfort in all his short life. Had he not tried to be a good boy? Why was the man poking at his hands with sharp needles? He turned his slanted tearful eyes to his mother and she staggered out of the room with Vera's arm around her shoulder.

"I think you should return later Dr Sigu," suggested the sister-in-charge.

"She is right my dear. Let's go home. His daddy can stay with him until they have finished with him."

Vera guided Wandia out of the hospital into the bright sun. When they were in the car Wandia turned suddenly and asked Vera:

"Where is your God?" A question as old as man's sojourn on this earth.

"Here with us in this terrible situation. Have no doubt."

"Then ask Him for the life of my son."

"I already have," answered Vera simply.

A couple of days later, it was confirmed that Daniel indeed had leukaemia — but it was not the most aggressive form, and there was even the possibility of a cure. On hearing that Wandia abandoned her agnostic stance and went to church, a place whose doors she had not darkened since her wedding day and to which only Aoro out of a sense of his strong religious inheritance rather than any clear belief, had hitherto gone with the children. Wandia went there specifically to bargain with this strange and terrifying God — which was the only concept she had had of him since the day she had watched her father's body being lowered into that gaping red hole.

"God, I know you and I have not been great

friends, but I have tried not to harm anyone and I have served many others. This is my son who was born maimed but whom I love dearly. It is said you are Love. If that is true, then you should understand how much I love him. Please let my son be cured and from now onward, I shall regularly go to church and see to it that all the four children know You." She could think of nothing else to say, but she stayed there kneeling for a very long time, head bowed before the tabernacle. Even she did not understand the significance of this act, for her knowledge of religion was almost non-existent.

Chapter 7

After the recovery of her son Daniel, it was only natural that Wandia's interest in pathology — the study of disease processes as a whole should find its fullest expression in haematology — the study of diseases of blood. Immediately after her second degree, she joined the university and became a lecturer and so became a teacher as well as a healer. She then got a scholarship to study haematology at Johns Hopkins Hospital in Baltimore, Maryland. This caused an agonized nail-biting session with Aoro. It is not easy to leave five children, the youngest of whom was only four years old — this was her younger son Mugo. The Courtney children had become so much a part of the family that Wandia never dreamed of excluding them from her calculations. Johnny, now a strapping lad of thirteen, was particularly close to her — not surprising for he had never had much of a mother or a father for that matter — John had disappeared without a trace. Daniel in his happy way would survive. Little Mugo already had a reputation for being a tough cookie. All Alicia wanted was to be like Vera — whose very feet she worshipped. Lisa was a highly strung, sensitive and extremely intelligent child. Like Daniel she was eight going on to nine. Lisa and Johnny were devoted to Wandia and did everything to make her happy. At the end of each term there was always a little ceremony that spoke volumes. Everyone arrived with his report card in hand. Little Mugo would start; his usually consisted of an orange or other fruit painted purple, pink or other similar blinding technicolour stimulus. On one side the teacher would have placed an A. His mother would admire it, exclaim over it and, gratified, he would move aside smiling broadly.

Daniel came next. He went to the same school the others went to and strangely enough managed to get the occasional C and once even a B- which feat of intellectual achievement had sent the whole family out to celebrate in style. They had all piled into the car and driven to the Safari Park Hotel for dinner. Most of Daniel's grades however consisted of 'D's and 'E's, but no one minded this particularly. He was doing very well considering his handicap.

Then Lisa would hand in hers and mother and daughter would exchange a look. Lisa had stayed at the top of her class since she first entered school and her mother fought constant battles to keep the teachers from promoting her too hurriedly. She had wisely decided that a good brain never rots and she hardly glanced at the grades — they were always 'A's. There was however a sub-column with grades for order, conduct, extracurricular activity and such like. Lisa's report was meant to be an accolade to her mother and therefore it had to be perfect. Unfortunately she had a hard time being orderly and she was not athletic. So there would be that condemning C for order which was not surprising. Although Lisa left the house looking spic and span with hair in a pony tail, well pressed tunic and clean white blouse, by the end of the day she would be in total disarray; clothes hanging anyhow, with hair in spikes, but her books would somehow survive — neat and clean enough to eat on. During games balls either rolled around her or landed smack on her tummy or other equally painful site. Her mind was always elsewhere.

Johnny was a son to make a mother proud. He was that rare thing — an all round student. He was now in class seven and was best student, class monitor and games captain and before his voice started breaking he, like his sister, sang like an angel. As he presented his shining report to his foster mother his eyes simply shone. And Wandia loved him for loving her so much.

Alicia now fifteen and in High School, preferred to discuss her report in private — adult to adult. Since they got on very well so long as it was understood that Vera had first place in her heart, Wandia agreed to most of her requests, which were always very sane and well thought out, without demur.

How could she leave all this and just go away? Aoro was very busy and had a tight operating schedule having decided to leave government service and go fully into private practice. But when she spoke to him, he was very encouraging.

"A year is not very long you know, honey. We will survive. I know you don't trust me — but do you have to show it so blatantly?"

"Of course I trust you! What a thing to say! It's just that you always seem to be having an emergency just when we need you most."

"OK. I'll tell all my patients to postpone their illnesses for one year — till you get back. How about that?" He smiled into her blazing eyes. "A joke — and not a good one, I can see. How about if I asked my sister Mary to come and live with us? It would be good for her too. I don't like the idea of her living in a poky flat in Eastlands with only a female room mate for company." To Wandia, it was like a light at the end of a dark tunnel. Mary had just completed a secretarial course and didn't have a well paying job yet. And she was a sensible young lady — thanks to Elizabeth who had acted as an antidote to Mark's brazen spoiling of 'his little girl'.

"You think she would want to come? She may not want to lose her independence you know."

"I am sure she'd be delighted to come."

"Maybe we should also get an extra house help to assist Tabu in running the house."

"Good idea," answered Aoro.

She was silent for a long time, then she shook her head a little and stood up.

"It's a long time since I saw Elizabeth. Would you drive us over there this weekend? I am sure she'd love to see the children and I'd like to talk to her."

Aoro looked at his wife with interest. The relationship between her and his mother was a constant source of amazement and amusement to him. In fact the two made him feel as if he was the outsider. Once he told her:

"I thought mothers and daughters-in-law were supposed to hate each other's guts?"

"Are you jealous?" asked Wandia cryptically.

"Of course not!" he had answered hastily.

So Aoro tore himself away from his work, got a colleague to answer his calls and drove his family to Njoro. Elizabeth was beside herself with joy. She was more lined and quite grey but otherwise still her active clear minded self. Mark on the other hand had lost his military swagger and was quite stiff with arthritis, but he was very hearty. Odongo, the younger twin whose schooling had eventually led nowhere was now the farm manager and was very useful — he had discovered a hidden talent for farming and especially animal husbandry — a streak probably inherited from his great grandmother Akoko who in her time had been a no mean cattle woman. He was in his element in the dairy. His twin Opiyo worked in Mark's former company and was now a manager. He was married and had a son — Mark junior and a daughter Elizabeth. He lived with his parents and commuted to Nakuru daily from Njoro.

As they piled into the sitting room, they found to their delight that Opiyo and his wife Edna were present as was, to Aoro's absolute joy, Father Tony himself! It was almost a family reunion. Everybody laughed and started talking at once—no one heard anything but no one minded in the least. Eventually all settled down and food was brought in staggering quantities.

"Hey, was an army passing this way, Mother?" asked Aoro.

"It is not everyday my grandchildren — *all of them,* come to see me; and I am a farmer; I have plenty of food — fresh from the garden, not like that frozen tasteless stuff you people eat in the city."

"Agreed! Agreed!" answered her eldest son waving a juicy looking drumstick in the air. She noticed with motherly approval that he had started to fill out and his eyes were happy and settled. For a while, she had feared that this particular son was headed for trouble. But that had been long ago in his boyhood. She had been mistaken — happy mistake. She noted with concern, however, that Wandia seemed to have little to say. Something was amiss. After the meal the children ran out to chase whatever farm animal they could find and to exercise their city cramped limbs. Aoro and Tony decided to take a walk together. Opiyo and his twin went to admire a herd of high breed cattle. Mark sat on the veranda admiring his scampering many-hued grandchildren and Elizabeth and Wandia went to the kitchen — the only place where a woman can expect not to be disturbed for a while, especially when all are well fed.

"Yes tell me. Is he giving you a hard time or something?" Elizabeth asked and Wandia looked at her startled.

"No! No! I mean — gosh — am I so obvious?"

"I can read you like a book, my girl."

"I have a scholarship to study in America for a year."

"And he is against it?"

"No! He is not. In fact he is all for it. But how can I leave him with five children?"

"Don't worry about him. You see if you don't go, it is something that will haunt you — a lost chance is very hard to live with. We will all chip in to give him a hand with the children. Mary is also there in Nairobi with absolutely no responsibility whatsoever. They will be OK. Just organise your affairs and go do what you have to do."

"Oh, thank you so much! Now I can tell the good news to my own family. I didn't want to have to disappoint them." The two women looked at each other with understanding. The leaving and cleaving was always more difficult for a woman who has to tear herself from so much, and give so much — which almost always went unnoticed.

The children, who apparently have some very powerful grinders in their tummies started rushing back into the house to ask for this, that or the other to eat and their solitude was broken as they attended to their needs, but Wandia was now at peace.

Father Tony and Aoro were reminiscing, about the escapades of their boyhood and each memory was punctuated by great gales of laughter. Eventually they got around to more serious talk.

"Great girl you have there." observed Tony.

"Yes. I am a lucky man. She does a wonderful job with the kids — Becky's as well as ours. How about you Tony? How's the priesthood? Are you happy?"

"Absolutely. It is my life and it fulfils me completely. You know the priesthood is quite like medicine. You deal with people in pain — a different kind of pain, but pain all the same. It can sap your strength if you don't know how to renew it. But then again there is always God."

"I wish I could believe that as absolutely as you do. By the way how's uncle Peter? It's years since I saw him. You men of cloth can get scarce!"

"He is OK — very strong. He'll outlive me. He says that I am a cerelac baby, while he himself was brought up on real African food. He is a great inspiration to me. I think you should go down to Kisumu to see him. Take the children — he'd be delighted — a vindication of his grandmother Akoko. He has told me so much about her, I believe I should write a book. To her, life was like a river, flowing from eternity into eternity. I believe it is because of the power of her faith that she is still remembered both in the blood and in the mind."

"It is strange you should say that. My wife is fascinated by that woman and asks endless questions about her. Sometimes I think that she wills herself to take over her spirit — if such a thing is possible."

"The believing human mind unleashes unimaginable power. I think your wife is a believer." He smiled enigmatically and Aoro who was a man very much bound to his five common senses and thus saw only what they could perceive, looked at his brother with total incomprehension. Tony laughed at him good naturedly and said:

"Oh forget it. Let's go home. It isn't everyday I get to eat food like mother's you know!"

"That's because you married the Church — you dummy!" His brother laughed with him. They regarded each other with affection then started running towards the house — for all the world as if they were boys again.

Chapter 8

The chairperson of the department of pathology in the University of Nairobi's School of Medicine, Professor Wandia Sigu slowly mounted the dais and knelt to receive the highest accolade possible in medical academics — a Doctorate in Medicine which was the medical equivalent of a PhD. Her husband, four children and two foster children watched in proprietary pride as the chancellor whose colourful academic gown and head gear bordered on the fantastic if not the bizarre, placed a wobbly looking academic hat on her head. He then intoned: "By the powers confered on me by the University of Nairobi I give you the powers to read and to do all that appertains to this degree."

"As if I have not read enough to last me two lifetimes!" she thought irreverently as the applause rose to a crescendo. She was the first Kenyan woman to achieve such a feat in medicine. As she rose to her feet, her little three year old daughter Kipusa could contain herself no longer and piped;

"That's my mummy!"

"We know, you dummy!" answered her brother Mugo. All eyes swivelled towards them and their father squirmed in his seat. Apparently, the professor had quite an ordinary looking family — was the approving verdict of those eyes. In Africa the greatest accolade is still the possession of children. As the clapping died down, Aoro whispered a word of congratulations to his wife.

"You sure earned it, my girl."

"Only with your help." And it was true. Without his constant encouragement, she would have faltered and maybe even given up. She knew that she was lucky to have him. He was big hearted and full of self confidence and begrudged her nothing. He had chosen one way and she had chosen another and each enjoyed what they did — he the cut throat world of private practice and she the equally competitive world of academic medicine. They had a good marriage, lovely children and professional satisfaction. It was a good life.

"You look very far away," he remarked looking into her eyes.

"Yes," she answered. "I was counting my blessings."

"Am I one of them?" He asked joking. He loved to joke.

"The best of them," she answered quite seriously and meant it.

Eventually the long ceremony ended and the sea of graduates in their black robes broke up. The Sigus rose and fought their way to the car. Back at home the whole extended family awaited them. The Mugos were there with their various spouses and their children as were the Sigus. There were also friends from either side. Wandia's mother who eventually had had to have an amputation and was a bit blind was nevertheless there for her daughter's big day. Vera had come up with her college friend Mary-Anne, her husband Matthew and their five active children. As was expected, Mary-Anne and Matthew were Supernumeraries, that is, married members of Opus Dei. Mary-Anne was in charge of the catering which released Wandia fully to enjoy herself. By nature she was a Martha — a worrier, but with Mary-Anne ably in charge, she could afford to be a Mary — relaxing with the guests. As was to be expected, Alicia — now an undergraduate student of Design and Music at Kenyatta University, was Vera's constant and bright eyed shadow. Johnny with Daniel in tow hovered between Aoro and Wandia. It was a foregone conclusion that he was going to the Medical School. Wandia had once tentatively asked him whether he might not want to fly—after all some of these things ran very deeply in the blood. Understanding the real implication of these words, Johnny had flushed; looking squarely at her he had answered:

"You know I never even knew him. If he were to walk in through that door this minute, I wouldn't even know what to say to him — that is if I could forgive him. You and uncle are all the father and mother I ever had and will ever need."

Wandia had answered, "You are almost a man now Johnny. You must realise how deeply your mother must have hurt him. You must learn to forgive for we all need forgiveness sooner or later." But when you are young with your unblemished youth ahead of you everything is either black or white and Johnny's answer had been:

"I can't see myself abandoning my children just because I disagree with my wife. They would just be the innocent victims. You may not realise it, but before I came to live with you I felt completely unlovable and unwanted. I thought it was because I was neither black nor white — but some horrible mixture; and now, Auntie, since we are talking heart to heart I would like to tell you that I want to change my name from Courtney to Sigu."

"Johnny, you are the most lovable person I know. I couldn't love you more if you were my own son, but never blame the colour of your skin for anything — that is just a crutch that some people use to cover up their weaknesses and short-comings. Stand up and be counted like a man — that is all that matters. Secondly never shut a door unnecessarily — and changing your name would do just that. You are a child of two worlds and I believe that somewhere within you, somehow, someday you will find that you have the best of both those worlds. Besides your father may come in search of you even after forty years if he is still alive somewhere. Keep the door open Johnny." Her eyes pleaded for the man she had never known, but his son just looked at her darkly and went to his room.

For young Johnny, now in late adolescence, was at a cross roads; most especially he felt keenly his total lack of an African name. His father in truth would not have minded, but Becky had not thought it necessary — and had given neither of her children an African appendage. Eventually at eighteen he would compromise and would take the name Sigu as a middle name — this, he felt would appease his African soul. Also Johnny was excessively fair with straight very light brown hair. People tended to take him for pure white, a thing he disliked and which he countered by speaking mostly Swahili, eating mainly African food, and having friends who were practically soot black. Wandia who was very observant, noted all this with great concern and asked Vera to write to John Courtney again — and to send him a photograph of his two children. Which father could resist or want to lose so fine a pair? And though Wandia did not know it, Johnny was the spitting image of his father.

The party swung on late into the night as the children dropped off one by one and were moved to the bedrooms and carefully placed on mattresses spread out on the floor to take as many as possible. The old folks then followed and only the young people remained — not so young anymore for many were in their late thirties and mid forties — the prime of life; and they wanted to dance and discuss the night away — a rare opportunity for they were all hard working, self driven people who rarely ever took a day off. Politics was particularly hot as the country was facing unprecedented economic decline with inflation spiralling completely out of control.

The recently concluded multi-party elections which many had hoped would usher in a new era had been characterised by confusion and cries of foul by the opposition and declarations of total transparency by the winners — who if they were to be believed, had turned from goat to guardians of the vegetable patch. Once again the people's dogged perseverance in the face of lies and bureaucratically engineered setbacks was something to behold: Kenyans — the common people, had come out shining. The donors, not particularly impressed by the capricorn turned guardian angel transformation of the rulers were still withholding aid and the country was going to the dogs, slowly but surely. These were the words in the mouth of all able bodied Kenyans these days and there was a fair representation of them in that room — from bankers to teachers, doctors to lawyers, engineers to architects: and each and everyone of them had an opinion to be voiced, preferably at the top of his or her lungs — with the assistance, of course, of some frothy brew or stinging distillate.

Elizabeth came out of a bedroom unobserved, stood looking at the noisy gathering below. These

Elizabeth her lips twitching. And, of course, there was a lifetime of memories with Mark Anthony — in her opinion still the best looking man around. She also remembered clearly the day Akoko had died and her conviction that it was all over. How mistaken she had been! For in truth it had only just begun and now she saw evidence of that great woman in so many of her grandchildren, but strangely enough most clearly in her daughter-in-law Wandia — the girl from the ridge country of the Kikuyu, who was no blood relative but who clearly if instinctively understood the true destiny of a woman — to live life to the full and to fight to the end.

In the small hours of the night, Elizabeth eventually slid into a fitful and disturbed sleep. Mark, being a very heavy sleeper stirred stiffly but did not wake up. The following morning everyone packed up and scattered to whatever direction they had come from — exhausted but happy.

Aoro and Wandia were dozing on the sofa when the phone started ringing insistently. It was Opiyo who had driven off with his parents and children earlier in the day. His voice shook a little as he gave his terse message: Elizabeth had fallen sick on the outskirts of Nakuru. Apparently she had had problems with breathing. They had rushed her to the hospital but to their horror and disbelief she had been declared dead on arrival. Would they please come immediately? He hung up with his brother's: "What! What do you mean...," still ringing in his ears.

They buried Elizabeth beneath her favourite grove of wildly branching Elgon teaks garlanded with vivid spray of purple bougainvillaea. A large crowd had come to say good-bye to *Mwalimu* — the teacher. Her children and her children's children and their spouses and friends stood still. There were the children she had taught at school so many years ago — now adults but still remembering with affection the gentle firmness with which she had guided them in their most formative years. There were fellow teachers and Mark's former workmates — now grizzled old men and women — the few who were still on their feet. Mark himself sat next to the coffin, rigid and mute, trying to grapple with the enormity of his loss and the magnitude of his loneliness. He himself would follow his wife within the year. She after all had been his life.

His Lordship Peter Owuor Kembo, bishop of the diocese of Kisumu now a stiff and grey old man, but still having the sparkle of youth in his eyes conducted the funeral Mass with the assistance of Father Anthony Sigu popularly known as Father Tony — who looked solemn and sad. He had been devoted to his mother. The Mass was beautiful and poignant and in the middle Wandia of all people fainted dead away, but on being roused refused to be helped away. She wept brokenly for her mother-in-law. No, rather for her friend Elizabeth. She would stay to the bitter end.

As the red earth rose to form a mound over the coffin, people began to wander away but her children hung on — forlorn and lost. But the dead have no use for the living who eventually have to tear themselves away to continue with the business of life. Even they finally had to wander away numb, but waiting for the healing touch of good memories; of love and laughter; which would eventually return to touch them with the breath of life once again.

Nearby was Becky's grave, covered with lovely flowers — as beautiful as she herself had been in this life…

The End